'Will *madame* ... ...'

'*Madame* would love to,' Ferelith replied and they made their way down the shallow, gently curving flight of steps to the garden below. Their way was no longer illuminated from the embassy but the moon was unobscured by clouds and gave enough light. Her escort reached up to one of the espaliered branches that disguised the harsh lines of the wall and brought down a peach. From somewhere beneath his servant's jacket, he produced a curved knife, its glinting blade barbarously efficient.

He slit the peach and detached a segment. 'Here, *madame*,' he said. 'Open your mouth.'

Ferelith did as she was bid and the slice, luscious and dripping with juice, slipped down her throat.

'Perhaps I should feed myself?' she suggested.

The footman laughed. 'No, *madame*. When they are as ripe as this, they need expert handling. You would ruin your gown,' and he pre-empted any further protest by feeding her the next slice. She took it without further comment and when the last piece had been swallowed she was laughingly grateful for the care with which he wiped her chin and lips almost, but not quite, as he might have done had she been a child, one finger holding her chin up while the other wiped away the juice with a fine linen handkerchief. His action made her feel suddenly both vulnerable and cherished. He paused briefly when his self-appointed task was complete, and frowned a little. Then he bent down and kissed her briefly, gently, on her upturned lips.

Janet Edmonds was born in Portsmouth and educated at Portsmouth High School. She now lives in the Cotswolds, where she taught English and History in a large comprehensive school before deciding that writing was more fun. A breeder, exhibitor and judge of dogs, her house is run for the benefit of the Alaskan Malamutes and German Spitz that are her speciality. She has one son and three cats and avoids any form of domestic activity if she possibly can.

Previous Titles

HIGHWAYMAN BRIDE
A CIVIL MARRIAGE
SCARLET WOMAN

FLIGHT FROM THE HAREM

Janet Edmonds

First published in Great Britain 1990 by Mills & Boon Limited

© Janet Edmonds 1990

Australian copyright 1990 Philippine copyright 1991 This edition 1991

ISBN 0 263 77149 0

Masquerade is a trademark published by Mills & Boon Limited, Eton House, 18–24 Paradise Road, Richmond, Surrey, TW9 1SR.

Set in Times Roman 10 on 10¼ pt. 04-9102-88165 C

Made and printed in Great Britain

HISTORICAL NOTE

WHEN Charles II married the Portuguese princess, Catherine of Braganza, she brought with her as part of her dowry the two great cities of Bombay and Tangier. The former became the foundation of the British Empire in India; the latter, despite its obvious strategic importance, was starved of funds, making it impossible to hold and we finally got out—blowing it up first—in 1684, after twenty-three years.

The present Medina—Old Town—of Tangier lies precisely within the boundaries of the seventeenth-century city but the resemblance ends there. The Dutch engraver, Wenceslaus Hollar, depicted the city in 1679 as characteristically Portuguese in style, with pitched and tiled roofs and gardens rather than courtyards—architecture which can still be seen elsewhere in northern Morocco, notably in Larache. The rest of Tangier now sprawls over the hills and valleys, making it impossible to visualise what it must have been like three hundred years ago, and I have drawn heavily on Hollar's engravings and Samuel Pepys's 'Tangier Papers'.

Pepys was given the secret mission of going to Tangier in 1683 in order to value property there so that owners could be recompensed by the English government, which had by that time decided to abandon it and intended to blow it up. His 'Tangier Papers'—which are not part of his better-known diary—contain much revealing information about life there and the personalities involved, particularly the notorious Colonel Piercey Kirke who was later, after his regiment's return to England, to round up with particular ferocity those who had participated in the Monmouth Rebellion of 1685. I have tried to depict Kirke and his wife as their contemporaries saw them.

It has been much more difficult to give an accurate picture of the Moroccan leader, Moulay Ismail, and his general, the Alcaid Ali Benabdala. This is because English histories see Ismail as the villain and describe his character accordingly, and I do not have the Arabic to read Moroccan accounts. He is, however, one of the great heroes of Moroccan history. He ruled for fifty-five years, during which time he is alleged to have sired a thousand children. More importantly, he drove the infidel out and united the country—at least during his lifetime. He was certainly ruthless and—by twentieth-century standards—cruel, though hardly more so than most monarchs of the time. His title was 'Sultan' but I have referred to him as 'King' because it more accurately reflects to a British reader his status. His 'Versailles' at Meknes is still there, though sadly in ruins, and my description of it is entirely imaginary.

Both Islam and Christianity are religions preaching tolerance, but there was precious little exhibited by either in the seventeenth-century. The terms 'infidel' and 'heathen' were the standard terms used by each of the other at that time and I have therefore used them in conversation. It is interesting to note that Christian converts to Islam were treated on an equal footing with other Muslims, but Muslim coverts to Christianity were not offered similar privileges.

I have used throughout the terms 'Moor' and 'Moorish' rather than Moroccan because the three races—Berber, Moor and Arab—were regarded as more separate than they are today. The boundaries were different, too, so I have used the Moroccan name for the country—al-Maghrib—rather than the modern English one.

Both sides used mercenaries. The Moors had their famous Sudanese, the English had the Scots and Irish. The Moroccan facility with languages was already well established in the seventeenth-century and, during the Siege of Tangier in 1680, when communications between the outlying forts and the city was either by messengers—who were killed—or through loud-hailers, the

English solved the problem of keeping their planned strategies secret by shouting across at each other in Irish! This idea was copied by the US forces during World War II when they used Navajo—though with more sophisticated techniques than loud-hailers. The brief history of our occupation of Tangier is full of similarly bizarre titbits.

My thanks to the many Moroccans who so kindly answered with great patience questions, the answers to many of which must have seemed self-evident, and not least to the real Ferelith who allowed me to use her name.

Finally, readers familiar with Morocco may wonder why there is no reference to the ubiquitous drink of that country—mint tea. The answer is quite simply that it was not adopted until the eighteenth-century.

CHAPTER ONE

FERELITH DURLISTON turned in front of the mirror, looking at herself doubtfully.

'Do you really think I should, Annie?' she asked the maid who was holding the large glass, raising and lowering it so that her mistress could observe herself from top to toe. 'You don't think it's too soon?'

Annie sighed with the exasperation of a trusted servant who no longer had to stand upon every point of ceremony. 'No, madam, I do not,' she said emphatically. 'It's been all of two years since Mr Durliston had his accident. Mourning is all very right and proper and I'd have been the first to tell you off if you hadn't gone into black straight away, but there's nothing to be gained by carrying these things to excess. You're a young woman, Mrs Durliston, and you should be thinking about the rest of your life—and that will include another husband in due course, I don't doubt, and perhaps some children this time. Besides, while black was quite becoming with your colouring, grey and lilac certainly aren't.'

Looking at her reflection, Ferelith was bound to agree with her maid. Of medium height and build, she had hair that was neither fair nor red, though its precise shade came closer to the latter. Ferelith had a pendant—a fly embedded in a piece of amber that someone had brought back from the realm of the giant King Peter of Russia—and it almost precisely matched her auburn curls. Her colouring was that associated with such hair, and deep mourning, particularly when it was demonstrated in the richness of black velvet, had flattered her far more than the heartbroken widow had ever realised. However, when the customary year was up Ferelith, instead of moving discreetly into other quiet colours before resuming the jewel-tones she adored, had made a deliberate decision to go into half-mourning for a further twelve months. Grey had made her look vapid and colourless and the various shades of lilac were little better. She had almost welcomed the insipidity that had looked back at her from her glass, because it showed the world—or such of it as she was likely to encounter—that her grief was too deep to allow for such superficial considerations as enhancing her appearance.

Her father, Major Hugh Melverley, had watched in dismay her gradual acquisition of a temperament to match her wardrobe and had eventually expressed his concern to Annie, the woman closest to his daughter since the death some ten years previously of Mrs Melverley.

'I know, Major, and it's been worrying me these many months,' Annie had told him. 'But she's made a vow to stay in half-mourning for a further year and I don't think there's anything you or I can say to make her change her mind. But when that year is up, I'll resist a continuance of it with all my might—and my chance of success will be the better if I know I've got your support, too.'

'You may depend upon it,' Major Melverley told her. 'Such behaviour as we are seeing goes beyond the natural.'

Ferelith's marriage to Francis Durliston had been that rarity, a love-match which had had the approval of both families. Major Melverley and Mr and Mrs Durliston had many times congratulated themselves that their respective offspring had chosen as well as they could have wished had they arranged the marriage themselves. Both families sprang from impoverished but respectable gentlefolk, the major having relieved his impecuniosity by joining General Monk's Horse Guards more than twenty years ago, a commission he had resigned a few months after the death of his son-in-law, without too much regret. There had been little chance of further preferment while the country was at peace and King Charles still reputedly desperately short of funds, even twenty years after regaining the throne. Alarmed at the continuing melancholia of his daughter, the major had felt he might be more usefully employed at home, where he had her under his watchful care. It would always be possible to buy himself back into the army should the situation both at home and elsewhere warrant it.

Thomas Durliston had gone discreetly but successfully into business as a ships' chandler and had warehouses in every major port from Bristol round to Tilbury. It had never been any part of his plan to have one of his sons follow in his footsteps. On the contrary, the wealth he had been steadily accumulating was to be used to enable them to regain the position in society to which their birth entitled them but which lack of means had prevented their father enjoying to the full. Francis had been a cleric and it had been everyone's opinion that he had had a brilliant future before him, until that fateful evening when his horse had stumbled on a loose cobblestone and fallen, throwing his rider, whose head had struck the wall of an adjacent house at such an angle that his neck had been broken and he had died instantly.

The marriage had been less than a year old and Ferelith herself only nineteen at the time. She had been inconsolable, her grief increased by the fact that she had not yet conceived and would therefore never have the satisfaction of seeing dear Francis live on through a son or daughter.

The very idea that she might some day marry again had been anathema to her, a concept she could barely recognise, and it was hardly less so now. Her dear Francis was gone, leaving a space that could never be filled.

Neither her father nor Annie wasted any time trying to convince her otherwise but both determined, in their own way, to use every stratagem at their disposal to ease the widow back into a life more fitting for a young woman so that there was a greater possibility of events pursuing a more natural course.

To this end, Annie saw to it that those garments which her mistress hadn't worn for two years were in good order and the major, as the two years drew to an end, passed the occasional comment which made it clear that he did not expect his daughter to extend her mourning.

'My dear,' he had said a few weeks previously, 'it will be a great source of comfort to me when you are able to run my household in a way that will enable you once more to be my hostess. Now that I've resigned my commission I must play a full part in our little corner of society or die of boredom.'

Ferelith had made no reply, a fact which had bothered the major not one whit. It had been enough to let the words sink in, to let her think he took it for granted that life would in many respects be much as it had been before her marriage.

His next foray into the minefield had been more direct, more specific. 'I wonder, my dear,' he had said at breakfast, 'whether you would have any very great objections if I invited a couple of old soldiers and their wives to supper in a week or two. I thought,' he added tentatively, 'it might be an acceptable gesture to invite Francis's parents as well.'

He knew that the last suggestion might be the more difficult one for her to accept and he found it hard to appear suitably nonchalant while he waited for her reply.

Ferelith considered the matter only briefly. Her father's words on the earlier occasion had made her realise that others might interpret a further continuation of her mourning as a form of selfishness, since she had become somewhat reclusive, rarely venturing out except to go to church. Her father had given up his career to ease her over this difficult time; she was honest enough to recognise that, in putting his daughter first, he had subdued his own gregarious nature in a way which he must find very difficult indeed.

She smiled fleetingly. 'No objections at all, Papa. It sounds an admirable idea and I'm sure my parents-in-law will appreciate the invitation.'

Major Melverley, who knew they shared his concern and had already plotted with them as well as with Annie, nodded. 'I think so, too. Shall we say in two weeks' time? Or is that a little too soon for you?'

It was, but she rather thought any time would be—sooner or later she must resume her place in her father's household and this was as good a time as any. 'No, Papa. Two weeks will suit me very well. It will give me time to get used to the idea as well as allowing me to plan. I'm quite out of practice, of course.'

So it was that she was standing in front of a glass trying to accustom herself to this 'new' reflection. Annie, who would have loved to put her mistress into a peridot-green satin gown that caught and enhanced the green of her large, long-lashed eyes, knew that this would not yet be acceptable. Instead she had produced this gown of bronze silk, always one of Ferelith's favourites. No one could condemn the colour as frivolous and the style was really quite plain, the overall impression of undeniable sumptuousness being achieved solely by the richness of the fabric.

'No jewels, I think,' Ferelith said, rearranging one long auburn ringlet over her shoulder.

'Nonsense,' Annie retorted briskly. 'That would look very odd indeed. The pearls Mr Durliston gave you will be most suitable—both the necklace and the ear-drops. Let them be the symbol of your continuing grief.'

Since pearls stood for tears as well as for purity, Ferelith was persuaded without too much difficulty and knew, when she looked once more in the mirror, that these most flattering of stones set the seal of perfection on the picture she presented. Such had not been her intention, of course, but there was no denying it was satisfying still to be able to produce such an effect. Ferelith knew she was no beauty: her mouth was too wide and generous and her colouring was not fashionable, but her wide-set green eyes gave her face a striking quality that was not far short of true beauty.

She turned to Annie with a smile that had in it something of her old confidence. 'I think we'll do, don't you?' she said.

'Indeed, I begin to think so, madam,' the maid replied with true satisfaction. She rather thought she would be able to report to Major Melverley that there was no need to despair.

The Durlistons were delighted to see their daughter-in-law beginning to come out of her shell of grief. It was very flattering to their son that she should have taken his death so hard, but it was hardly practical. Any young woman should have a husband and a family. Fate had deprived Ferelith of both and it was incumbent upon her, as upon any young widow, to remedy that deficiency as soon as she decently could. It was at last beginning to look as if Ferelith herself had recognised that fact. They greeted her with affection.

'I'm so glad to see you taking up the reins of life again, my dear,' Mrs Durliston said as she kissed her daughter-in-law. 'You always did dress to advantage, and Francis's pearls are very fitting.'

Ferelith smiled acknowledgement of the tribute and led them into the salon where the other guests were already assembled. Major Melverley had extended his original modest suggestion by one couple. Mr Pepys was a relatively recent acquaintance and his associations, which were with the civil arm of the Navy, made him more closely acquainted with the Durlistons through whom he had been introduced to the major. Mrs Durliston and Mrs Pepys knew each other well but Ferelith's self-imposed seclusion since the death of her husband meant that she had never met either the husband or his wife before. Mrs Pepys seemed a pleasant enough woman, though Ferelith suspected she must find her husband something of a tribulation: he had gazed into Ferelith's eyes a little too deeply and had held on to her hand a little too long to permit his hostess to feel entirely at her ease in his company.

Conversation was general and desultory until the second course was on the table.

'Tell me, Major,' Mr Pepys began, helping himself to a generous portion of squab pie as he spoke, 'how do you find your retirement?'

'A trifle irksome now that the novelty has worn off,' the major admitted. 'I listen to Colonel Dean here and sometimes I itch to be back in that particular saddle.'

His guest nodded. 'My own retirement is of too recent a date for that feeling to have surfaced yet, but I don't doubt it will. For the time being I'm content with the coffee-houses but too much political converse will soon have me wishing I could be back in the thick of it.'

'Were you a politician?' Ferelith asked, surprised. 'Forgive me—I had thought you were a civilian servant of the Crown.'

'As I was, my dear, as I was. However, Secretary to the Admiralty is a post that gives one the ear of the politicians and, while that can be a most frustrating situation—particularly when they don't listen—it can also be very useful. Either way, it gives one the feeling of being very close to the shaping of events and that is the element I fancy I shall come to miss.'

Mr Durliston robustly declared that he couldn't see himself in retirement at all. 'I should sit at home biting my nails to the quick, totally convinced that no one would run my business as well as I did, and longing to interfere.'

Colonel Dean and Captain Spelsbury were of much the same mind.

'The Army becomes a way of life,' the latter said, 'and, now that King Charles seems tacitly to have accepted the need for a standing army, it has become an area in which one may build a good career.'

'The major is an experienced officer and a great deal younger than I,' Mr Pepys commented. 'I'm sure that if he desired to return he would have little difficulty in obtaining a commission, though not necessarily in his old regiment.'

Major Melverley hastened to disclaim any ambitions in that direction and the conversation returned to the general.

Ferelith found the evening a strain, but only because she had been unused to social gatherings for so long. Accustomed as she had been all her life to hearing important matters discussed and to being allowed to add her contribution without invoking scorn even when her ideas had been immature or impractical, she had enjoyed converse which, while far from deep, had ranged beyond the price of mutton and the unreliability of younger servants these days.

When their guests had gone, she and her father enjoyed a final cup of chocolate in the small parlour at the back of the house.

'I don't think you will be sorry to see your bed tonight,' Major Melverley commented shrewdly.

'It becomes more appealing by the minute,' his daughter replied. 'That need not be a reason for not entertaining again: I'm tired but I have also enjoyed this evening. The company made me forget my own sorrows for a few hours. I feel almost guilty at admitting that Francis has not dominated my mind this evening, but I must admit to feeling the better for it.'

'I'm glad. Oh, I've no desire to encourage you to forget your husband. You never will—and never would, even had you not married for love. But sooner or later you do have to move him to one side a little so that you have space in which to go on living. I think for you that time has come and I'm glad to see it. I was beginning to worry about you.'

'Perhaps it's I who should be worrying about you, Papa,' she said. 'I know you left the Army mainly on my account. I've been so wrapped up in myself that I've never stopped to think that perhaps you would rather still be a soldier. Would you wish to return to Army life if the opportunity arose?'

'I gave it up willingly enough. There's no need for you to blame yourself on my behalf. To tell you the truth, I had envisaged the delights of the life of a gentleman of leisure without appreciating that when one is unaccustomed to a disproportionate amount of leisure its appeal tends to wear thin. I like to be doing; I'm accustomed to it, and, yes, time does occasionally hang heavy. The answer is undoubtedly to find something with which to occupy it and, now that I perceive you to be less intensely wrapped in your natural grief, I shall pursue more active steps in that direction.'

'Are you inclined to take up Mr Pepys's suggestion of returning to the Army?' Ferelith asked.

Her father considered it for some while. 'No, I don't think so,' he said at last. 'There's no denying I've a fondness for the life, but I don't think one should try to retrace one's steps. Better by far to move on to something else.' He leant forward and patted her hand. 'Don't you worry about it, at all events. I shall hit upon something.'

In the ensuing months Ferelith gave little further thought to her father's words. She gradually assumed more positively than hitherto the role in her father's household that she had occupied prior to her marriage. She made a conscious decision not to return to the home she and Francis had set up together: it was too lonely and the memories that thrust themselves at her from every room were too recent for her to feel inclined to live among them just yet. So the house continued to be let and Ferelith became once more as much her father's housekeeper as his hostess. By degrees she resumed the role in society that her position expected of her, and if she suspected that the inclusion by both her father and her parents-in-law in their invitations of unattached and therefore by definition eligible men of various ages and conditions had an ulterior motive, she gave no sign of it. She gave such gentlemen no encouragement, either, and did so to such effect that even those who felt within themselves the stirring of an interest soon proved disinclined to pursue the matter.

She was embroidering one afternoon by a fire of sea-coal when her father came into the parlour and hovered as if he had something to say but wasn't at all sure how to start. Ferelith gave him a minute or two and then looked up, smiling.

'Won't you sit down, Papa? You look most uncomfortable and it is your house, after all.'

'I'm not disturbing you?' He sounded anxious.

'Not at all: needlework is something one can pick up or lay down at will. One can also ply a needle and hold an intelligent conversation at the same time. Is that what you want to do? Talk?'

'Well, yes, there is a matter I wanted to raise,' the major said, perching on the edge of an ornately carved chair in a way which looked extremely uncomfortable.

Ferelith expected that statement to be followed by an exposition of what it was he had wanted to say, but nothing seemed to be forthcoming.

'And what is that, Papa?' she asked helpfully, wondering what it could be that was so serious that her normally articulate father was lost for words.

'I wonder if you recall a conversation we had some time ago?' he began and then stopped again.

'Quite possibly,' Ferelith said, trying to keep a hint of sharpness out of her voice. She found it unnerving to have her father so obviously unsure of the reception his words were likely to have. 'Perhaps if you were to pinpoint more precisely which conversation you had in mind I could more accurately tell you if I recalled it.'

Major Melverley smiled wryly. 'Your mother had just such a sharp turn of phrase on occasion,' he said. 'She always said it went with the hair. You're right, of course—I'm hedging. It was a conversation we had when the guests had gone on that occasion when Mr and Mrs Pepys were here. About the Army and whether I regretted having resigned.'

Ferelith's needle was plied with a little less vigour. 'I remember it very well, though perhaps not the precise words. I formed the impression that you didn't regret it, precisely, though you were feeling the lack, but that, having taken the decision to leave, it would be unwise to consider trying to resume a military career. Would you agree with that summary?'

'Faultless,' her father admitted.

'Let me guess, Papa,' Ferelith went on, seeing that he had hesitated once more. 'You have changed your mind since then. You are now inclined to rejoin General Monk.'

'Not exactly.'

' "Not exactly"? Surely, Papa, you either repurchase your commission or you don't. I can't see how there can be any ambivalence about it.'

'My attention has been drawn to the fact that my experience as an officer in an infantry regiment could be extremely useful in certain circumstances, and it has been suggested that an application to join a regiment of foot could be very well received, given a recommendation from the right quarter. But it wouldn't be my old regiment.'

Ferelith looked at him in amazement. 'Why? Won't they have you?'

'No, no, nothing like that,' he assured her hastily. 'I haven't even approached them. This suggestion came from Mr Pepys, who is himself prepared to recommend me.'

'But he is—or was—Admiralty!' Ferelith exclaimed. 'Will his word carry much weight in Army circles?'

'Don't underestimate Mr Pepys,' her father warned. 'In this particular case I think his opinion, placed in the right ear, will be all that's needed. There is a strong Naval connection, you see.'

'No,' Ferelith said baldly. 'I don't.'

'He has in mind the Tangier Regiment of Foot,' Major Melverley said apologetically.

'That ill-paid, ill-disciplined rabble!' Ferelith had given up all pretence at embroidering. 'Who is their present commander?'

'Piercey Kirke—and it's hardly the regiment's fault if their pay doesn't arrive on time,' her father pointed out. 'If it did, I dare say their discipline would improve a hundredfold overnight.'

'By all accounts, it has need to,' Ferelith said bluntly. 'Kirke's lambs! Do you see yourself as one of that flock, Papa?'

'I never have done,' her father conceded, 'but you must admit it offers a challenge.'

'Indeed, it does! A challenge offered by a combination of no pay, inadequate and foreign food, incomprehensible customs and a number of diseases none of which you are likely to encounter in this country. Is that the sort of challenge you had in mind?'

'I was thinking more of the challenge of instilling a little discipline despite the problems,' he told her. 'Couple that with the satisfaction of humbling the Moors and there would be a job well done—and well rewarded by His Majesty when we returned.'

'Papa, you delude yourself. Tangier has been ours for...what? Twenty years? Since Queen Catherine brought it with her as part of her dowry. Perhaps it is longer than that. I know very little about it, of course, but I have gathered that the Moors do not welcome our presence; that the city is in a more or less permanent state of siege from the landward side and that we are no further forward in securing it than we were when the Portuguese parted with it.'

'That's all very true, my dear, but there are compensating factors. The climate is said to be delightful—neither too hot nor too cold, though it does rain quite heavily in the autumn, and the garrison is supplied from the sea without too much difficulty. The harbour has always presented something of a problem, being far from ideal in its natural state, but the building of a mole is almost complete and that will provide a safe anchorage that will make a world of difference.'

'You mean the pirates that are said to abound in those waters will only be able to attack ships as they approach and leave?' she said sarcastically.

'Privateers,' he corrected her. 'Or corsairs. Not pirates. It means that we could keep a sufficiently strong fleet at Tangier to patrol the waters on either side of the Straits of Gibraltar and thus protect our merchant shipping.'

'Then why wasn't the mole built before?'

'Money,' he said succinctly.

'By which you mean the lack of it. Presumably the same lack which leaves its soldiers unpaid for months on end. Papa, do you really want to go?'

Major Melverley shifted uneasily. 'I know it sounds most unpromising, but it also sounds rather exciting, and excitement is something that's noticeably lacking in civilian life. Oh, I'm not going to be able to change the habits of a regiment. I know that. All the same, I should enjoy trying and if there is substantial prize-money at the end of it all, so much the better. Yes, I think that, on balance, I should like to go.'

Ferelith looked at him in some surprise. 'Then why the hesitation, Papa? If that's what you want to do, then you must do it. How can you doubt that?'

'I think you have perhaps missed the point,' he said ruefully. 'The question isn't really whether I want to go. It's whether you wish to accompany me.'

'To Tangier? Is it a suitable place for a woman?'

'Probably not,' he told her cheerfully. 'That hasn't prevented most of the officers' families accompanying them. Colonel Kirke's wife is there, I know. The houses are said to be charming and with pleasant gardens, though in the Portuguese style, naturally, not the English, and the city itself is well protected behind its wall, so the families are perfectly safe.' He hesitated, as if unsure how to broach some other consideration. 'I've no wish to put undue pressure on you, Frithy, and I know the Durlistons would be happy to have you live with them if you prefer to stay here, but it has crossed my mind that it might be a very good thing for you to have a few months—maybe even a year or two—in completely different surroundings.'

Both his voice and the light in his eyes told Ferelith that her father was indeed excited by the prospect that had been offered. She was less sure. His career had never before taken him away from England and he could no more have a real appreciation of the implications than she had herself. She probably had the power of dissuading him but it would be the height of selfishness to do so, especially in view of the fact that he had given up his career in the first place for her sake.

She was not obliged to go with him and he would entirely understand if she decided to stay, but if she did what would life hold for her? No doubt her father was right when he said the Durlistons would be happy to have her live with them, but she was accustomed to being mistress of her house and would find it very difficult to become a permanent guest. She could remain behind, in either her father's house or her own and in Annie she had a chaperon of sorts, but she would be able only to entertain women similarly placed to herself; she would have no opportunity of mixing with society in any broader sense, though probably the Durlistons would take pity on her and invite her from time to time.

No, life would suddenly become unacceptably narrow, and just when she was beginning to enjoy it again. Besides, Tangier would be an adventure and a part of her was beginning to long for something a little more exciting than the life she was currently living. She felt guilty for feeling like that because so many people had gone out of their way to help her through a difficult time, but she was an honest woman and had to admit the feeling was there.

'Yes, Papa,' she said. 'I think I'd very much like to come too.'

CHAPTER TWO

FERELITH began to regret her decision when the *Pelican* entered the Bay of Biscay. She had been congratulating herself on proving to be a born sailor, feeling none of the indisposition experienced by some of the other passengers. The savage waters of the Bay soon demolished that conceit and, as the ship dipped and rose while simultaneously rolling from side to side, the decks periodically disappearing under great swathes of sea-water, she formed the opinion that death, provided it was quick, was infinitely preferable. Major Melverley was no less incommoded and they were both grateful for the news that the planned two or three days' anchorage in Lisbon would have to be extended to enable repairs to be carried out as well as replenishing the stocks of fresh water, fruit and meat.

When they stepped on to the jetty, Ferelith had the disconcerting sensation that it, like the skiff that had ferried them from the *Pelican*, was rising to meet her, and it was several minutes before the sensation steadied down to an occasional quiet undulation, thus enabling the major and his daughter to walk without each other's support.

'I'm not sure what image we must present, my dear,' the major commented. 'I feel as if I'm drunk; I hope I look nothing worse than foolish.'

'No one seems to be taking a great deal of notice,' Ferelith replied. 'Perhaps they are so accustomed to seeing people in our condition that it no longer attracts attention.'

There were certainly plenty of people about. The harbour was prosperous and bustled with life, all of it looking very strange to Ferelith, especially since much of the labouring work seemed to be carried out by black slaves who had, they were told, been brought back to Portugal from its dominions in the New World. The harbour was haven to boats from all over the maritime world and the faces, the languages and the clothes seemed very strange indeed to someone who, although she had lived in London most of her life, had never ventured into those parts of the city that fed the docks. It was hot, too. Hotter than Ferelith had imagined, and she was grateful for the breeze that blew in from the ocean. Major Melverley told her that they were a little past the halfway mark on their journey, and she wondered how tolerable the heat of Tangier would prove to be.

Away from the harbour area, the streets were as narrow and twisting as those of London and even more crowded with a milling, shouting throng, all the more bewildering because she could understand nothing that was said. She was, however, fascinated by the wares on offer and in particular by such fruits as oranges and lemons being sold here as cheaply as apples and pears at home. She bought a quantity of the former and a beautifully woven basket to put them in and then spotted a woman selling remarkably fine linen.

'I shan't be a moment, Papa,' she said, turning aside to examine the cloth. A narrower, crowded lane opened behind the linen-seller and Ferelith realised that this woman was just the first of many. In no time, she was in her element, turning over linen and lawn, lace and embroidery, and exclaiming over each new discovery so that she, in her turn became the centre of an interested audience. She did not, however, have any money with her, the major having taken the precaution of secreting it about his person where it would at least have the protection of a sword and a soldier's arm, and when she looked around to ask him for the wherewithal to buy the item on which she had finally determined, he was nowhere to be seen.

'Papa...? Papa!' she called. She looked this way and that but there was no sign of him. Surely it had been only a few moments ago that she had spoken to him? It was easy to understand how they could have become separated but how could he have disappeared so completely in such a short time? Nevertheless, he had undoubtedly disappeared and now that it became apparent that she had wasted everybody's time by selecting goods for which she lacked the means to pay, the mood of the crowd around her changed. Instead of giggles and conspiratorial nudges, there were low, ugly murmurs and frowning brows and she felt people plucking at her cloak as if searching for something of value hidden in its folds which would be acceptable in place of silver. The worst thing about it was that she was quite unable to explain the situation or to understand precisely what was being said, although she could form a shrewd idea of its gist. She glanced back to where she thought she had entered the lane and found she was about halfway along it and had turned this way and that so many times in examining the goods thrust at her that she was not entirely sure from which end she had entered it. Of her father there was still no sign whatever.

By now Ferelith was really frightened. She needed to get away from here as quickly as she could and must take a gamble as to which end of the lane to head for. She handed the lace she had hoped to purchase resolutely back to its vendor with a firm, 'I'm awfully sorry but I'm afraid I really don't have any money with me at all,' and turned to walk in as determined a manner as she could in her chosen direction.

The crowd was not letting her go that easily. The lace-seller shouted abuse at her in tones which made Ferelith privately very grateful that she couldn't understand a word, and the lace-seller had the sympathy of the crowd. Ferelith guessed they were waiting for her to display the first sign of overt fear and she suspected that it would not be long before she did so. A burly man placed himself squarely in front of her, blocking her path. He said something incomprehensible to Ferelith but obviously approved of by the mob, and drew a wickedly gleaming knife from its sheath at his waist. There was nothing incomprehensible about that gesture, she thought.

The only item of any value was the betrothal ring she wore beneath her gloves. It was the last thing from which she wanted to be parted but it began to look as if it was the only thing that would extricate her from this increasingly ugly situation.

At the precise moment that she decided it would have to be sacrificed, she was aware that the crowd behind her was falling back—or, at least, pressing forward less determinedly—and the burly man's attention had been diverted to a point just over her shoulder. Assuming Major Melverley had found her, Ferelith turned with a smile of relief but it faded almost before it had flowered.

By comparison with the burly individual, the newcomer seemed slight. He was neither particularly tall nor particularly broad though he somehow conveyed an impression of suppressed strength. He did not look like a Portuguese either in his dress or his physiognomy. To be sure, his hair was black and somewhat curled but his skin was much lighter than that of those he confronted. His eyes were disconcertingly pale—hazel, Ferelith thought, though it was difficult to be sure without staring. He wore a long, loose robe, the hood of which was thrown back, and Ferelith put his age at about thirty. He might not look like a Portuguese, but he appeared to be fluent in the language.

'There is a problem, *madame*?' he said in heavily accented English.

Ferelith's feeling of relief returned. At least she would now be able to make herself understood. She smiled—more than a little tremulously. 'Thank goodness you speak English,' she said. 'You will be able to explain to these people. I set out with my father who, for safety's sake, has all our money with him. When I turned down this little lane, I somehow became parted from him but I didn't realise that until I had decided what to buy and turned to where I assumed he must be for the wherewithal. When it became obvious that I had, in effect, been wasting these people's time, they became angry. I should like to apologise and be allowed to go on my way but I speak no Portuguese.'

The man nodded and Ferelith had the uncomfortable idea that he was laughing at her. Be that as it may, he spoke rapidly to the assembled crowd, apparently relaying Ferelith's words because some of them threw up their hands in exasperation while others nodded knowingly. By the time he had finished most of them had drifted away in search of more certain excitements and her rescuer turned back to her with a small bow.

'And now for you, *madame*. We must reunite you with your father. Since you do not know where he is, the best solution would perhaps be to return you to the place at which you are staying.'

Ferelith smiled ruefully. 'An excellent idea, sir. Unfortunately I have no idea in which direction that might be.'

He held both his hands out sideways and shrugged. 'No problem, *madame*. Give me the address and together we shall find it.'

'We're passengers on the *Pelican*,' Ferelith told him. 'I'm sure Papa will return there when he realises he has mislaid me.'

She thought he cast her a sharpened glance at mention of the ship's name but all he said was, 'Then it becomes a simple matter to return you to him. You won't object if I accompany you?'

'Certainly not,' Ferelith assured him warmly. 'I shall be most grateful for your escort.'

The stranger had an air of the sort of authority that made its way through the throng of buyers, sellers and onlookers with nothing more than a tap on the shoulder here and a small bow there and, somewhat to Ferelith's surprise, they were very soon back on the quayside with the *Pelican* ahead of them.

'And I thought I was miles away from here!' Ferelith exclaimed.

'I expect you merely miscalculated the length of time you had spent turning over merchandise rather than walking,' her escort suggested.

'I think you may be right,' Ferelith laughed. 'However, I should never have found it on my own, much less extricated myself from that crowd whose mood was rapidly becoming ugly. For that I must thank you.' She caught sight of a familiar figure looking out over the wharf from the *Pelican*'s deck. The figure simultaneously saw her and waved energetically before running down the gangway to meet her. 'There's Papa,' she went on. 'I know he will wish to add his thanks to mine.' She waved to acknowledge Major Melverley and turned to introduce her escort.

There was no sign of him. One minute he had been standing so close behind her that she could feel his warmth; the next he had vanished as completely as had her father earlier on. Her gaze scoured the dockside crowds but there was no trace of the robed stranger and she felt disproportionately sorry that he had gone so suddenly. Why, she didn't even know his name!

Because the *Pelican* was carrying victuals and armaments for the Tangier garrison as well as a few replacement officers and men, the ambassador felt it appropriate, in view of the ship's extended stay, to entertain the higher-ranking officers to what he described as 'a modest banquet in the Portuguese style'.

Ferelith studied the invitation with amusement. 'I wonder it didn't occur to His Excellency that there is a degree of inconsistency between "modest" and "banquet",' she remarked.

The major frowned and tut-tutted. 'Keep such observations to yourself, Frithy,' he rebuked her. 'Those in exalted positions do not customarily appreciate having their inconsistencies pointed out to them.'

'Papa, I'm really not so foolish as to say such a thing to the ambassador himself,' Ferelith protested.

'I'm sure you're not, but if you should make such a remark to someone else you might find it repeated either by its recipient or by someone who happened to overhear it. Do, please, be careful.'

'Very well, Papa, I promise to be suitably subdued—but perhaps you can advise me whether to dress to the "modest" or the "banquet"?'

The major smiled wryly. 'I think it would be wise to assume that when the ambassador describes it as "modest", he is being deliberately self-deprecating. I very much doubt whether it will be any such thing.'

Major Melverley was entirely correct, and as they ascended the steps of the embassy and entered a banqueting hall ablaze with candles Ferelith was heartily glad to have gone to the trouble of extricating from her trunks one of her more magnificent gowns. The richly brocaded silk damask was in one of the shades of green that Ferelith knew set off her hair to its best advantage and, instead of following the current fashion for pearls, she chose to pick up the auburn tints with a collar of Baltic amber, from the centre of which depended that huge polished amber pear-drop, imprisoned within which for all time lay a delicately winged insect. Smaller drops of clear amber hung from her ears and Ferelith did not need the mirrored walls of the banqueting hall to tell her she presented a striking picture. She recalled that it was not so very long ago that she had abjured such worldly vanity and she felt briefly guilty that she had slipped back into such considerations with remarkable ease. She knew that it did not mean she loved Francis any the less, but she was more than a little afraid that that was how others might interpret it. It was some comfort to be able to remind herself that there was small likelihood of anyone present being aware of her changed appearance.

The ambassador and his lady stood at the top of the magnificent staircase greeting their guests and assuring them that it was really quite an informal little get-together with perhaps some dancing later on for those who were of a mind for it. Ferelith guessed that His Excellency's use of "informal" might be comparable to his use of "modest". She was soon proved right, and privately concluded that if this was a banquet in the Portuguese style it differed very little from those she was used to. There was rather more plate, that was all.

She took her allotted place and glanced across the table as she did so to see who was seated opposite. It was an elderly man—a Portuguese, she guessed—and his wife, but she noticed no more than that, for her attention was drawn to the footman guiding his chair. She had no idea what made her notice the servant—except in one's own home, one regarded them in much the same light as the wall-hangings or the furniture: essential for one's comfort but only meriting comment if they failed to be there. Perhaps this one had been staring at her until his attention had been needed elsewhere. Whatever the reason, she found herself looking at him sharply and when, his immediate task concluded, he too glanced up, she recognised the man who had come to her rescue in the street of linen-merchants. She was puzzled. There had been nothing of the servant in his manner on that occasion. On the contrary, he had had all the hallmarks of one accustomed to being obeyed, and so great was the contrast in his manner that she frowned. Perhaps she had been mistaken. The hint of a smile told her that she was not and that he had recognised her. Ferelith looked for her father. The major had been unable to thank the stranger for his kindness and she was anxious that he should have an opportunity to do so. But Major Melverley had been seated several places further down the table and when she glanced back at the footman opposite she found him still regarding her, this time with an infinitesimal shake of the head, as if he had read her mind.

Ferelith tried to give her full attention to the guests on either side of her but she knew her responses to their courteous enquiries about her voyage and her initial impressions of Lisbon sounded vague and unsatisfactory and suspected that, had they not been compelled by circumstance to maintain a conversation, they would have drifted away to find more forthcoming company. A part of her attention remained very conscious of the footman opposite and she began to wonder whether her earlier assessment of him as a leader was attributable to nothing more than her own gratitude for his timely arrival. She could not delude herself that he was anything other than a perfect footman: unobtrusively attentive and subservient without being servile. Surely only a man trained in domestic service from an early age could execute the task so admirably?

When the banquet was finally over, the doors to an adjacent room were flung open and the guests invited to enter. Here a small orchestra played for those who wished to dance, while others could take advantage of the opportunity to circulate and converse. Ferelith noted with some relief that the long windows leading into the warm night air were open. The combined heat of so many people and so many candles had meant that she had risen from the table feeling a little unwell. The soft breeze blowing in from the sea quickly cleared the muzziness from her head and she was conversing quite animatedly with the ambassador's daughter when Major Melverley joined her.

After exchanging pleasantries with Lady Margaret, he turned to his daughter. 'Would you mind very much, Frithy, my dear, if I made the most of this opportunity to find out what I can about the situation in Tangier? There are several people here with more up-to-date information than was available when we left home, but I would not want you to feel neglected.'

Ferelith laughed. 'That's not very likely, Papa. No, you talk to whomever you need to. I'm entirely happy as I am—there's really no need to give me a second thought until you want to return to the *Pelican*.'

'You won't hesitate to let me know if you decide you're ready to return before I am?'

'Not for one second.'

With that assurance, the major left her to pick Lady Margaret's greater experience as to which of the city's impressive warehouses was the most satisfactory to deal with.

Ferelith declined, without too much reluctance, two or three invitations to dance. She was not yet ready to discard all remnants of her grief, though naturally this was not an explanation she offered to the young officers who asked her, and, when she found herself briefly without a conversational partner, she moved quietly over to the long windows and peered out, enjoying the fresh breeze and waiting for her eyes to become accustomed to the darkness.

'If *madame* wished to walk on the terrace, I shall be happy to safeguard her,' said a familiar voice behind her.

She turned quickly, an uncertain half-smile on her lips. An English footman would never have said such a thing, but this was not England.

'And beyond the terrace?' she asked.

'A formal garden. Very Portuguese, they say, but they err. It is entirely Moorish.'

'Then, since I'm on my way to Tangier, I ought to see it, don't you think?' she replied lightly. She was more than ever sure that this was a conversation which should not be taking place but he had already proved himself a reliable escort and she would much rather see the garden than make social chit-chat.

The footman bowed and guided her in the most unexceptionable manner over the low sill. The terrace was wide, and because every room in the embassy was ablaze with light the formal parterre below was well illuminated.

'Will *madame* venture further?' he asked.

'*Madame* would love to,' Ferelith replied and they made their way down the shallow, gently curving flight of steps to the garden below. 'Why should you consider the garden to be Moorish rather than Portuguese?' she asked, privately considering that, apart from the use of fountains, it did not differ greatly from similar formal gardens in England.

'Did you not know that Portugal, like most of Spain, was once part of a huge Moorish empire? These gardens were one of the legacies left behind.'

Ferelith had not known that and said so, allowing herself to be guided along the intricate paths, the rustle of her skirts echoing the sound of gently falling water. She realised that there must be a high wall round the garden because there was no hint here of the sea-breeze that had cooled the embassy salons.

Her guess was vindicated when they reached the end of the garden. Their way was no longer illuminated from the embassy but the moon, though only at the crescent, was unobscured by clouds and gave enough light to cause Ferelith not to notice the lack of a torch-bearer. Her escort reached up to one of the espaliered branches that disguised the harsh lines of the wall and brought down a peach. From somewhere beneath his servant's jacket, he produced a curved knife, its glinting blade barbarously efficient. Ferelith did not need to test its edge to know that this was no ceremonial ornament and it crossed her mind briefly to wonder what sort of footman it was who wore such a weapon on duty.

He slit the peach and detached a segment. 'Here, *madame*,' he said. 'Open your mouth.'

Ferelith did as she was bid and the slice, luscious and dripping with juice, slipped down her throat almost before she had time to close her teeth on it. The next piece she made sure she bit in half first and, as she did so, she felt the juice on her skin. She held out her hand.

'Perhaps I should feed myself?' she suggested.

The footman laughed. 'No, *madame*. When they are as ripe as this, they need expert handling. You would ruin your gown,' and he pre-empted any further protest by feeding her the next slice. She took it without further comment and when the last piece had been swallowed she was laughingly grateful for the care with which he wiped her chin and her lips almost, but not quite, as he might have done had she been a child, one finger holding her chin up while the other wiped away the juice with a fine linen handkerchief.

This, Ferelith knew, was not the way footmen customarily behaved. She told herself that this was Portugal, where things might well be different, but she knew that was self-delusion.

His action made her feel suddenly both vulnerable and cherished, feelings she had not experienced for a long time and, as she stared up into his eyes, she was entirely unaware that the yearning she felt but had not yet acknowledged even to herself was revealed in her eyes to anyone with the wit to see it. He paused briefly when his self-appointed task was complete, and frowned a little. Then he bent down and kissed her briefly, gently, on her upturned lips.

Ferelith eyes widened in genuine surprise but, although she knew she should at the very least immediately demand to be taken back to the reception and perhaps even to strike him for his impertinence, she did neither. Footman notwithstanding, there was something in his manner which precluded any charge of impertinence, and she suddenly had no wish to return to the others.

It was the footman himself who dictated her next move. He took her gently by the arm. 'Come, *madame*, I must return you to your compatriots. They will be wondering what has befallen you.'

'My father may be worried. I doubt whether anyone else will have noticed my absence,' she told him.

'Then we must allay your father's anxieties.' He hesitated before continuing. '*Madame*, is it imperative that you go to Tangier?'

'My father has taken up a commission there.'

'I know that, but must you accompany him? Can you not return to England?'

A brief, irrational hope that he had been going to ask her to remain in Lisbon flickered into life and died. 'I suppose I could, but we are both agreed that the change of scene will be beneficial to me.'

'Tangier is under more or less constant siege,' he pointed out. 'That can hardly be considered a beneficial atmosphere for a lady.'

'I understand there are plenty of ladies already with the garrison. I imagine life there may well be more restricted than it is at home, but it will at least be different.'

He bowed. 'I can't deny that,' he said. 'Come, before you catch a chill.'

He accompanied her to the terrace and Ferelith was conscious—very conscious—of his hand guiding her back through the tall window, but when she turned to thank him there was no sign of him. He had vanished as completely as if he had never been there. The sense of loss was disproportionately great and during the rest of their brief stay in Lisbon it was as if, for Ferelith, the sun was in eclipse. Wherever they went, whatever they did, she found herself constantly looking for the lean figure with its dark hair and hazel eyes, but there was no sign of him at all.

CHAPTER THREE

FERELITH studied the city before her. That was to say, she studied the vast grey walls surging up from the ocean bed and topped with ornate crenellations so different from the plain and functional ones on similar fortifications in England. She had seen this style before, though, in Lisbon, and she wondered how much more of the Portuguese way of doing things would have survived the city's change of ownership.

Once they had left the Portuguese capital, the lookouts had been doubled and the atmosphere on board had become increasingly tense as they moved into the waters where privateers were said to abound. A sail on the horizon was the signal for gun-ports to be opened and they remained so even when the ship had been identified as belonging to a friendly power. Privateers were not above sailing under a flag to which they owed no allegiance if, by doing so, they could lull likely quarry into an entirely false sense of security.

She had learnt the difference between privateers and corsairs on the one hand and pirates on the other and, although her fellow passengers seemed to set great store by the difference, Ferelith privately thought it was a matter of pure semantics, since both varieties seemed equally undesirable. Privateers and corsairs were licensed by their ruler to pillage and plunder on the high seas and were obliged to hand over a proportion of their prizes to that ruler and another percentage to the church or mosque, depending upon the faith of their country. The only exceptions to this rule of thumb were the Maltese corsairs who were licensed by the Knights of St John, but in other respects operated under all the same restrictions relating to ships of friendly nations, and the complications that arose when the ship was of friendly origin but some of the cargo or some of the passengers were not—and vice versa. Pirates were licensed by no one and shared their spoils with none save their own crew. This might have been expected to make piracy the more attractive pursuit, but it meant that there were no harbours where they could expect guaranteed sanctuary and they were therefore much more vulnerable.

The corsairs of the Mediterranean were restricted by the shores of that sea, rarely venturing into the Atlantic, but the privateers of the Barbary coast, and in particular the notorious Sally rovers, had no such limitations. The great port of the Moorish privateers was Sallé and from here they ventured even as far as Iceland and had on occasion tackled the treacherous waters off Ireland and Cornwall.

It was no wonder that merchantmen and men-of-war alike kept a sharp watch out for them and Ferelith almost wished they had encountered one on the voyage. Almost, but not quite: she had no wish to spend the rest of her life a prisoner of some Moorish king and that, since she could think of no relative who was likely to pay a substantial ransom for her, would be her most likely fate. No, upon reflection, she was quite glad that the Bay of Biscay had offered the sum total of excitement on the voyage.

Several ships rode at anchor in the shelter provided by the unfinished mole, and while their own vessel was manoeuvred into a favourable position Ferelith passed the time watching an army of labourers toiling to tip baskets of stone into the sea at the end and sides of the steadily lengthening arm. Many of them were soldiers but there were plenty of civilian workers of indisputably European origin and almost as many who seemed to be Moors. This puzzled Ferelith, who had been expecting to find the city prohibited to what she, as an Army daughter, thought of as 'the enemy'. There were two substantial sentry-posts along its length in addition to the temporary buildings where some of the workforce lived and a flotilla of small boats—bum-boats, Ferelith supposed, though their shape differed from those she had seen in English harbours—crowded round the ship as it made its way cautiously past the new mole towards the remains of the old, beyond which would be found the most convenient anchorage.

The bum-boats were manned by Moors, or so Ferelith assumed from their fairly uniform manner of dressing, their physical appearance being very varied indeed. Some looked more like the black pageboys who were currently essential accessories to the more fashionable elements of English society; some had the olive skin and hawk-like features of the Arab, and some came into neither category, combining the aquiline handsomeness of the Arab with disconcertingly hazel eyes that seemed at variance with their black hair. These reminded her inescapably of the embassy footman and she wondered whether he had originated here.

As one of the besieging boats, larger than most and carrying a lateen sail as well as a considerable number of oarsmen, drew alongside, she saw something that made her feel as if the deck had suddenly disappeared from beneath her feet. Several men stood along the deck of the smaller vessel waving items they presumably wished to sell, though Ferelith could make out nothing of what they shouted. There were lengths of cloth, bowl-shaped baskets of dates, leather slippers and strings of beads that she took to be amber. But immediately beneath her and gazing straight up at her, the hood of his *djellabah* having slipped from his dark hair, was none other than the footman from Lisbon. The intensity of his hazel eyes had taken her attention, drawing her green ones to them, and she knew he had recognised her. Indeed, since he had been aware of her ultimate destination, he must have been expecting to see her.

Their eyes locked and held and continued to hold even as the *felucca* moved away in response to the shouts of *'Imshi, imshi!'* from those seamen who had picked up a few Arabic phrases in the course of their careers, and the total lack of response to their attempts to sell merchandise.

Ferelith watched them go, disturbed by the encounter. There was no doubting their mutual recognition, yet he had not spoken—indeed, had given no sign. Was it possible that she was mistaken? That he was just a stranger who bore a remarkable likeness to that other man? She dismissed the possibility. She was not—could not be—mistaken. His presence here raised all sorts of questions, not least among them that of whether he had come here simply to pursue their acquaintance. It was an appealing theory but Ferelith was honest enough to accept that it was the least probable, even though she could formulate no better ones to take its place. Whatever had brought him here, the encounter had been a disconcerting one. It was best put out of her mind. Accordingly, she moved to the other side of the ship and took a very concentrated interest in the techniques of seamanship and in the approaching city.

The city road rose up from the harbour in a straight line across the foreshore and through the gate into the city itself. This was situated on steadily rising ground so that the green and terracotta tiles of the pitched Portuguese roofs could be clearly made out. Ferelith found the sight of pitched roofs surprisingly comforting, simply because they seemed less strange than the flat ones she had observed distantly as they neared the Barbary coast.

Despite its city status, Tangier was, so far as Ferelith could judge, no larger than a small country town in England. If she was correct, then it would also share the characteristic whereby everyone not only knew everyone else, but was acquainted in some depth with everyone else's business. The accuracy of her judgement was confirmed when they were finally rowed ashore with their baggage, and the first man Major Melverley stopped with a request to be taken to Colonel Kirke glanced from him to his daughter and said, 'Ah, you'll be the one they've taken a house for just off the marketplace, across from the Head Court of Guard. Do you want a guide?'

Rightly interpreting this as indicating that, if he did, he'd have to pay for the privilege, Major Melverley fished in his pocket and found a sixpence, enough to buy a quart of wine at Tangerine prices. 'If you'll take the bags as well,' he said.

The man looked doubtful. 'Not on my own, I won't, and it'll not be safe to leave some of them sitting here to be fetched later. Tell you what, Major: double it in small change and I'll get a little caravan of bearers to follow us up.'

Major Melverley found another sixpennyworth of pence, ha'pennies and farthings and handed them to the man, who jingled them in his hand and called out to the world at large something that was quite unintelligible to Ferelith and her father.

No one else suffered from the same disability, it appeared, for in no time they were surrounded by shouting figures and grasping hands.

With a quick, 'You, you, you and you,' their guide selected some half-dozen would-be porters, allocated them trunks and chests and then led the procession through the streets to the two-storeyed, narrow-fronted house he said was theirs. A tattoo beaten on a neighbouring door produced the heavy iron key and, once they were inside and the baggage placed neatly just inside the door, the guide paid off the porters, leaving himself, Major Melverley noted, with a profit amounting to about half of the second sixpence. He didn't begrudge it, knowing that he would never have been able to organise the removal so quickly himself and that while he had been trying to much of their baggage might well have walked away of its own accord.

'Thank you, Mr...?' he began.

'Lew, sir. Corporal Lew. Think nothing of it. Happy to oblige.' With these words he managed a rough and ready salute and backed hurriedly out of the door.

'An obliging man,' Ferelith observed.

'Obliging? Nonsense. That was a man who hasn't been paid for twelve months and will go to almost any lengths to earn the wherewithal to stay alive.'

'That's as may be, Papa, but there's no denying he obliged us and I'll not be too churlish to acknowledge it.'

The house was a reasonable size but only sparsely furnished, a fact for which Ferelith felt they should probably be grateful, since neither the mattresses nor the bedding were as clean as she was accustomed to. One oddity which struck her at once was the absence of fireplaces, explained, no doubt, by the Moorish climate which was said to be infinitely warmer than that of England. Only in the kitchen was there a hearth but, search as she might, she could find no sign of a bread oven.

When her brief tour of discovery was over, she returned to the main saloon where her father was relaxing in a heavily carved chair. He looked up as she entered.

'How is everything? To your satisfaction, I hope? Do you know, I have the oddest sensation in this chair: it feels exactly as if I were still at sea.'

'I imagine a long sea-voyage is much like a long carriage-journey,' Ferelith said. 'At the end of it your head knows you've stopped moving but your senses tell you otherwise. As for the house, it will do very well but I advise you not to sleep on the mattress tonight. Tomorrow I'll try to get some fresh straw or—better still—some feathers. Otherwise we shall both of us be bitten to death. The bedclothes, too, are none too clean but soap and water will soon correct that.'

The major looked doubtful. 'Tangier is a city under virtual siege,' he told her. 'I shall be surprised if there is any straw available and I can't imagine feathers will be in very great evidence. We may have to make do with what we have.'

'Nonsense,' Ferelith told him briskly. 'There were chickens all over the place as we walked here. Some of them must be killed and eaten from time to time. There must be a supply of feathers even if we have to keep our own hens. There's a pleasant garden behind the kitchen. It's not large but I'm sure it could accommodate a hen-coop.'

Major Melverley forbore to point out that it would take the feathers from a sizeable flock to fill even one mattress, much less two, but, since his daughter must be as well aware of that as he, he guessed that she was deliberately taking an optimistic tone. 'So apart from that, you're quite happy?' he said.

'I think so, Papa. Just one thing puzzles me—there seems to be no bread oven. Do these people not eat bread?'

'They must do. Everyone does. Besides, bread is mentioned in the Bible so it must be known even though we're a long way from the Holy Land. The Spanish eat it, and they're only a few miles away. No, there must be bread. Tomorrow we must find ourselves some servants. Will you be able to manage in the meantime?'

Ferelith assured him she would: there was plenty of flour in the provisions they had brought with them and if he would but find some kindling she would produce some griddle-cakes.

In the event, neither was necessary. The key had been held by the wife of a captain and when Imelda Kilcummin judged her new neighbours had had time to find their way around their lodgings she knocked on the door.

'I dare say you're finding it all very strange,' she said. 'Patrick and I wondered whether you'd do us the honour of having supper with us. It won't be anything very grand, you understand,' she added hastily lest their expectations should reach too great a height, 'but it will be wholesome and hot, and fill you up.'

'We can ask no more than that,' Major Melverley told her. 'Ferelith, have you any objection?'

'None in the world, Papa. It's the answer to a prayer.'

The meal was certainly both hot and filling but Ferelith had reservations as to how wholesome it might be. Boiled salt beef should be so, of course, though it was hardly a great delicacy, especially when there was an after-taste about it that suggested it had been none too fresh when cooking began. It was accompanied by pease pudding and a vegetable that was not unlike turnip but which

Mrs Kilcummin told them was a local one called simnel.
There was only one other dish in this, the only course,
and that was a salad of oranges and spice which, delicious in itself, also cleansed the palate from the heav-
iness of the accompanying dishes.

'How difficult is it to live well here?' Ferelith asked.

Their hosts exchanged glances. 'It depends upon what
use you intend to make of your garden,' Captain
Kilcummin replied. 'Your private means have some
bearing on it, too. Those who are dependent upon their
pay have no option but to buy from the Army, because
credit is extended to them while they await their pay—
and that's most of the time. Unfortunately, the food that
is imported is chosen more with regard to the victuallers'
pockets than the men's needs, so we get salt beef and
pork, pease, oatmeal, ship's biscuit, weevily cheese and
rancid butter. They don't even send us the best: we once
had a consignment of salt beef that was three years old
when it left England. Add to that the fact that the soldiers' rations are calculated at fourteen ounces in the
pound instead of sixteen, and you'll realise that life is
very bad here for anyone dependent upon the Army for
survival.'

From the bitterness in his voice, Ferelith guessed that
he and his wife, despite his commissioned status, might
well come close to that category. It made the meal they
had just eaten all the more one to be appreciated. 'Do
you make use of your garden?' she asked.

'We have only a very small one,' Mrs Kilcummin told
her. 'It has one old orange tree in the middle, which we
cherish, and I grow some food in the spots that aren't
overshadowed by the tree: a few peas and beans, some
lettuce and cucumbers. Yours is much larger and you
have an olive tree and a fig. I hope you won't cut them
down.' She sounded wistful at the thought of such
bounty and Ferelith hastened to reassure her.

'Indeed, no! That would be a foolish thing to do!
Perhaps we may effect an exchange from time to time:
some of your oranges for some of our olives and figs?'

Mrs Kilcummin's face lit up. 'That would be marvellous. I'm afraid a lot of the soldiers do cut down the trees for firewood. So foolish when one considers that among them are also apricots, lemons, mulberries, limes and peaches—all that food sacrificed for a fire on which to cook salt pork!'

Her mention of fire reminded Ferelith of her kitchen's deficiency. 'We have no bread oven,' she said. 'Have you?'

Her hostess shook her head. 'It's not the custom. The housewife makes the bread each day and takes it along to the bakehouse in much the same way as they do in the poorer parts of London. Prick every loaf in a uniform pattern so that you can distinguish your bread from everyone else's. Have you brought no servants with you? You'll need a woman in the house and a man to do the heavy work—to till the garden and an allotment of land outside the city walls.'

'Is it possible to go outside them?' Ferelith asked, amazed. 'I assumed we would be restricted to the city itself.'

'You must walk on the ramparts tomorrow and then you'll understand,' the captain explained. 'We have a row of forts about a quarter of a mile beyond the walls and in that intervening space the enterprising grow crops either for their own use or for sale. There's hay in May and barley and wheat in June. Wild asparagus grows in the fields and calabashes and simnels are good substitutes for cabbages and turnips. The only hindrance is finding either the time to work the land yourself or the money to pay someone to do it for you.'

Since the Kilcummins clearly did not have such an allotment, the Melverleys correctly deduced that they had neither. The major tactfully changed the topic under discussion.

'We left our household, such as it is, behind,' he said. 'I told my daughter there should be no difficulty finding someone here. Perhaps some soldier's wife will welcome the chance of employment?'

Imelda Kilcummin sniffed. 'Quite possibly. Whether you would be pleased with the result is another matter. You would be better advised to go to the *bagno*—the barracks where captive Moors are kept pending their ransom—and see what you can find. They will only need to be fed during the day because they have to be returned to the *bagno* each night. It is possible to get special dispensation for them to stay with you, but it's rarely given. You should be able to find a maid for Mrs Durliston and a man to do the rest of the work.'

'Will such a captive be allowed to work outside the walls?'

'Oh, yes: the sentries on the forts keep a close watch on them.'

Ferelith and her father spent an uncomfortable night curled up on the floor of their respective rooms, wrapped in blankets they had brought with them and with only their own pillows to relieve the hardness beneath. Mrs Kilcummin had undertaken to escort Ferelith round the city on the morrow where, she said, clean straw would be more easily come by than clean feathers.

Little had struck Ferelith on the day of their arrival in Tangier other than an overall sense of the strangeness of the place. Now, the fatigue of the journey somewhat abated, she was better able to take in the sights and sounds, not to mention the smells, that assailed her from all sides.

Two things struck her in particular. The first was the sheer filth of the place. Imelda Kilcummin had advised her not to forget her wooden pattens and it was advice she was heartily glad to have followed. The streets were strewn with heaps of rotting refuse mingled with the discarded contents of chamber-pots, and among all this debris scurried some of the largest and healthiest rats Ferelith had ever seen.

She held her handkerchief to her nose. 'Is nothing ever done about this?' she asked.

'The citizens complained and a city scavenger was appointed to keep the streets clean but, as you see, he has had little effect.'

'Perhaps he should be given help. They could appoint some assistant scavengers,' Ferelith suggested.

'They could,' Imelda agreed, 'but if they spent as much time in the ale-house as their superior, I don't suppose any more would be achieved.'

The other thing that struck her, also through her nose, so that she wished there were some way of disentangling it from the stench of the streets, was the smell of spices. Accustomed as she was to spices being rare and expensive commodities to be kept in small containers under lock and key, Ferelith was astounded to see them brought into Tangier by the donkey-load, each animal carrying panniers loaded to the gunwales with one spice or another, a small fortune often spilt in the refuse-tip of the streets as an animal was nudged or bumped. There needed be no excuse for the taste of rotten meat being undisguised.

Mrs Kilcummin took her on to the ramparts and showed the newcomer the vista of green hills rolling away into the distance. Closer to hand she could make out the wooden forts, each on its small eminence, that defended the landward approaches to the city, and expressed surprise at the sight of a small band of horsemen whose clothes proclaimed them to be from the garrison, riding beyond that protective ring. Of the Moors there was no sign.

'They will be there, somewhere,' Mrs Kilcummin told her. 'We have an agreement with them to ride a certain distance from the city, and since we aren't actively engaged against them just now there's no danger in going beyond the forts provided one takes care not to stray beyond the limits set by Moulay Ismail.'

'Is that their general?' Ferelith enquired.

Mrs Kilcummin shook her head. 'Their king. It's fashionable to sneer at him as a heathen and a savage but Patrick says he's no savage and we underestimate him at our peril.'

On the coast to the west of the city itself and situated between the city walls and the fort known as the Devil's Drop was a little township known as Whitby. Here,

Ferelith learned, were quarters for workmen and their families together with some ninety strong workhorses and a number of storehouses. The people of Whitby were not military. They were miners and quarrymen whose task was to quarry the local stone from which the mole was being built. One of the reasons this protective arm into the sea was costing far more than King Charles had allowed for was that the stone was softer than had originally been thought and the dimensions of the mole had therefore had to be increased to compensate for its erosion by the pounding waves.

'With these quarries to hand,' Ferelith asked, 'why are the forts made of wood? Surely stone would be stronger—even soft stone?'

'Of course, but they would take longer to erect and Moulay Ismail is hardly likely to sit in one of his palaces and let us get on with making our position easier to retain.'

When Ferelith returned to the house, having extracted from a merchant a faithful promise that not only would the straw he supplied be from wheat and not barley, but it would arrive that afternoon without fail, she found her father had also returned and had spent his morning to advantage.

He had found two servants.

'This is Amin,' he said, pushing forward a man of uncertain age with a grizzled beard and a wiriness about him that suggested that he might be a great deal tougher than his age and otherwise slight build might lead one to expect. 'He was taken from an Algerian corsair galley and has rowed in our galleys since then. He's unlikely ever to be ransomed and doubtless will find the sort of work we expect from him a great deal easier than what he's used to. I'm told he speaks French and Italian when it suits him as well as Arabic. This is Latifa.' He pushed forward a girl who was probably younger than Ferelith but tall and slim and, unlike any of the Moors that Ferelith had so far seen, she was very black. 'Her father was one of Moulay Ismail's Sudanese soldiers,' the major said. 'He was killed during the siege three years ago and

she and her mother were captured. Her mother sub-
sequently died and although her relatives have been invited to ransom her there has been no response so far.
I'm told she's a good hard worker and a first-class cook.
She speaks Arabic, of course, but she's picked up a lot
of English. She will be entirely answerable to you.'

'Then the first thing she can do is empty the mattresses and burn the straw,' Ferelith told him. 'Then between us we'll wash the covers.'

'We're invited to break bread with Colonel Kirke this
evening,' the major warned her. 'I accepted, of course,
so at least you won't have to provide a meal as well.'

'How did you find the colonel?' she asked.

'He was well.'

It seemed a rather brusque reply to a question which
had not been intended to elicit an answer regarding the
governor's health. 'That isn't quite what I meant, Papa.
How did you like him?'

The major chose his words with care. 'A man
somewhat given to an excessive use of oaths,' he said
finally. 'Doubtless he knows better than to employ them
in front of ladies, however.'

Ferelith laughed. 'You didn't like him. Never mind,
Papa. Perhaps he improves on acquaintance.'

By the end of the evening, she felt bound to admit
that he did not. Colonel Piercey Kirke was a big, blustering man with more brains and organising ability than
were immediately apparent. If her father's assumption
that his language would be moderated in the presence
of ladies were accurate, Ferelith dreaded to think what
it must have been like in their absence. 'God damn me,'
was the expression that most often passed his lips and
it did so with such frequency that Ferelith thought it
might well prove to be as much a prognosis as an ex-
pletive. His wife, Lady Mary Kirke, was a direct contrast, being quiet to the point of self-effacement, with
a pallid, drawn, unhealthy look about her. She greeted
her guests with a murmured welcome but, after intro-
ducing Ferelith to the wives of some of the other officers, clearly considered her duty was done and

contributed little more to the conversation except when she was addressed directly.

Her husband made up for the deficiency and Ferelith wished he were a little less obviously pleased to find what he evidently regarded as a new flirt in the garrison. When they were seated at table precedence distanced him far enough for him to be able to do little more than catch her eye and wink significantly, but when he was not so restricted he seemed to find a multiplicity of opportunities to brush up against her or to rest his hand absentmindedly on her waist and he several times complimented Major Melverley on the possession of a daughter so beautiful and dutiful as his. It was a form of attention and compliment to which Ferelith was quite unaccustomed and she neither liked it nor wished it to continue. Several times a cutting remark occurred to her but she reminded herself that this was her father's commanding officer and she might be better advised to ignore it for the time being and keep well out of his way for the future. So she bit her tongue and said nothing.

The meal that was placed before them was a revelation after the one the Kilcummins had provided the previous day and Ferelith began to appreciate the difference made to any officer by the existence of private means which had no dependence upon the Army. There were good anchovies and potted wild boar, a side of roasted venison and pickled oysters and the whole was washed down with good claret and Rhenish wine. Although Mrs Kilcummin had told Ferelith of the vegetables that were grown in and around the city, only some artichokes and beans appeared on the table, the garrison obviously preferring to keep to the English habit of providing so much meat and pies that vegetables became superfluous. Remembering the sharp clarity of the orange salad, Ferelith thought this was a pity. None the less, she was curious to learn the explanation for such plenty.

'Papa and I hadn't realised there would be such a choice of meat in Tangier,' she said, addressing the officer on her left. Her words were picked up by the governor.

'God damn me, Mrs Durliston: you don't expect His Majesty's representative to make do with salt beef, do you?' Kirke threw back his head and roared with laughter. 'We hunt, my dear. The hills outside the city are alive with game: boar and antelope, hare and plover, curlew and bustard—they give us good sport and enable us to keep a good table. Then for those who enjoy fishing, they can go out in a boat or—more wisely, perhaps—fish from the mole. There's gurnet and turbot, mullet and lobster, shrimps and cod, old-women and bonitos. And, if that palls, there's always hawking and the small game that brings in. We live well enough.'

'Yet you are surrounded by the enemy,' Ferelith remarked. 'Do the Moors let you have so much freedom outside Tangier?'

The officer to whom she had addressed her original question pre-empted his superior. 'We may ride out and hunt providing there are fewer than twelve in the party and providing we stay within certain limits,' he told her. 'Do you ride, Mrs Durliston?'

'Not often, but I am quite competent,' she said.

'Then you and Major Melverley must borrow horses and engage a guide and have a small exploration. It breaks the monotony of the city wonderfully.'

Ferelith nodded. 'I can imagine it would. I had no idea Tangier was so small. Perhaps I should ask Papa whether he can't buy me a horse and then I can enjoy a daily ride.'

'I fancy that will prove well-nigh impossible,' her neighbour told her. 'There are very few horses here: those brought out from England have tended to sicken and die. Spanish ones survive and do quite well but the authorities in England don't share our belief that horses are essential here and would be a great military asset, so they won't advance the money to purchase them. Does your maid ride, too? It is most important to have a female chaperon once you leave the confines of the city:

the heathens form their own opinion of women who venture out without.'

'I've no idea whether she does or not,' Ferelith said. 'Father selected her from the *bagno*. She's Sudanese. Is she likely to?'

He looked at her in polite horror. 'You didn't bring your maid with you? In that case I suggest you only ride if you have your father's escort.'

'Annie is a determined woman,' Ferelith told him. 'She has been with the family a long time and has always resolutely resisted any attempt to persuade her to leave England and, since we needed to leave the house in the hands of someone we could trust implicitly, neither Papa nor I tried too hard to persuade her, though I own I should have liked some English-speaking female company with whom I felt at ease on this, my first visit abroad.'

'God damn me,' Kirke broke in across the table. 'If this is your first time out of England, Mrs Durliston, we must make it a visit to be remembered.'

Ferelith could only thank him aloud and privately hope he left that to others. She rather suspected that the very strangeness of the place would be enough to imprint it forever on her memory.

One Tangerine custom she was very happy to adopt was that of lying down within the cool walls of the house when the sun was at its hottest in the early afternoon. There was little point in doing anything else, for all the merchants shut their shops and the Moors from outside the city who had ventured in to sell their wares covered them over and curled up beside them in the shadow of a wall and slept for two or three hours. Latifa introduced her to the custom, making it abundantly clear that she expected her mistress to sleep—possibly, Ferelith suspected, so that she could do so herself. It took a day or two to get used to the idea but once she had, to Latifa's obvious satisfaction, she took no further persuading.

She had just woken up from one such afternoon nap when Latifa came in to say that the major was below and would speak with his daughter. Ferelith hurried to

the hall and found that her father had managed to
borrow two horses and was hoping to take her for a ride
if she was interested in seeing rather more of their surroundings than could be glimpsed from the ramparts.
She was, and hastened back to her room to change into
a severely cut riding-habit of clear green broadcloth, its
facings, hem, pockets and cuffs trimmed with gold braid.
A severe cravat and a black bicorne profusely trimmed
with ostrich feathers completed the picture.

Both horses were of the heavy-headed Andalusian
breed and even Ferelith, who did not regard herself as
a judge of such things, recognised that they were not
outstanding specimens of the type. The major threw her
into the saddle and appeared relieved that the animal
did no more than twitch an ear in recognition of his
load.

'I was told he was a placid beast, and it seems to be
true,' he said.

'Not too placid, I hope,' Ferelith said sharply. 'I'll
not get much enjoyment from a mount that is only happy
plodding along and has to be beaten into a faster gait.'

Her father, who had mounted by this time, permitted
himself an uncharacteristic grin. 'Don't speak too soon,'
he warned her. 'This is the first time he's carried a lady's
saddle. You could end up measuring the ground yet.'

Ferelith gathered up the reins with some caution. Her
mount seemed unperturbed by the unfamiliar distri-
bution of weight on his back and his rider's confidence
increased as he progressed through the narrow streets,
unbothered either by his rider's unfamiliar style or the
noise and bustle of the city as it resumed its business
now that the worst of the day's heat was done. They
had reached one of the gates before she realised that
they were alone.

'Should we not have a guide, Papa?' she asked,
drawing rein at the Old Gate.

He shook his head. 'I don't think so: I've been taken
out a couple of times to familiarise me with our lines
and the limit put upon us by the Moors has been pointed
out to me. I'm confident enough and, besides, the Moors

do not seem anxious to tangle with us for the time being. The general feeling is that they are waiting for their spies to report back.'

'What can their spies see from outside the city?' Ferelith asked.

'Not very much, I imagine. It's what they find out from inside that's useful to their generals.'

'From inside! Do you mean there are spies creeping about in Tangier?'

'Of course there are—just as we have some in their encampments. Among the spice merchants and fruit sellers will be some who aren't what they seem and they certainly won't be "creeping about", as you put it. They will be behaving like any legitimate trader.'

'If that is known, why doesn't the governor stop them all from coming in?' Ferelith demanded.

'My dear girl, stop and think,' her father advised her testily. 'The garrison is dependent upon two sources of food: that which is shipped from England and that which is grown outside the city. The first source is unreliable both in terms of supply and quality, and the amount we grow ourselves is insufficient. We must do business with the Moors to stay alive.'

'Then why don't they simply starve us out and then they can have their city back?'

'Two years ago they nearly succeeded after a seven-month siege. The garrison rallied in one last, desperate charge which took them by surprise and they could not withstand it. Both sides needed a temporary truce after that, for the garrison was too weak to press home its advantage. For some reason it suits them not to try again just yet. I'm too recent an arrival here to understand all the implications. I only know that what goes on here is very different from anything I've been used to.'

They rode south between the hill that held Fountain Fort—the city's only supply of fresh water since the English had failed to keep clean the conduits that, under the Portuguese, had piped fresh water to every house—and its neighbouring eminence upon which stood Bellesizes Fort. Then they headed southwest along the valley between Bellesizes and the more massive bulk of York fort at the westernmost end of a long escarpment. In this part of the landscape, every hilltop held an English fortification of some sort, the whole presided over to the south-west by the more impressive forts named after King Charles's brother James and that royal duke's daughter, Anne. It was, Ferelith reflected, a fortunate aspect of the topography that it enabled each fort to be within hailing distance of another and it gave her a great feeling of security to know that they were surrounded by English bastions. She was therefore a little uneasy when her father headed to the north of Anne Fort, where the valley was broader, and into the open countryside beyond.

'Is it safe to go beyond our forts, Papa?' she asked.

'Perfectly, so long as our present agreement with the Moors lasts,' he told her. 'The good hunting is to be found out here. Let's see whether we can get that great, lumbering brute of yours out of a trot.' With these words, he set his spurs into his own mount's sides and was soon cantering beyond the English lines.

Ferelith was unsure whether her horse responded to her whip or had a constitutional dislike of being left behind but she was pleasantly surprised when it broke into a canter with unexpected alacrity and proved at this pace to be a much more comfortable ride than it had previously demonstrated. It soon displayed a competitive edge she hadn't suspected and, since it also had the cavalry horse's hard mouth and a thick neck that would have done justice to a stallion, she had some difficulty holding him. There was no suggestion that he was bolting; he was merely determined to overtake the horse in front at whatever speed it was necessary to do so, and equally determined not to be deflected from his purpose. Once they had overtaken the major, he slowed of his own accord and appeared more responsive to the rein, though Ferelith noticed that his eyes continually checked to ensure that his companion was not getting too close. Conversation became difficult and any communication between Ferelith and her father had to be shouted.

Ferelith could only hope he would shout loudly if she seemed likely to lead them beyond the permitted bounds.

There was no denying the sheer delight of being away from the noisy, malodorous city and out in the fresh air. It was hot, too hot for anyone to be comfortable in a habit of broadcloth, and Ferelith felt a twinge of envy of the loose robes of the Moors. Flocks of white egrets lifted into the air as they pounded past, settling again a few yards further on.

She glanced back to see how close her father was and realised that she could no longer make out any of the English fortifications with which the landscape had previously appeared to be littered. She drew rein.

'Have we gone too far, Papa?' she asked. 'If we can't see the forts, then they can't see us.'

'No, we're still all right,' he assured her. 'I've been further than this on two or three occasions. If you're unhappy, however, I've no objection to our returning.'

Ferelith thought of the city and grimaced. 'Not yet— not until we have to. So long as we're safe I'm not at all anxious to return.'

Because he was leading, her mount was less willing this time to be pushed into a canter and only agreed to it when he saw the major's horse out of the corner of his eye bidding fair to overtake him. Then he took the bit between his teeth and went at a strong, if not headlong gallop, ignoring both rein and voice. A glance over her shoulder told Ferelith she was leaving her father's horse behind, a possibility that had certainly not seemed very likely when she had first taken stock of the two animals. She knew she was no expert horsewoman and could only pray that no unforeseen obstacle should make her horse swerve suddenly, because if he did they would undoubtedly part company.

There was no swerve. Instead, he threw up his head, stretched out his forelegs and slid to an unexpected stop so suddenly that Ferelith was first thrown forward on to his mane and then, thoroughly off balance, she slid slowly and none too gracefully to the ground.

When she got to her feet she found she was surrounded by a contingent of heavily armed and beautifully mounted men. They were black and their features were similar in a general sense to those of Latifa. Ferelith deduced that they were therefore Sudanese. She was not sorry to realise that her father was beside her. She was less happy about the very obvious interest they exhibited in herself. There was less novelty about Major Melverley.

'Do you speak English?' he asked the group at large.

Ferelith thought this a singularly pointless question and was taken aback when one of them asked, in guttural French, whether they spoke that language.

The major did, and proceeded to explain that he did not think they were outside the limits set down by Moulay Ismail but that, if they were, it was an unintentional trespass and they would be happy for an escort to the correct boundaries.

It was difficult to tell whether they found the major's accent incomprehensible or whether their French was too limited to permit them to follow so involved a speech. Whatever the explanation, they looked totally bemused. Some words passed between them and then one of them rode off at a handy gallop. Ferelith and her father had no choice but to remain where they were, their captors holding the reins of both horses.

It seemed a very long time before the horseman returned and, when he did so, he was no longer alone. At his side, mounted on a small but wiry grey, was a man who, even from a distance, much more resembled the Moorish traders and merchants Ferelith had seen around the city.

The encircling band of soldiers parted to let the newcomer and his escort through, and when he drew rein before her Ferelith found herself looking up into the disconcerting hazel eyes of the man in the *felucca*—the footman from the Lisbon embassy.

Unaccustomed to any need to dissimulate, Ferelith guessed that her recognition and the shock it induced raced across her features for anyone to discern. The face of the Moor gave nothing away; only a barely perceptible stiffening of his back hinted that he might be as surprised as she, though he might simply be surprised at finding a woman riding this far from Tangier.

His eyes met hers briefly and then passed on to her father. Ferelith could detect no flicker in that passing contact and was disconcerted to find herself put out by that circumstance.

He addressed her father not, as she expected, in heavily accented English, but in flawless French. She wondered why but noted that at least his tone was conciliatory.

'I am Benani,' he said. 'I am what you would call an aide to Moulay Ismail. You are obviously from Tangier. What is your standing there?'

'I'm Major Melverley, recently attached to the garrison. This is my daughter, Mrs Durliston.'

'Is Mr Durliston also attached to the garrison?'

'Mr Durliston is dead. My daughter is a widow. That's why it was possible for her to accompany me and run my household.'

'What are you doing so far from Tangier?'

'Giving my daughter an opportunity to see more of the country than she can from within the confines of the city. This has been her first chance to take some exercise.'

'Did no one tell you of the limits set by Moulay Ismail?'

'Of course. I wasn't aware that we had transgressed them, but if we have done so it was inadvertent and I shall be happy to apologise. My daughter, of course, was simply following my lead and can in no way be held responsible if she is out of bounds.'

Benani's interest in Ferelith seemed so small that even when she was the subject of the conversation he gave no glance in her direction. 'You say she was following your lead? I was given to understand that she was very much leading you.'

Major Melverley was better aware than his daughter of the dangers of having appeared to lie and hastened to set the record straight.

'It must certainly have appeared so. Her horse has never carried a lady before and is far too strong and hard-mouthed to be a suitable lady's mount. He got the bit between his teeth when he thought my horse might draw level. We are grateful that Moulay Ismail's troops were here to stop him.'

The major had hoped that that interpretation of the appearance of the Sudanese warriors would be sufficiently diplomatic to defuse the situation. Benani's next words told him that his line of thought had not been missed.

'With respect, major, she appears to have been taking the lead for some considerable time past.'

'Only because that brute won't allow himself to be overtaken. I assure you it was I, not she, who set the route and directed her when a choice of path offered itself.'

Benani looked Ferelith's horse over with a dispassionate eye. 'An ugly brute with little to commend him except an ability to carry weight. Certainly not one upon which I should choose to mount a woman of my own household.'

'Nor should I, given a choice. We brought no horses with us and have therefore been dependent upon the kindness of fellow officers to lend us theirs.'

The man turned to his fellows and began to speak rapidly. Ferelith assumed he was explaining the conversation to them, an assumption that was confirmed when the listeners studied both their captives and the horses, nodding knowingly at intervals in the explanation. This exchange was followed by a more acrimonious one between Benani and the man whom Ferelith had taken to be the leader of their captors. Finally Benani turned back to Major Melverley.

'I have persuaded my friend that on this occasion we should escort you until you're within sight of your own fortifications. This is a gesture of courtesy to two newcomers to our land, you understand.'

'A courtesy of which we are fully conscious,' the major told him.

Benani bowed and translated the major's words, which
obviously met with the approval of the Sudanese captain.

'Mount up, Major,' Benani told him and turned to
Ferelith, acknowledging her existence for the first time.
'Permit me to help you, *madame*,' he said.

He cupped his hands to take her foot and threw her
into the saddle with an expertise that surprised her, since
the few Moorish women she had seen mounted had sat
astride their donkey or mule. Once she was in the saddle,
his hand rested on her horse's neck. Ferelith smiled down
at him rather diffidently. He seemed so uninterested in
her existence that she almost hesitated to speak to him.

'Thank you,' she murmured, in English.

He inclined his head. *'Mraba,'* he said. 'Perhaps
madame should take the opportunity to learn something
of our language, since we make it our duty to learn those
of Europe. "Thank you" is a good beginning. In Arabic,
"Barakallahufik" or "shokran".'

Ferelith repeated the phrase hesitantly and self-
consciously.

For the first time, he smiled, revealing white teeth in
his tanned face. 'Good. You must practise it on the ride
back. And *"mraba"*, of course. It means "you're
welcome" or "it's a pleasure". Should we ever meet
again, I shall expect you to be word-perfect.'

Ferelith laughed, her spirits suddenly lightened by the
prospect he had held out, even though she knew it could
be nothing more than a simple courtesy.

Benani did not accompany them. The Sudanese had
their instructions and presumably could be trusted to
follow them. Moulay Ismail's envoy remounted and was
soon lost to sight in the hills beyond them. He gave no
backward glance, nor did he draw rein to look back
before he disappeared. Ferelith was disappointed: it
added force to her suspicion that his final words had
indeed been nothing more than politeness. Even so, it
couldn't entirely dampen her spirits and she was perfectly content to allow herself to be herded along in a
phalanx of horsemen. Their escort was not giving them
any opportunity to break free until it was permitted. She

therefore had plenty of time to ponder the intriguing question of why an aide to Moulay Ismail should have been a footman in the English embassy and why he should later appear as a bum-boat trader. His acceptance by the Sudanese indicated that he was, indeed, a man of some standing. Then why the humbler roles? Perhaps it was something she should mention to her father, but that would be difficult without saying something of that walk in the garden. How else could she convince him that she was not mistaken? That brief encounter was one she wished to treasure in private. No, she would have to solve the puzzle on her own.

'Papa,' she began after a while, 'do you think we——?'

'Wait until we're alone,' he interrupted. 'We'll talk then.'

Ferelith glanced at the men surrounding them. 'But, Papa, they don't speak English.'

He smiled a somewhat grim-lipped smile. 'They don't *appear* to speak it, certainly. Perhaps they don't but, even if that's so, they may well understand. As our friend from Moulay Ismail said, the Moors make it their duty to learn European languages and, since Tangier has been ours for twenty years, it would be wise to assume that far more people understand us than we realise.'

Ferelith, recalling that she knew Benani to speak very good English and that he had chosen not to do so even though he knew she would not be deceived, was silenced.

When Anne Fort was just visible on the skyline, their escort without a word reined back before wheeling and galloping off in the direction from which it had come, leaving Ferelith and her father to go on alone.

'Papa,' Ferelith began again, 'do you think we had gone beyond the agreed bounds?'

'I don't think so but I can't be sure. I think we must have been a quarter of a mile within them, but I have to accept that I may have been mistaken.'

'I noticed that that man—Benani—never did actually say we had overstepped the mark. You indicated that if we had, it had been unintentional and he said nothing to disabuse you of the assumption.'

'You noticed that? So did I. We may assume Mr Benani is an honourable man who prefers not to give a direct lie. I should have asked a straightforward question. However, the fact that he chose not to confirm my assumption or to say by how much we had strayed inclines me to the opinion that it was the Sudanese who were beyond the bounds. It crossed my mind at the time but their numbers were such that it seemed inadvisable to risk putting them at a disadvantage. Colonel Kirke must know, however. As soon as we get back, I must report to him.'

The governor of Tangier frowned when he heard Major Melverley's story. He led him into his map-room and demanded to be shown exactly where they had ridden, a demand with which the major was both willing and able to comply.

'And you're quite sure you went no further than this?' he demanded.

'Absolutely certain, sir. The terrain is unmistakable. I told my daughter I thought we were a good quarter of a mile inside the boundary. That was a guess, of course, but I don't seem to have been all that much out.'

'In which case we must assume they're not keeping to their part of the bargain. The question is, why not?' The colonel lapsed into silence and paced the room for some time, weighing up the implications of the news he had just heard. 'And you say this man introduced himself as Benani?' he said at last.

'That's right. Just "Benani". I took it to be a surname.'

Kirke nodded. 'It would be. The men rarely give you their Christian names—I mean their given names, of course,' he corrected himself. 'Describe this Benani,' he went on.

The major did so. It was probably not so detailed a description as his daughter could have furnished, but it was sufficient for Governor Kirke.

'Light eyes, you say? Then he was a Berber. We think of them all as Moors, of course, be they true Moors, Arabs or Berbers, but they draw a clear distinction between them. It matters little to us in the ordinary way because they're all vassals of Moulay Ismail; however, in this case, I think we may have something rather more serious to worry us. A certain Rashid Benani is a Berber chieftain of considerable influence in the Rif Mountains. He has a son called Hassan, who may well be the young man you met this afternoon. He described himself as an aide to the Moorish King, you said? That suggests that the Berbers of the Rif have been persuaded to play a very much more active part in trying to force us out of Tangier than they have done hitherto.' He resumed his pacing. 'If they choose to invest the city again, I doubt the garrison can hold out as long as it did last time. If only the King and his Parliament would spend money on this place! They won't send us horses, they send us too few men, they expect us forever to cut the costs of the mole—though without sacrificing its effectiveness, you understand; above all, they send no money to pay the garrison and food which is inadequate and of appalling quality. I'm only surprised that more men don't turn renegade. Those that do live a great deal better as heathen Mohammedans than they ever will as good Christians in this benighted hole,' he concluded bitterly.

Major Melverley made a non-committal reply. The governor's words indicated an appreciation of the situation of an astuteness which his normal blustering, oath-laden manner belied, and the major began to feel that perhaps Piercey Kirke had not been so disastrous a choice of governor as he had thought.

'Get back to your daughter, Melverley,' the colonel said, 'but don't breathe anything of this outside these walls. I'll not disguise from you that your experience this afternoon worries me greatly, but I'd rather not let it worry anyone else just yet.'

CHAPTER FOUR

WHATEVER shortcomings there might be to life in Tangier—and there were many—lack of social intercourse was not one. The governor's house in one corner of the Upper Castle—so named because it stood at the highest point within the city walls—was the scene of many supper parties such as that which Ferelith had already attended. Other officers returned the governor's hospitality and when foreign dignitaries arrived the entertainments were extended to include concerts and balls. There was rarely an evening when Ferelith could expect to stay at home.

The social distinctions were far more clearly marked in Tangier than they were in England and it took Ferelith some time to become accustomed to the rigidity of the artificial barriers between the citizens which among so small a population seemed ludicrously restrictive. At the top, the circle to which Major Melverley and his daughter were admitted was composed of the governor and his family together with the principal officers of the garrison, the chief engineers working on the mole, and their families. This amounted to some twenty families in all and the only other people admitted to their entertainments were the occasional distinguished visitors such as commanders of Mediterranean fleets and the gentlemen captains of the King's frigates. No merchants, however rich or influential, ever penetrated this circle, a fact which made Ferelith alternately chuckle and fume, depending upon her mood, for under the unwritten rules of Tangier she was admitted because her father was an officer, but her Durliston parents-in-law would not have been because, though of better birth, Mr Durliston was indisputably a merchant by choice. They would have had to be content with the company of the municipal dignitaries, the doctors, the schoolmaster and various minor officials of the mole office, to say nothing of the governor's secretary and a few subaltern officers who preferred the less rarefied air at that level of society.

Below the merchants came the much larger group composed of the private soldiers and their families, the mole workmen, the poorer shopkeepers and the garrison's hangers-on, while the shifting population of foreigners kept themselves quite separate from the English and had—or so Ferelith was told—their own social distinctions which they observed with as much punctiliousness as their rulers. The Jews, both from Barbary and Europe, had their own *mellah*, or quarter of the town, complete with its synagogue, and lived their own separate life, to be called upon occasionally to act as mediators between the English and the Moors, being accepted by both sides as impartial in that they accepted neither Christianity nor Islam and were accepted by neither. The slaves, mainly Moors and Turks, formed their own group. Some were privately owned but most were employed in His Majesty's galleys. It was estimated that they numbered some three hundred and fifty and most of them returned to the *bagno* at night, though the governor had the power to waive this provision if he could be convinced it was advisable. Amin and Latifa came into this category and Ferelith, like the rest of her circle, had no contact with them except in the course of their duties. She had far less personal association with them than she would have had with any servant at home and knew nothing of their lives outside her own house. At the very bottom of the ladder and despised by everyone above them came the sailors from visiting ships of any nationality.

Not all officers had brought their wives and many of the younger ones were as yet unmarried, so the arrival of a young and striking widow was an event that provoked a noticeable flutter in the pigeon-loft as those eligible to take advantage of her presence preened themselves with more than usual care. The news that she was no impoverished widow swept through the garrison within hours of her arrival and her beauty increased with the reported size of her fortune.

When dancing was the order of the day, Ferelith was never without a partner and was never obliged to dance with the same man twice. Since to do so would have been to give a particularity to the partnership which would have given rise to just the sort of gossip and speculation she was anxious to avoid, this situation suited her very well. She would have been unnatural if she had not enjoyed the attention she received and Annie would have been gratified to have seen how far her former charge had come from the deep mourning that had so concerned those about her. Certainly, none of her present admirers would have guessed how much she still grieved for Francis, and when Lieutenant Newlyn paid a morning call on Mrs Durliston it was with every expectation of a happy outcome.

Frederick Newlyn was a thoroughly nice young man. The younger son of a country gentleman, he had his own way to make and had chosen the Army as his vehicle. There was no denying that a wealthy wife—even if her wealth had been somewhat exaggerated in the telling—would be a great asset in obtaining his preferment. The fact that Mrs Durliston was also a considerable beauty, if not precisely in the fashionable mould, and one with whom conversation could pass beyond a discussion of the weather and one's fellow guests, made her all the more attractive as a prospective wife. Furthermore, although she had never given the gossiping tongues the smallest hint of any preference for his company over that of his fellow officers, she had always greeted him with evident pleasure that rather exceeded, in his judgement, that with which she greeted others. He did wonder whether he should first approach her father but decided her widowed status made that unnecessary. He would have to tackle the major, of course, but it might be wiser to have the widow lending her weight to any argument that might ensue. Fathers were inclined to be over-protective and the lieutenant suspected that Major Melverley might be unable to see beyond his relative penury and might therefore fail to recognise the very real esteem in which the younger man held his daughter.

It was not usual for unmarried officers to pay morning calls on their own and it certainly did not occur to Ferelith to leave Latifa outside the room. The girl stood quietly inside the door while her mistress went forward to greet their visitor.

'Why, Lieutenant Newlyn! This is indeed a pleasure. May one enquire its purpose?' were Ferelith's opening words.

The young man glanced past her at the maid and frowned. He should have foreseen there would be a chaperon present but there was no denying that the fervour of his feelings—or rather, the fervour with which he might express them—would be seriously inhibited by the attendance of a third party, even if that third party would almost certainly be unable to comprehend a word of what he was saying.

He hesitated, 'I had hoped to speak to you alone, Mrs Durliston,' he said.

Ferelith smiled kindly. 'Surely not, Mr Newlyn? In the absence of Papa, you would not, I know, wish me to lay myself open to the sort of censure that would inevitably be my lot once it became known that no chaperon had attended our meeting.'

'No, no, of course not,' he hastened to assure her though he did wonder how details of an entirely private meeting could possibly reach the ears of the gossiping tabbies of Tangier. Besides, the girl probably wouldn't understand a word.

All the same, it wasn't easy to decide where to begin. It had seemed easy enough in the solitude of his lodgings. Here it was less so and not made easier by the expectant smile of his hostess.

'The thing is, Mrs Durliston,' he began awkwardly, very conscious that somehow the words were not emerging as smoothly as he had anticipated, 'the thing is, we've known one another for some time now.'

Ferelith considered. 'Something in the region of four or five weeks, I think,' she said.

'Is that all? I had thought it to be much more.'

'Thank you,' Ferelith commented, unable to repress a small smile. She was sure he meant it as a compliment but it was at best a two-edged one.

The irony escaped him. 'Not at all,' he said politely. 'I feel I know you so well, you see, and you have to admit we get along famously together.'

If Ferelith had been unsure of his purpose before, she thought she had a good idea what it might be now, and decided that a little not-too-cruel deflation might give a broad enough hint to deflect him from his purpose.

'I have to admit that we dance well together,' she said, 'and we have never quarrelled in public. Would that be your definition of "getting along famously"?'

'You have it precisely, Mrs Durliston. Not that I would expect anyone to quarrel in public, of course, but you must admit we've never had the slightest disagreement.'

'We have certainly never voiced one,' Ferelith conceded. 'That's not quite the same thing.'

'Perhaps not, but you'll admit it's a very good omen.'

Ferelith sighed. Lieutenant Newlyn was not very good at seeing hints. 'For what?' she asked, resigned to the inevitable.

'Why, for marriage, of course! What else?' He threw himself down on one knee at her feet in the time-honoured, if somewhat mythical manner that was said to derive from the days of chivalry, and seized her hand. 'Mrs Durliston, will you do me the honour of becoming my wife?' Without waiting for an answer, he pressed her hand to his lips as if to demonstrate the determination of his suit.

Ferelith disengaged her hand with equal determination. 'I'm flattered by your proposal, Mr Newlyn. Flattered and honoured. Nevertheless, I fear I must decline.'

He stared up at her, open-mouthed. 'Decline? But why? Surely you can't be indifferent to me?'

'Indifferent?' she echoed. 'No, I don't think I'm indifferent: you are a charming young man, an able officer, I'm told, and very pleasant company. These are hardly adequate qualities upon which to base a marriage.'

Aware that he must now look faintly ridiculous on one knee, the lieutenant rose to his feet. 'But they're not a bad starting-point,' he said reasonably.

'That's very true. However, before I remarry I shall need to be far better acquainted with my future husband than I am with you and, besides, there's one thing you've overlooked.'

He cast about in his mind but could think of nothing. 'What's that?' he asked.

'My husband died just over two years ago,' she told him. 'Mr Newlyn, I may have abandoned the outward trappings of mourning in order the better to serve my father's present interest, but my love for my late husband is in no way diminished. I know it's unreasonable to measure every man against the memory of Francis, but that's precisely what I do. I mean no disrespect to you when I say I have not yet met his equal.'

The young officer looked suitably abashed. He felt he could refute most objections she might put forward but no man could refute comparison with a dead husband, and no man of honour would try.

'Is that your last word, Mrs Durliston?' he asked.

'For the foreseeable future, yes,' she told him. 'You would be best advised to seek a wife when you next return home. I'm sure so personable a man as you will not have too much difficulty. Good morning, Mr Newlyn.'

He hesitated. 'I hope your father won't——'

'My father will know nothing of this interview unless you tell him,' Ferelith said and was rewarded with a broad, boyish smile.

'Thank you, Mrs Durliston—and good morning.' He swept her a profuse and rather over-stated bow before departing through the door that Latifa was now holding open for him.

Ferelith saw him leave and sighed. He was probably four or five years older than she, yet she felt inde-

scribably the older of the two. She went over to the
window that looked out on the garden which now bode
fair to becoming a flourishing source of vegetables and
herbs. She guessed that Lieutenant Newlyn's was only
the first such declaration she might expect. There was
no conceit in this assumption, simply an acceptance of
the fact that she was living in a garrison town where men
outnumbered women and most of the men were unmarried. Any eligible woman was a rarity. One with a
fortune at her disposal, even if the fortune was smaller
than rumour would have it, was a prize of the first order.

She was glad to have discovered that Francis was the
ultimate deterrent, the argument to which there was no
counter, but she was a little shocked to discover that,
when she thought of him, his features had become a
little blurred, like the reflection in a misted glass. She
tried to clarify the picture, as one rubbed the water-
vapour from a mirror, but there was only a brief lifting
of the haze. It was very disturbing, the more so because
another face came unbidden and with startling clarity
into her mind in its place. It was an olive-skinned face
with white teeth and hazel eyes, and it had no right to
be in her mind at all. She pushed it resolutely aside and
made her way to the kitchen. There was plenty to do
there before her father came home and conversation
could preclude thought for a few hours.

Colonel Piercey Kirke was much more difficult to deal
with. Discussion with Imelda Kilcummin soon told
Ferelith that her original impression of Tangier's governor had been entirely accurate. Colonel Kirke was one
of those men to whom any woman under the age of thirty
and passably pretty was a challenge to be grappled with—
sometimes quite literally—and beaten. It was believed
never to have crossed his mind that most women found
his charms resistible and those that did not submitted
for purely practical considerations such as the fur-
therance of their husband's careers and even, in one or
two cases, as a means of punishing their husbands for
neglect, whether real or imaginary.

'I must warn you, Mrs Durliston, the bets are already being laid on whether you will succumb or not.'

Ferelith had laughed. 'Then I hope those who think I shall will wager a great deal of money. Nothing would give me greater pleasure than to see them lose it all.'

Mrs Kilcummin looked doubtful. 'I've heard others say the same thing with equal vehemence,' she said. 'I'd not be too sure of myself if I were you.'

Ferelith wondered what her neighbour's experience of the colonel had been but they were not on terms of sufficient intimacy yet to permit of her asking, so she stilled her curiosity and tried to dismiss the knowledge that she was the subject of such garrison-wide speculation.

It would have been easier had she not been obliged to attend the numerous social functions that were conducted at one house or another. The colonel was invariably present, though Lady Mary as often as not cried off, pleading ill health with, according to gossip, good reason. The climate of Tangier did not agree with her ladyship. Ferelith, who found it rather agreeable, suspected that the noise and smell and general feeling of constraint that attended life in the city might have more to do with it. It also occurred to her that it must be galling to witness one's husband continually flirting with other women and that ill health might be a very useful excuse to remove oneself from exposure to its continued repetition.

The governor had set his sights on the major's widowed daughter and did nothing to disguise the fact. Protocol insisted that he open every ball by being the first to take to the floor and, naturally, his partner would be his wife—if she was there. Since she was absent more often than not, he was obliged to find another partner and for the time being that partner was Mrs Durliston. It was simply not possible to decline his invitation to join him at the head of the line for the first dance but Ferelith stood firm on refusing him any further dances, something which was most easily achieved by the expedient of making sure she already had partners for them. When she did not, she had recourse to bluntness.

'No, Colonel,' she said on one occasion, to the delight of those within earshot, 'I will not dance with you again, conscious though I am of the honour. It is not at all the thing to dance more than once with a man to whom one is neither betrothed nor married and it would look very peculiar were I to accept. It would give the event a particularity which I'm sure you would wish to avoid since it could only occasion the sort of comment which might distress Lady Mary.'

'Lady Mary isn't here and will know nothing of it,' he protested.

Ferelith gave him her sweetest smile. 'Come, come, Colonel. You know as well as I do that if we were so very indiscreet she would learn of it before morning.'

This was so incontrovertible that he could only snort and bluster, 'And if she did, she'd think nothing of it.'

'Quite possibly, but I've no wish to put her to the distress that might ensue if you're wrong.' Ferelith spoke with a finality which even Piercey Kirke could not ignore and several people who overheard the exchange, to say nothing of several of those who heard about it later, decided to hedge their bets.

Even so, there was always one dance with the governor that invariably led to her fingers being pressed more firmly than was entirely acceptable or being held a fraction longer than was quite necessary. At supper parties and concerts, where rooms were often quite crowded, he displayed a genius for finding himself close enough to Ferelith to breathe into her ear, to squeeze her waist, or for his hand to just happen to brush against her breast. Her only uncertainty was whether her father was aware of it. She found it hard to believe that he had heard none of the gossip, that no hint of the wager had reached his ears, but at no time did he refer to it. Ferelith guessed that, while he would act if she asked him to, he would much rather not. He was a good soldier and an excellent officer but had always avoided confrontations in his personal life as much as possible. She knew he would be similarly content to leave this matter to her to deal with and, although that realisation made her feel a little bitter and she experienced a renewed pang for Francis, who would certainly have acted without being asked, she supposed that it would probably be very good for her to have to discourage the colonel's attentions on her own. After all, her father would not always be there and by the very nature of his calling he could be taken from her at very short notice. No, she would contrive.

The opportunity to do so came sooner than she anticipated.

Major Melverley having expressed a wish that the Tangerine cook he had taken on should be taught to make a good pie, Ferelith was engaged in doing so when Latifa appeared in the kitchen to tell her mistress that a gentleman had arrived to see her. Ferelith dusted the worst of the flour from her hands and was about to remove her apron when a thought struck her. 'Is it that same young man who was here last week?' she asked.

Latifa grinned. 'No, madam. Far more important. It's the governor.'

Ferelith hesitated. Anyone as prominent as the governor of Tangier merited a quick removal of any evidence of work and common courtesy demanded that there should be no hint that he had interrupted his hostess. On the other hand, she had no wish to appear too welcoming lest he should assume a repeat visit would be well received.

'Is he alone, or is Lady Mary with him? Or perhaps an aide-de-camp?'

Latifa's grin grew wider. 'No, madam. He's alone.'

Correctly deducing from the girl's grin that Latifa knew of the wager, Ferelith coloured and instead of removing her floury apron tightened it. 'Very well,' she said. 'You'll come with me, Latifa, and you will remain in the room.' She picked up the rolling-pin and dabbed some flour on her face so that it looked as if she had passed the back of a floury hand across her forehead. 'Not the most subtle of gentlemen,' she went on. 'I'd not want him to think I've nothing better to do than receive him.'

Thus unconventionally equipped, she went through to the little saloon where Colonel Kirke was waiting for her.

If her appearance struck the governor as at all out of the ordinary, he gave no indication of having noticed it. Ferelith was unsure whether this showed an unexpected exhibition of good manners or betrayed a sad lack of observation. He swept her a gallant bow before replacing his hat and then glanced towards Latifa, standing demurely beside the door, and—like Lieutenant Newlyn before him—frowned. Unlike his subordinate, he knew very well how to deal with chaperons, especially when they were servants or slaves. It was dowagers who tended to be recalcitrant.

'You may go, girl,' he said. 'You won't be needed.' He waved his hand towards the door in a gesture of dismissal whose meaning was unmistakable.

Latifa looked uncertainly at her mistress.

Ferelith shook her head. 'Latifa remains, Colonel,' she said. 'You would not, I'm sure, wish to give rise to the sort of gossip there would be were we to converse without a chaperon.'

'Nonsense, Mrs Durliston. Why, I'm old enough to be your father—and married, into the bargain. Let us not forget that. It must render a chaperon superfluous.'

'Indeed, Colonel, I hope neither of us forgets those facts,' Ferelith said with heavy emphasis. 'All the same, I should prefer her to remain.'

He frowned. 'But I should not.' He turned to Latifa. *'Imshi, imshi,'* he said in his most ferocious voice, and bore down upon her as if he would physically remove her from the room. Latifa fled. 'That's better,' he remarked as he turned back to Ferelith.

'On the contrary, Colonel, it is inexcusable—and you know it. I have no choice but to ask you to leave.'

'Come, come, my dear. You don't mean that. After all, you don't know what has brought me here yet.'

'No, I don't, and if this is your manner of telling me I don't think I have very much curiosity about it, either.

I suggest you leave and, if the purpose of your visit is so important, return when Papa is at home.'

'That would render my purpose pointless,' he said and added inconsequentially, 'I do admire a woman of spirit.'

Since he could obviously not be shamed into leaving and since she clearly lacked the physical ability to force him to do so, Ferelith decided she had better resign herself to being told his purpose so that she could then get him out of the house with no further delay.

'Then I suggest you come to the point as quickly as possible, so that I may return to the kitchen. It's Papa's expressed wish that the cook learns to bake pies and I was engaged in teaching her the art of pastry-making when you arrived.'

'God damn me, Mrs Durliston, I'll wager the best pastry in Tangier will be had here. I don't doubt the cook has an excellent teacher.'

'Your point, Colonel.'

'Ah, yes, the purpose of my visit.' He edged a little closer and Ferelith edged a little further away. 'Young Newlyn was here last week, I gather. Pressing his interest, no doubt. Been going around with a face as long as a fiddle ever since, from which we all conclude you turned him down.'

He paused and Ferelith reflected bitterly on the impossibility of keeping anything quiet in this town—an impossibility that would certainly encompass the unchaperoned visit of the governor.

'I have to admit that I was not altogether surprised that you turned him down,' he went on smugly. 'I've been very conscious that there is a certain rapport between us.'

'Indeed?' Ferelith said frostily. 'I was unaware of it.'

He shook his head. 'No, no—you can't have been. I assure you others have noticed it.'

'And is that why I'm the subject of wagers?' Ferelith asked.

'You know about that, do you? Not very admirable, of course, but I advise you not to let it worry you. I ignore such things.'

'As a man, you can probably afford to do so,' Ferelith
pointed out. 'Colonel, if you are aware of the wagers
being laid, I'm all the more shocked that you should
come here as you have, dismiss my chaperon and pursue
a line of conversation that is, to say the least, indelicate
between a man and a woman who are virtual strangers.'

He moved rapidly closer, pinning her between a san-
dalwood court-cupboard and the wall. 'When two people
are as closely drawn to one another as we are, who can
call them virtual strangers? Mrs Durliston, from the
moment you arrived in Tangier—well, from the moment
I first saw you—I felt as if I had known you forever. I
felt that here, at last, was the soulmate I had been
searching for.'

Ferelith tried to wriggle out of the corner into which
she was pinned. She failed, so she looked him straight
in the eye. 'What a remarkably bad judge of character
you must be, Colonel! It makes one wonder why you
were ever elevated to your present position.'

'Is that the way to speak to your governor?' he asked.
His tone was jocular but Ferelith sensed she had disconcerted him. He pulled her roughly towards him and
sunk his mouth on to her neck while the hand that was
not restraining her in a far from gentle hold fumbled
with the tempting curve of her bosom upthrust, as was
the fashion, by the cut of her bodice. His lips followed
his hand and, the next Ferelith knew, he was fumbling
with her skirts.

No man had ever treated her in this outrageous
fashion. Even Francis, who of all men had the right to,
had behaved with delicacy and with sensitivity to her
own response. Ferelith's grasp of the almost-forgotten
rolling-pin tightened. She was at least as much angered
as outraged but nevertheless she tried once more to let
reason prevail.

'I insist that you let me go, Colonel,' she said.

Her demand was ignored. If anything, her adversary
became more determined.

She forced herself to relax in his hold so that she appeared to be submitting to his will and, as she had hoped,

that hold was itself relaxed as he felt her opposition melt away. That relaxation gave her room to manoeuvre, at least to the extent of raising her arm. The colonel was considerably taller than she but his head, being occupied with her bosom, was level with her shoulder, his neck exposed.

Ferelith, determination clenching her jaw, rammed the blunt round end of the rolling-pin into his neck and then, having pushed him off balance and taken him by surprise, she brought it down on the side of his head. The angle from which she struck him and the limited space she had in which to strike precluded her using much force but it was enough to send the King's representative tumbling to the floor where he lay very still.

She stood looking down at him for a moment, more than a little afraid that she had killed him. Common sense told her this was unlikely—that she had only been as successful as she had because surprise had been on her side. She bent down quickly and felt the pulse in his neck. It was beating quite distinctly. She thought quickly. A small vase of wild flowers stood by the window. She picked it up and emptied some of the water on the floor by the colonel's feet, then she replaced the flowers and the vase and left the room, calling for Latifa.

'Fetch Amin,' she said when the girl came, 'and then join me in the saloon. Colonel Kirke has had a fall.'

Ferelith did not actually return to the room before Amin arrived because she had no wish to be alone with even an unconscious governor and she certainly wanted company when he came round.

Amin was soon fetched and in a very short time the colonel was sitting up looking very angry indeed. He opened his mouth to give vent to his feelings but Ferelith raised a cautionary hand.

'Don't try to speak, Colonel. You've had a nasty fall.' She turned to Latifa and pointed to the water on the floor. 'You really must be more careful, Latifa. The colonel slipped on that small pool. I imagine it must have come from the vase. I don't know whether you spilt some or whether it was over-full and spilt inadvertently.

Either way, it should have been noticed and mopped up. Do you understand?'

'Yes, madam,' Latifa said. She understood very well indeed.

'Then the least you can do is fetch the colonel some Madeira. I fancy he will need it. And don't spill that,' she called after her.

By this time Amin had got the colonel on to a chair, and the latter was sufficiently in command of his senses to realise that if the truth of this escapade leaked out he would become the laughing-stock of the garrison. Mrs Durliston's explanation at least had the merit of saving his face.

'I am so sorry,' Ferelith told him as she handed him the goblet Latifa had brought. 'This will make you feel very much more the thing and I assure you the girl will be soundly beaten. That will teach her to take more care in future.'

He sipped the Madeira and nodded approval. 'You have to be careful with these natives. They can be very slack if you're not behind them every minute of the day. It doesn't do to leave them unsupervised even for the simplest task.'

'As I'm rapidly learning,' Ferelith told him apologetically. He has already almost succeeded in convincing himself that he really did slip, she thought. Good. Maybe within a day or two that's all he will choose to remember. 'Colonel, I hesitate to leave you but you are in good hands with Amin and I really should return to the kitchen. As you so rightly say, these people do need constant supervision. If there's anything you need, you have only to ask and it will be brought. Will you excuse me?'

He graciously agreed to do so, his self-esteem almost restored by her very proper subservience to his wishes. Latifa followed her mistress out of the saloon and closed the door behind them.

'Do you intend to beat me, madam?' she asked uncertainly. One never knew with Europeans.

'Certainly not. Why ever should I?' Ferelith asked. 'Mind you, it would do no harm if your demeanour over the next few days suggested I had.'

'Yes, madam,' Latifa said, and grinned.

Three frigates put into Tangier, the escort for two large merchantmen whose masters had refused to sail into corsair-infested waters with so valuable a cargo as supplies of both food and cannon for the garrison. Their arrival was particularly welcome and the captains of all five vessels were naturally to be entertained to the best of the garrison's ability during their brief stay. A banquet was to be the highlight of the visit, to be followed by an 'impromptu' ball, though, from the preparations being made and the decorations being erected in the great hall of York Castle, Ferelith felt that 'impromptu' was not perhaps the most apposite word.

Hunting parties were dispatched and returned with antelope and wild boar, while the local fishermen were commissioned to bring back the largest turbots and the best sardines they could find. Magnificent silk rugs covered the long banqueting tables down which stood at regular intervals ornately embossed silver bowls piled high with the fruits of the countryside. Between each bowl of fruit stood a silver *toubak* of flat, Moorish bread, its contents hidden by the dish's tall, conical lid. Several of the boars were potted, like hares, and two of the antelopes had been spit-roasted. The others had been transformed into game pies to supplement pigeon pies that were a more usual dish behind the city walls. There was boiled mutton for those with a taste for it and the ducks unique to Tangier in both colour and taste because they were kept away from dirty water and fattened on oatmeal and pease.

A Moorish envoy arrived at the Catherine Gate early in the morning of the day preceding the planned climax to the visitors' stay. He was admitted at once and led before the officer of the day, Major Melverley. He listened to the man's message in silence and then instructed his adjutant to take him into another room and to treat him with the utmost courtesy, which, the major suggested, should include coffee and sweetmeats, while he consulted with the governor.

Colonel Kirke also listened in silence.

'I don't believe it,' he declared when the major had finished. 'God damn me, I *can't* believe it. The man's a lot of things but he's not a fool, and that would be foolish beyond belief. You mark my words, if we agree to this, we'll end up with someone else on his behalf and the city full of Moors who, at the very least, will be poking around to find out what the fleet has just brought in.'

'That was my initial reaction,' the major agreed, 'but I'm not so sure: this place is a hotbed of spies. There are traders from outside coming in and many of the foreign traders resident in the city have no compunction about selling outside any information they can glean from within the walls. I very much doubt whether there is so much as a single nail in this last cargo that Moulay Ismail isn't already aware of. Why should he take the risk—the enormous risk—of sending his chief general?'

'Whatever it may be, I think we can discount the one we've been given. The King of al-Maghrib has never indicated any great respect for King Charles and even less for his representative in Tangier. Why, after all these years, should he suddenly decide to show a respect he doesn't have?'

'Perhaps he is encountering his own difficulties—difficulties of which we have no idea,' suggested the major.

The governor paced up and down, his head thrust forward, his brows drawn together. Then he shook his head. 'It's possible, but I don't think so. His own troops are loyal, his Sudanese mercenaries must be assumed so because if they weren't they'd have disappeared in the night, and if the Rifi tribesmen had decided to call an end to their co-operation with their King I think our own spies would have brought word.'

'So what are we going to do? The envoy is expected back by tonight.'

'And back he must be: I've no wish to give the Alcaid Ali Benabdala an excuse to descend on Tangier in force.

He's a devious man and I dare not overlook the possibility that he may be depending upon this whole proposal giving us so much to talk about that we keep the envoy longer and give the but Alcaid a pretext he not only wants but has manoeuvred us into giving him. I'd like to confer, but there isn't time.'

Together with the major, he pored over the maps and charts on the table against the wall, seeking an answer and finding none. Finally, he turned to his officer of the day. 'Right, Major. There's only one thing we can do. We take the message at face value and send a message back welcoming Ali Benabdala's initiative and inviting him to the banquet and ball. Better get the wild boar taken off the menu: no need to give unnecessary offence.'

'He'll not come alone,' Major Melverley pointed out. 'The invitation must be extended to cover his officers, little though one wants to see them in the city.'

Kirke grinned. 'God's teeth, now, that gives me an idea! If we could but get the Alcaid and *all* his officers within the walls, there would be an end to King Charles's problems forever!'

'As you pointed out yourself, sir, the man isn't a fool. He'd never agree to that. I think we can safely leave the number of accompanying officers to his discretion. If he comes,' Major Melverley added.

'If, indeed,' the governor agreed. 'We must work on the assumption that he will. Tell them to send the envoy back to me.'

As soon as the envoy had been released to carry his message back to his general, the governor and Major Melverley climbed to the top of the Peterborough Tower to watch his progress. The man rode as fast as he could across Whitehall, the broad and roughly level expanse of ground in front of the walls at that point, between Charles and Kendal forts and then, as soon as he was clear of the garrison's outer fortifications, the rising ground on either side of his route was suddenly edged with a solid phalanx of horsemen whose weapons glinted as they were caught in the rays of the setting sun. Gazing into the west as they were, it was impossible for the two men to estimate with any precision the number of Moors who had thus appeared so unexpectedly and so close.

'Thank God we sent the man back before dusk,' Major Melverley commented.

'Amen to that,' the governor agreed, for once not taking refuge in one of his more forceful oaths. 'We have less than two thousand men, not counting the workmen from the mole—who are quite useful fighters when they have to be—and the visiting sailors, who are undoubtedly good at sea, but usually prove useless in land battles against the heathen. I don't suppose we've just seen the half of the Alcaid's army. At least as many again will be lying out of sight but poised to join their fellows. A surprise attack after dark might well have done for us, Melverley.'

The governor might have had to make a decision on his response to the envoy without consulting his officers, but he made very sure the situation was clearly explained to them before the banquet and instructed them to see to it that all members of their families who would be present also knew how important it was that nothing should go wrong. His definition of 'going wrong' ranged from the improbability of someone's misguidedly releasing the Alcaid from the troubles of this world to the far greater likelihood of his unwittingly being given offence.

When Major Melverley explained it to his daughter, Ferelith listened carefully. 'One must just hope that the Alcaid is himself prepared to take the benevolent view,' she said. 'If he is *looking* for offence, he is likely to find it. Take myself, for example: I can only be as well-behaved as I would be in a similar situation in England. If I say or do the wrong thing, he must make allowances.'

'That necessity is precisely what the colonel wants to avoid,' her father said sharply. 'Fortunately, he's unlikely to expect a woman to know precisely how to behave, but you would be well advised to keep your distance if you're unsure.'

Ferelith chuckled. 'Don't worry, Papa. I have no interest at all in the Alcaid and his entourage beyond pure curiosity, and that can be satisfied by standing the other side of the room and staring out at him from behind a pillar.'

Her father sniffed disapprovingly. 'You may choose to make a joke of it,' he said. 'You won't find it a joking matter when you're incarcerated in some Moorish *bagno*—or worse, some tribal chieftain's harem.'

CHAPTER FIVE

THE ALCAID brought with him a rather larger entourage than made the garrison's senior officers feel entirely comfortable, and he left an army of well-mounted and well-armed men conspicuously encamped in a long arc that precisely followed the Moorish lines of the siege some three years earlier. The message was apparent to all: if the Alcaid and his officers did not leave the city safely, the encircling troops would enter.

The Catherine Gate was opened with due ceremony to admit them and a mounted escort led them through the city to the Upper Castle. The citizenry went about its business for the most part appearing uninterested in the presence in its midst of the military leader of its enemy, but surreptitious glances were cast at the party while, in the houses along the route, the women peeped from behind the shutters to determine the nature of their visitor.

They learned very little. The small, wiry, high-tailed, dish-faced horses were very different from the heavy, cloddish English and Andalusian ones of the escort and had more vitality. The women, accustomed to seeing soldiers more heavily mounted, thought they looked odd. The men, who knew how perfect such animals were for a quick, slashing charge, admired their proportions and could understand why the late Lord Protector, Oliver Cromwell, and the present King of England both went to extraordinary lengths to procure such animals, the latter for their speed, the former to lighten and improve the heavy destriers that his more lightly equipped modern army had had no further need for. The riders were robed and turbanned, the hoods of their *djellabahs* thrown back. The Alcaid looked straight ahead but it was noticed that his officers' eyes were everywhere and missed nothing. More than one spectator expressed the opinion that if the Moors hadn't had a map of Tangier when they entered the city they would certainly be able to make one when they got back.

They were taken directly to the Upper Castle where the governor was awaiting them and where they were served tea in the English style to underline the fact that, while Tangier might be part of the landmass the Moors called al-Maghrib, the land of the west, it was an English possession. The Alcaid must get no hint that His Majesty was fast coming to the conclusion that it was more trouble than it was worth and that only the fact that he who commanded Tangier also commanded the entrance to the Mediterranean, that rich trading sea, induced King Charles to retain it. It was not the Moorish custom to come crudely to the point or to come to a quick conclusion once it had been mooted. A meeting such as this was as much an opportunity to assess the character of those with whom one was discoursing as to make decisions or reach agreements and the Moors were in no hurry: al-Maghrib had been theirs for a thousand years and more, and doubtless would be theirs again, even this small piece of it. Sooner or later, the English would go, taking their Scots and Irish mercenaries with them. The Moors would prefer it to be sooner and talked with that in mind, but they also talked with the knowledge that it was inevitable and speed was not the first priority.

The first Ferelith saw of the Alcaid and his party was at the banquet. The route from the Catherine Gate to the Upper Castle had not gone past their lodgings, and although she had felt a certain curiosity as to what the visitors looked like she resisted any temptation to rush out and stare. The man was their enemy. She was disinclined to pander to his self-importance, however justified. Besides, she would see him at the banquet.

This, too, was arranged in the European style, men and women alternating down the table in order of precedence. Imelda told Ferelith that the Alcaid and his men were likely to be discomposed by this, since it was said that their custom was for the men to eat together in one room while the women's meal was served in another.

Well, Ferelith thought, if the Alcaid is discomposed, he hides it very well. He seemed entirely at ease, conversing in good, if not fluent French, and it seemed as if his officers had themselves been selected for their ability to converse in that language. None of them appeared to speak English and Ferelith, remembering her father's words, wondered if any of them did but chose not to, or whether they perhaps understood the language of their hosts better than they spoke it. It was hard to believe that none of them had any knowledge of it at all.

Casting her eyes down the table she was completely taken aback when they encountered and were held by the hazel ones of Benani. He inclined his head in acknowledgement that the recognition was mutual and Ferelith almost immediately dropped hers in confusion. Happily they were seated at opposite sides of the table and so could not have conversed even had they been close enough to do so. She wondered wistfully if he might later wish to resume their slight acquaintance: in a room full of strangers, and those mostly hostile, it would not be unreasonable for him to seek out the one person with whom he had already established a rapport. Ferelith, recalling the walk in the embassy garden, was not at all sure how best to deal with that situation, especially under the gaze of the other guests. Nonsense, she told herself. You will behave as you would if he were an English officer—with courtesy and circumspection.

When the meal was eventually concluded, the participants moved into the smaller rooms leading off the great hall, which had been prepared for this brief interval so that the tables could be stripped and moved to clear the floor for the ball. The orchestra was larger than was usual, the handful of soldiers and workmen who normally fiddled, piped and drummed being supplemented by some of the visiting sailors with their own instruments.

While everything was being prepared and, as always happened on such occasions, taking longer than had been anticipated, Ferelith and her father were chatting with one of the visiting Naval officers when Captain Kilcummin came over and tapped the major on the arm. He was accompanied by the familiar robed figure.

'Excuse me, Major,' he said, 'but Mr——' his tongue grappled with the unfamiliar word '—Benani tells me he would like to resume your acquaintance.' The captain spoke in French so that the guest might not imagine anything untoward was being said. It was the first time Ferelith had heard French spoken with an Irish accent and she wondered how difficult the Berber found it to understand.

The major turned to the visitor and smiled. 'Of course, Mr Benani, I remember you well. I've good cause to be grateful to you. You recollect my daughter, Mrs Durliston, perhaps?' The words were unexceptionable and Ferelith suspected it was only her better knowledge of her father that enabled her to detect the the hint of caution in his tone.

The Berber bowed, Moorish fashion, and then, to her surprise, took her hand and raised it to his lips. It was the accepted gesture of any European but his unfamiliarity with it gave it a certain awkwardness.

'Of course I remember *madame*.' He smiled at her and there was no awkwardness in the smile or in the words that followed. 'Permit me to say, *madame*, that you are as beautiful in the ballroom as on horseback.'

Ferelith blushed and thanked him and then in her turn introduced him to the Naval lieutenant to whom they had been talking. The conversation was general and had not had time to become stilted when Colonel Kirke announced the commencement of the ball, expressing the hope that their Moorish visitors would engage the ladies of the garrison to instruct them in the English dances. The protocol attendant upon such a function was fraught with problems on this occasion. Strictly speaking, the ball should have been opened by the Alcaid and Lady Mary Kirke, while the colonel followed with the Alcaid's wife or, in the absence of one, with the next most senior lady present. However, since the Alcaid was not conversant with European dances this was scarcely feasible, so a hasty conference had been called at which it had been decided that the Alcaid and the governor should be seated on a low dais at one end of the hall while Lady Mary opened the ball with the most senior of the visiting frigate captains. It was also decided that only the most simple of dances should be performed for at least the first two hours, and that these should not progress: it was felt that the Moors would thereby be able to master the steps with a constant partner if, indeed, they chose to dance.

Most of them did, though the idea of dancing with other men's wives was clearly one to which they found it difficult to become accustomed. Benani seemed less concerned than some of his colleagues, possibly because he knew Ferelith was widowed and that therefore there was no need to fear the knife in the ribs that would have ensued had her husband been a Moor.

'Will you obey your governor and teach me the steps, Mrs Durliston?' he asked.

Ferelith smiled. 'It will be my pleasure, Mr Benani. The pavane with which they are opening the ball will not tax your abilities too far, I'm sure.'

He proved to be light on his feet and to have a natural aptitude so that he was soon able to give a little of his attention to his partner instead of his feet. Since the dance must have struck him as very strange, Ferelith could only admire the speed with which he became familiar with the steps.

'You are an excellent teacher, Mrs Durliston,' he remarked once he felt his attention to his feet need be less concentrated.

'I have an apt pupil, Mr Benani,' she replied politely.

They continued in silence for several minutes before he spoke again. 'You have come a very long way to be with your father,' he commented.

'Papa needed someone to keep house and to be his hostess,' she said. 'Who better in the absence of a wife than a daughter?'

'May I enquire whether your mother died or did your father put her aside?' he asked.

Ferelith was shocked. 'She died, of course—some years ago. A gentleman does not put his wife aside, as you call it, in England. Well, not very often,' she said honestly, thinking of a certain notorious monarch, 'and I believe it is very difficult to do.'

'Is it not the custom for Englishmen to remarry when their wife dies?' he asked.

'Very much so, but Papa chose not to. I've never asked him why, but he seems content enough.'

Her partner shook his head uncomprehendingly. 'It seems very strange,' he said.

Ferelith decided it was her turn to ask questions. 'Is it true that Moors may have several wives at the same time?' she enquired.

He smiled. 'Do you know, that's the first question captive Christians always ask? The Koran permits us up to four wives at a time but only if we can support them adequately, each in her own quarters, undertaking to treat each wife equally.'

'One hears of sultans and pashas having hundreds of wives,' Ferelith said doubtfully.

He laughed. 'Not wives. A man may well have several concubines though I imagine very, very few could number them in hundreds—after all, they will all expect to be fed and clothed and few men could afford that.'

'A king could, I suppose. What about yours—Moulay Ismail?'

'He has an extensive harem,' the Berber admitted, 'but then, I understand your own King is no sluggard in that respect.'

Ferelith giggled. 'Very true, though it is generally held to be rather shocking, not so much because he has so many mistresses—concubines, I think was your word— but because he makes no secret of it.'

'Why should he?' Benani was genuinely puzzled. 'It can only reflect to his advantage, particularly if they have children.'

'Which in his case they do,' Ferelith agreed. She laughed. 'We seem to have discovered one of the great differences between our societies,' she went on. 'In England such openness is tolerated only in the King. Lesser men would find themselves ostracised from decent homes.' She concentrated on the dance for a few minutes before continuing. 'That doesn't mean that decent men don't have mistresses—though I imagine they have rather fewer than the King—but they don't *flaunt* them. It's a matter of discretion, you understand.'

'I suppose discretion is one word for it,' he said, unable to keep the disapproval out of his voice.

'What word would you use?' Ferelith asked, intrigued.

'Hypocrisy,' he said shortly.

Upon a brief reflection, Ferelith thought he might have a point but, since the whole topic was not really one suitable for discussion between an unrelated man and woman, she decided to change the subject and enquired into the nature of the hunting in the countryside to the south of the city. Her partner seemed perfectly willing to follow her lead and the rest of the pavane was danced with less interest but more propriety.

The Berber shook his head when Major Melverley suggested an introduction to another of the garrison's ladies for the next dance.

'Thank you, Major, but I think I should prefer to stand and watch for a dance or two. Our dancing is nothing like this and I shall enjoy watching the overall shift and change of the pattern of the dances on the floor.'

'If you're sure...?' the major said doubtfully, but perfectly willing to stand with him while the Naval lieutenant led Ferelith on to the floor.

The dance after that was a simple branle rendered even more simple by the removal of any progression. It was an ideal dance for someone new to a ball in the English style and Major Melverley suggested to the Berber, who seemed in no hurry to become acquainted with anyone else in the room, that he might like to tackle it. He had intended to introduce him to Mrs Kilcummin who stood near by but before he could do so Benani had jumped

to the conclusion that it was with Ferelith that her father
intended him to dance.

'If Mrs Durliston has the patience to teach me once
more,' he said, 'it would give me much pleasure.'

Ferelith shot a look at her father. Two dances with
the same man could lead to a number of misapprehen-
sions on several people's parts, not least that of the man
concerned. Major Melverley was as fully conscious of
that as his daughter but guessed—correctly—that the
man in question was unaware of the possible implications. He trusted that those who might otherwise begin
nudging and whispering would in this instance at least
appreciate that it was nothing more than good manners
and preferable to the insult a refusal would certainly be.

'There you are, Ferelith,' he said. 'Your powers of
instruction are sought once more. I can see Mr Benani
will soon be the most accomplished of his countrymen.'

Ferelith smiled. 'How can I refuse?' she said, laying
her hand upon the sleeve of the Berber's robe. 'Come,
Mr Benani, but you will find this more fatiguing than
the pavane, I promise you.'

As they left the spectators to join the ring of dancers,
he lowered his voice. 'Mrs Durliston, you seemed not
altogether pleased. Would you have preferred not to undertake my further instruction? The truth, please. No
diplomacy, no discretion.'

'The truth? Very well, then. No, Mr Benani, I've no
objection to teaching you any number of dances. My
hesitation wasn't on that account at all.'

'It was there, nevertheless, and it seemed to me you
sought your father's approval.'

'You're an observant man. I did, but not for that
reason. We have a convention of which I imagine you're
unaware. It isn't usual for a lady to dance more than
once—twice, in the case of a very long family acquaintance—with any one man. To do so is to indicate that
there is...' she hesitated, seeking the right phrase that
would express the correct degree of indication '...an
understanding between them.'

'An understanding?'

'Yes. That it is tacitly understood they will eventually marry, even if no formal announcement has been made. If one exceeds the conventional limit without such an understanding, one is considered fast.'

'And the gentleman?'

The question took Ferelith by surprise. 'I don't think it alters the way people think of him one way or another. It is for the woman to protect her name, after all.'

'Or the men of her family, I presume.'

'Indeed, but Papa wouldn't have wished you to feel offended by my refusal—and nor would I,' she added honestly. 'Now, come, Mr Benani. To the dance.'

He found the branle, though relatively simple, undoubtedly energetic. It was in any case not the sort of dance that gave its participants much chance to talk to one another, unlike the stately pavane, and by the time it was finished any further questions about the ways of the English where their womenfolk were concerned seemed inappropriate.

Ferelith, too, felt it was a subject best not revived. This was a pity because she was intrigued by considerations as to whether Mr Benani himself had four wives—or, if the truth were told, even one. It was, of course, no more her business than the number and quality of his concubines, assuming he had any, but, even so, Ferelith felt a distinct curiosity on the matter. She also felt a distinct regret when the branle was over. Having explained to her partner the significance some might read into their second dance, he was unlikely to suggest a third: the subject of their conversation might have been one that would have shocked an eavesdropper, but, all the same, she rather thought him to be a man of honour, something that could hardly be said of the governor, she thought as she saw Colonel Kirke bearing down upon them.

The colonel, very much alive at a time like this to the importance of a correct observance of protocol, had explained the situation to the Alcaid and had, with that gentleman's concurrence, been dancing with the lady of each of his senior officers in strict order of their husbands'—or, in Ferelith's case, father's—seniority. Ferelith's turn had now come.

In normal circumstances, Colonel Kirke would have been perfectly happy never to see Ferelith Durliston again. Unfortunately, Tangier was never 'normal circumstances'. In the first place, it would look far more odd, on an occasion such as this, if he didn't dance with her than if he did. In the second, that wager was still being bandied about and word of his visit to the Melverley house had leaked out. As far as he knew no hint of his humiliation there had accompanied the leak and he had a perverse desire to consolidate his reputation. Besides, he thought, watching Ferelith across the ring of the branle, she was a damned fine woman, a sight too good for that heathen she seemed so taken with. The man was a handsome enough devil, he supposed, but it was hard to believe any Englishwoman could actually *enjoy* the company of such a one. She was probably just being diplomatic and, of course, since she must know she would come under the governor's scrutiny, there was the strong probability that she hoped to make him jealous. Yes, that was it: the resistance to his advances that she had so recently shown—a very violent resistance, it must be admitted—had almost certainly been nothing more than a ruse to increase his interest.

Colonel Kirke was amazed that this had not occurred to him before since it was blindingly obvious, but then, he had had other things on his mind, especially in the last few days. He smiled with satisfaction and made his way across as the branle came to an end.

'Mrs Durliston, your next dance must be with me. Do you minuet?' The French dance was a very recent introduction to the English court and, although courtiers were reasonably proficient at it, one could never be quite sure how far it had filtered down through society—and it was a very complex dance.

'I do, Colonel, but with only modest ability,' Ferelith said truthfully. She and Francis had employed a dancing-master to teach them but she had naturally never danced it with another partner and, while she felt she was competent at the basic measures, she knew she would not be able to invent the intricate variations which proclaimed the accomplished minuettist.

'Then, as we must lead, I undertake to keep to the simpler steps,' the colonel told her. His tone was so benign that Ferelith, who remembered all too clearly the circumstances under which they last parted, glanced at him suspiciously, expecting to detect a hint of irony in his expression, and when she saw nothing she was simply puzzled.

The minuet was a dance unusual in that each couple performed in isolation, watched with admiration, envy or satisfaction by an interested crowd of fellow guests. Depending upon the number of couples participating, a minuet could last a very long time indeed and it was said that at the grander functions at Versailles it was often necessary for those not actually on the floor to adjourn to another room for refreshment in the course of the dance. In England it was customary as a matter of courtesy to watch the couples preceding and following oneself but then one might unobtrusively withdraw. It was, however, unthinkable that a couple should go their separate ways before the whole dance was completed.

Colonel Kirke was true to his word and kept to a very basic interpretation of the minuet which Ferelith had no difficulty in following and then, the next couple having taken the floor, she stood with him at the end of the great hall furthest from her father. She glanced across and saw that Benani, the Berber, was still close to her father, though he appeared to be conversing with someone else, and she felt a quite unjustified desire to know what they were discussing. As this thought struck her, to be instantly dismissed, he glanced away from his companion, across the hall, and caught her eye. Ferelith immediately let her glance fall, disconcerted at having been caught staring so overtly at him, but not before she noticed a faint smile cross his lips before he, too, turned away. Then she was aware that the governor was speaking.

'Come, Mrs Durliston: after such energetic activity, I think we both deserve refreshment. Orgeat and lemonade, as well as wine and ale, are set out in the governor's antechamber. Permit me to escort you.'

Ferelith hesitated. She had no desire to be escorted anywhere by Colonel Kirke, least of all to a side-room. On the other hand there would at the very least be stewards present, so even if there were no other guests in the antechamber she would not be alone with him. Convention and courtesy demanded that she stay with him until the minuet was over and, besides, it was hot in the great hall and she was very thirsty. She glanced round as if hoping there would be someone near by— her father, perhaps—who would need no more than a speaking glance by way of a hint to come with them, but there was no one.

She smiled perfunctorily. 'Thank you, Colonel. Some orgeat would be most welcome.'

He bowed and offered her his arm. Ferelith laid her hand upon it and they made their way through the spectators by means of a touch on the shoulder here and a bow there.

Three couples came out of the antechamber as they entered and the room proved to be empty save for the two stewards.

Colonel Kirke paused by one of them. 'Rhenish, Mrs Durliston? Very revivifying.'

'Thank you, Colonel, but orgeat is more to my taste.'

Upon a nod from his commanding officer, the steward handed Ferelith a glass of the refreshing mixture of almonds and orange-flower water and then a goblet of the Rhenish wine to her escort. She had tasted no more than a welcome sip when she felt the colonel's hand under her elbow guiding her towards the door of his office.

'Come, my dear,' he said in a low voice. 'Let's go where we may be comfortable.' He reached out to turn the handle.

Ferelith drew back. 'No, Colonel, it wouldn't be at all *comme il faut*. We will take our refreshment here, in the room set aside for the purpose.'

'Nonsense, my dear. What could be nicer than to sit down and have a pleasant chat while the rest of them sweat themselves to a frazzle on the ballroom floor?'

His hand became more insistent and Ferelith knew her instincts were right when she caught sight of an imperfectly disguised grin on the face of one of the stewards.

She decided to abandon tact. 'I'm astonished at you, Colonel. To be frank, I'd have thought I had made my feelings perfectly plain to you on the occasion of our last meeting. You seem to have an exceedingly short memory—or perhaps it's merely very selective.'

The colonel's naturally high colour deepened. 'Mrs Durliston, I'm not one to pull rank and I am reluctant to remind you that I am your father's commanding officer.'

'Not too reluctant, it would seem,' she snapped. 'To draw my attention to the fact that Papa's preferment depends very much upon your good will is both unnecessary and uncouth, and I suspect my father rates his daughter's honour rather higher than his own preferment.'

The colonel snorted. 'How like a woman to jump to that assumption! I fancy the major might view it differently. However, enough of this.' He lowered his voice to a more confidential level. 'You needn't worry about them, you know,' he said, indicating the stewards with a nod of his head. 'They know how to be discreet.'

'I should prefer them to have no call to exercise their undoubted discretion,' Ferelith said sweetly, and was about to ask the colonel to take her back into the great hall when another voice broke in.

'Ah, Madame Durliston—here you are! Your father was concerned that you were not to be seen and I offered my services as a search-party. Taking refreshment, I see. I dare say after such an energetic dance as this minuet seems to be it is needed.'

The governor was furious at the interruption but impotent to do anything other than invite the Alcaid's aide to partake himself.

Benani smiled and declined. 'Thank you, but no. I shall, however, be happy to restore *madame* to her father. You have other guests, Governor, and I'm sure he will understand that something has arisen which needs your attentions.'

Thus saying, he somehow interposed himself between them and unobtrusively guided Ferelith back into the ballroom. Once through the door, she turned to him and smiled gratefully.

'Papa must be a mind-reader,' she said. 'I had only minutes before been wishing he were there.'

Benani smiled grimly. 'I have a confession, *madame*: the major had no idea what I was doing. I happened to notice that you seemed a trifle unwilling to accompany the colonel and thought it might be prudent to follow— and, I'm afraid, to eavesdrop.'

'I'm glad you did,' Ferelith assured him. 'The governor is a very good soldier, I believe, and in many respects a good administrator, but his sense of honour where women are concerned is not always what it should be.'

'So I observe. It makes me realise our own good sense in not allowing our womenfolk to be put in such an awkward situation. Tell me, *madame*, did your husband have no brothers?'

'Why, yes—two.'

Although her answer was a statement, there was a question implicit in her tone and Benani chose to answer it. 'Yet neither of them married you when you were widowed?' he asked.

Ferelith stared at him. 'Good gracious, no!' she exclaimed. 'For one thing, they're both married—though I suppose that wouldn't be regarded as a bar here,' she added, recollecting their earlier conversation. 'Apart from that little snag, it would be illegal, anyway: one simply may not marry a dead spouse's brother or sister.'

He looked mystified. 'Then what provision is made for widows?' he asked. 'Someone has to look after them, surely?'

Ferelith had taken the technicalities of widowhood so much for granted that at first she was at a loss how to reply. 'Usually she has her dowry to fall back on together with whatever was settled upon her at the marriage,' she said. 'That ensures her financial security. She may be able to return to the parental home, as I have done, or she may choose to live with her parents-in-law. Older widows generally continue as they were, but without a husband.'

'And with no male protector,' he concluded. 'Doesn't such a woman become prey to men who are more interested in her fortune than her character?'

Ferelith laughed. 'Frequently. Few widows are so completely separated from their families that their male relations can't take up the cudgels on their behalf, however.'

He shook his head. 'It sounds most unsatisfactory to me,' he said. 'The differences between our people go deeper than I'd realised.'

'I wonder...' She hesitated. 'Mr Benani, may I in turn ask you something similarly personal?'

He stiffened, and although he smiled it was a polite rather than a warm smile. 'Of course,' he said. 'Understanding goes both ways.'

In other words, Ferelith thought, it's all right for you to pry but not for me. Very well, I'll tread carefully. Aloud, she said, 'Would you marry your brothers' widows?'

'Of course—as they would marry mine.'

Ferelith was not sure she was very happy about the implications of that rider, but she persisted. 'What would happen if you already had four wives when one of your brothers died?'

He shrugged. 'Another brother would marry her.'

'But let us assume all of you were, so to speak, fully booked. What then?'

He smiled, a genuine smile this time. 'This eternal fascination with our marital arrangements,' he exclaimed. 'Very few men—ordinary men, I mean—are likely to be "fully booked", as you so engagingly put it. If they were, then there would have to be a family meeting at which something would be decided. It might be divorce. More probably a dowry would be provided to ensure another husband for her. Does that answer your question?'

Ferelith supposed it did. 'How much weight would be given to the widow's preference?' she asked.

'That would depend upon the family—and the widow,' he said.

Thinking about it, Ferelith supposed it would. 'In that respect, at least, our two societies are not so very different,' she remarked.

Major Melverley, assuming that his Berber companion had moved off to talk to someone else, had himself moved on by the time Ferelith and her rescuer returned to his end of the hall and it was two or three minutes before they could make him out some way along the other wall.

'There he is,' Ferelith said, pointing with her fan.

'Good. It's time his daughter was restored to him.' He guided her through the bystanders, but just before they were within earshot of the major Benani stopped. 'Perhaps as a courtesy I should answer the one question you didn't ask,' he said.

Ferelith's startled gaze flew to his face. 'Is there one?' she said.

'Most assuredly there is. I have no wives, *madame*, though my father tells me it's time I remedied that. Nor do I have any concubines.'

Ferelith was completely taken aback at so unexpectedly accurate a reading of her thoughts and, because of their nature, she coloured in a confusion that was further increased by the quite disproportionate pleasure his revelation had given her.

'A matter of so personal a nature is none of my business,' she protested.

'It was none the less in your mind,' he replied. He paused and raised her hand to his lips once more, his eyes glancing up at her under his necessarily lowered lashes. 'You have no idea, *madame*, how much I regret that there is here neither terrace nor garden. I should have enjoyed finding an excuse to explore it together—in the moonlight. As it is, I must content myself with returning you to your father. Major Melverley—your daughter.'

The major turned, surprised, but thanked the visitor who then tactfully faded from their side. Ferelith caught a glimpse of him from time to time, conversing with this officer and that, occasionally exchanging words with one of his fellows and once in apparently deep discussion with the Alcaid Ali Benabdala. She tried not to watch his progress but her eyes were drawn to him and it was a source of some exasperation that she did not seem to exercise a similarly magnetic effect on him. Several times she vowed she would not glance in his direction again, that if he chanced to look across he would find her engrossed in converse with someone else, but each time the vow was broken. Only when it was time for the Moorish guests to leave did he look towards her and it was with the unerring aim of one who knew exactly in which direction to glance. Their eyes locked and held and Ferelith was aware that her heart was behaving in a most extraordinary way, hammering against her ribs as if she had been running uphill. He smiled, his teeth gleaming against his tanned skin, and he inclined his head in the only farewell possible across the great hall.

Ferelith, confused by her own confusion, could only similarly incline her own in reply and then took refuge behind her fan. His last impression was of long lashes fluttering over those large green eyes. It was not, he decided, so very different from the effect achieved by the veil.

For several days after the departure of the visitors, the garrison buzzed with speculation. Why had they come? What had they discussed with the governor behind closed doors? Above all, what had induced the Alcaid himself to come? The citizens would have been only slightly more amazed had Moulay Ismail himself walked through the Catherine Gate. There were those who thought the governor a fool to let so important a man go when he could have been held to a ransom from which everyone in the garrison could have benefited. There were others who recalled the silent crescent of men ringing the landward approaches to Tangier while Ali Benabdala was within, and were very glad the governor had been so wise. Those armed horsemen had enveloped their leader and his entourage when it reached them and together they had faded into the warm, soft blackness of the night. In the morning, cautious parties of scouts rode out from the outlying forts. They found nothing but trampled vegetation. The Moors had disappeared as rapidly and unexpectedly as they had arrived. It was all very unsettling.

Ferelith felt particularly unsettled after the visit but for different reasons. She had met Benani several times now and could not deny that she felt drawn to him far more strongly than was proper. Whenever she thought of their stroll in the embassy gardens, a part of her yearned for its repetition even though she knew such emotions were reprehensible. She told herself that he represented some sort of constant in a world of new and strange impressions, and the argument was almost convincing.

Aspects of Benani—she found herself wondering about his given name—kept infiltrating her conscious mind: the sound of his voice with its gutturally accented French, his smiling teeth, the disconcerting eyes. The mind's image was a very positive one, as clear-cut as if he stood before her. There was nothing wrong with that, of course, but when she later found her mind wandering to the memory of dear Francis it seemed as if that image were a little blurred around the edges, and that worried her. It was as if she had been unfaithful to him, though she knew she had never even contemplated such a thing. As she sat at her embroidery-frame, she turned their conversation over in her mind. Perhaps the most bizarre aspect of it was the suggestion that she should have married one of Francis's brothers. She recalled pompous, boring Oliver and the pleasant but ineffectual Edwin and almost laughed aloud. Even had such an alliance been permissable, she would infinitely have preferred to be alone and unprotected than married to either. It was but a short mental step to the contemplation of the expression

on the faces of their respective wives at the news that
Ferelith was to join their household—or rather, she reminded herself, to have her own household adjacent to
theirs. They would not have been pleased and would undoubtedly have lent their very considerable combined
weight to her entreaties to remain single. The scene had
its comical aspect and she set her stitches with the smile
its contemplation provoked.

Almost a week had gone by before the speculation
over the Alcaid's visit died down to be replaced by a
more ominous concern.

The normally steady stream through the city gates of
native merchants with fish and fruit, spices and vegetables, all for sale in Tangier's marketplace, slowed to
a trickle and then dried up like a water-course in summer.
Did this mean the siege of three years before was being
reinvested?

Troops rode out to the limits of their permitted territory and reported no sign of the Moors. Scouts ventured further and returned with the news that Moulay
Ismail was said to be in his new capital of Meknes, some
two hundred miles south as the egret flew. Too far, in
Piercey Kirke's opinion, to be of undue concern. The
Alcaid was halfway between his King and Tangier, at
Ouezzane, but even that was too far off to enable him
to march on the city in the night and a prolonged approach over several days would throw up dust clouds
that would be clearly visible from the higher fortifications guarding the city. The scouts hazarded a warning
guess that there were very likely small groups of Moorish
troops lying in wait for any ill-advised foraging party
that went beyond the agreed limits. The governor and
his officers were inclined to agree with them.

There was no immediate risk of starvation: the plots
outside the city walls and the gardens within provided a
limited supplement to the quite appalling stores landed
by the now-departed merchantmen, and the guard on
the water-supply at Fountain Fort was doubled. These
precautions gave the garrison a breathing-space, time
within which to secure an alternative source of food, but

there was one major snag: the only possible alternative source was from Europe and to get to Europe it was necessary to sail into either the Mediterranean or the Atlantic. It was, as Major Melverley pointed out to his fellow officers, a matter of Scylla or Charibdis. Both seas were infested with corsairs who paid tribute to various rulers on both sides of the water as well as some of the islands in between. In addition, neither the French nor Spanish king was particularly charitably disposed towards the English, Spain being openly hostile in part due to the continued harassment of its treasure ships in the West Indies by English pirates, and France through fear of the growing power of its old enemy. Portugal, the home of King Charles's wife, was a more likely supporter and Piercey Kirke decided that it must be to the Regent Pedro, likely soon to become King Pedro II, that they must apply. It was a pity the merchantmen and their accompanying frigates had gone. There were smaller, less well-armed sailing ships in the harbour as well as several English galleys. There was also a galeasse: more manoeuvrable than a man-of-war, but with more fire-power than a galley, though with less room for cargo than the governor would have liked. Still, food did not keep indefinitely and there was always the possibility of chartering something more in Lisbon. The choice of envoy presented few problems.

'Major Melverley, you're an experienced soldier senior enough to represent the governor. Furthermore you've a God-damned diplomatic way of putting things when it suits you. You'll take the commission, of course?'

'I shall be honoured,' the major said and then hesitated. 'May I presume to ask you to take care of my daughter in my absence?' he asked. 'Nothing obtrusive, you understand—she prides herself on a degree of independence and is a remarkably capable young woman. All the same, I would feel happier if I felt that someone was keeping a watchful eye on her.'

The governor bowed. 'I, too, shall be honoured,' he said, smiling.

Glances were exchanged between some of the other men present. Surely Melverley had heard of the wagers? Few of them would have been happy to give the colonel such a brief. On the other hand, Kirke would have been rightly offended if a subordinate had been asked to perform that duty. The next three or four weeks could be very interesting indeed.

CHAPTER SIX

FERELITH was aghast when she heard the news.

'I accept that you must obey orders, Papa,' she said. 'But to make Colonel Kirke responsible for me! Whatever induced you to do so?'

'Not responsible, Frithy,' he protested. 'I asked him to keep an eye on you. That's not the same thing at all. You will be as independent as ever but if you need anyone to turn to for help the colonel will be there—and in a place like this you can never be sure that everything will always go smoothly.'

'Papa, I've no objection to your asking *someone* to keep an eye on me, but why Colonel Kirke? I can think of few men less suitable.'

'Nonsense. Who could be more suitable than the governor himself? Besides, he'd be deeply offended if someone of lesser rank were asked when he is willing.'

'I don't like the man,' Ferelith said, unwilling to say more and thus place her father in an invidious position.

'I'm aware of that, my dear. I can't truthfully say he's the sort of person with whom I'd wish to associate very much myself were he not my commanding officer, but I think you refine too much upon garrison gossip which certainly doesn't flatter him. You have to remember that the commander of any garrison is invariably slandered by those beneath him. It doesn't mean anything. It's simply a way of venting pent-up feelings about life in general, rather as a child will complain that its parents are unfair or that the cook never serves some dish that happens to be its favourite. Colonel Kirke is a good soldier and is best placed to look after your interests in my absence.'

'I can't argue with either of those statements,' Ferelith said, 'but whether being best placed is necessarily best suited is another matter. However, it's done now and can't be undone, so I must make the best of it. Don't worry about it, Papa. I'm quite sure I shall have no cause to require the colonel's help. I shall quite simply avoid him if I can do so without being too pointedly rude—which is precisely what I do anyway. I'm far more concerned for your safety. Your mission wouldn't be an easy one at the best of times, and if the Moors really are behind the cessation of food from outside they will be expecting something like this, won't they? It must mean there's a very real risk of the ship's being attacked.'

'It's a possibility,' her father admitted. 'We shall be fully armed, however, and both captain and crew are mightily experienced in these waters so we must put our trust in God, knowing that he will favour the just cause.'

Ferelith agreed, but frowned. It was an argument she had heard many times in her life and had never queried until they came here, but Latifa believed in a single god and from something she had once said Ferelith had deduced that she held exactly the same view—except that Latifa saw justice on the opposing side. The arguments were mirror images of each other—and they couldn't both be right. It made Ferelith wonder whether neither was, but she knew better than to say so. She was unsure whether to voice the possibility was heresy or blasphemy, but both were crimes and such views best kept to oneself.

By morning, Major Melverley had gone. The quicker the party set sail for Lisbon the less chance there was of word of their intent reaching either Moulay Ismaii or Ali Benabdala and the greater their chance of success. Ferelith knew he would be away at least four weeks—more if the weather was unfavourable or the Portuguese proved difficult to convince. She resigned herself to a more constricted life in the absence of an escort and found the Kilcummins to be true friends. It was Imelda who suggested she apply to have Latifa sleep in the house rather than return each night to the *bagno*. The case was put by Captain Kilcummin on the grounds that Major Melverley would almost certainly have requested it

himself, had there not been so much urgency attached
to his departure. The governor hummed and hawed but
it was an entirely reasonable request and to decline it
would be to give rise to the most unwelcome gossip, so
Ferelith acquired a chaperon for twenty-four hours in
the day and Latifa gained a comfortable bed and two
rather squarer meals than she was accustomed to.

So far as the governor was concerned, Ferelith
managed to stay out of his way. True, he did pay a
morning call on one occasion but he was accompanied
by Lady Mary—a rare event in itself—and it so happened that Imelda was visiting at the same time, so no
awkwardness could possibly attach to that encounter.
The governor's wife commented vaguely that when they
next held a supper party she would be sure to send Mrs
Durliston an invitation, to which Ferelith had no option
but to reply that she would be happy to accept. However,
the fourth week came and went with no such party's
being arranged and Ferelith was optimistic that her father
would be back before the need to accept arose.

The fifth week followed the fourth with no news of
either the major or his mission. Midway through the sixth
week a *felucca* put in to Tangier, having previously called
at Lisbon and Cadiz. Its captain was escorted to the
Upper Castle for questioning. All he could tell his in-
terrogators was that he had seen no galeasse such as they
described in Lisbon harbour. Quick calculations indicated that he had possibly left the city before the galeasse
had arrived but there was no denying that the complete
absence of any sighting of the major's ship was very
worrying.

Ferelith heard that the *felucca* captain was being questioned and prevailed upon Captain Kilcummin to bring
word to her of the outcome, but when he had done so
she was uncertain whether to be glad she had made him
or not.

The sixth week came to an end and the *felucca* left,
and as the seventh week rolled inexorably on Ferelith
became increasingly anxious. In vain her neighbours assured her that eight weeks was 'nothing' where a ship

on the high seas was concerned. In vain was she repeatedly told that no news was good news. Even Latifa was concerned for her mistress's peace of mind.

'I'm sure you need not be so anxious,' she told her. 'The major is a good man and Allah will surely protect him, even though he be an infidel.'

Ferelith forced a tight smile. 'I'm sure you're right, Latifa,' she said, but she was not convinced.

'I have a feeling about it,' she confided to Imelda. 'I can't explain why but I just *know* something has gone wrong. I just want to know what. If only I knew, I should be easier in my mind.'

'Of course you would,' Imelda told her. 'But it doesn't do to be paying too much heed to hunches. More often than not they prove to be misplaced.'

The eighth week was nearly at its end when a Moorish horseman galloped up to the city walls and demanded an audience of the governor. His request having been granted, Colonel Kirke and his aides heard him out in silence, their faces carefully schooled to betray nothing of their thoughts or emotions as they listened to the message he brought.

'Is that all?' Colonel Kirke asked when he appeared to be done.

'It is, Excellency,' the man said, bowing.

'We shall consider the news you bring us and will give you our reply in the morning,' the governor told him. 'In the meantime, you will enjoy our hospitality though not, I fear, at liberty. I'm sure you understand.'

The man did, but if all he lost was his liberty for a day and a night he would not think himself hard done by. The colonel gave orders for his accommodation and, when the guards had taken him away, followed them up with further orders that the man was to be fed with the best available food, and plenty of it. 'When he gets back to his King, I want him to be able to describe a garrison flowing with milk and honey. Make sure his guards don't watch him eat with their tongues hanging out. Now, gentlemen,' he went on when the door had closed behind the recipient of those instructions, 'what do we do about this?'

'What do we tell Mrs Durliston?' someone was heard to remark in an undertone.

The governor's eyes flashed. 'We tell Mrs Durliston the truth,' he snapped. 'But we don't tell her anything at all until we've decided what to do. Comments, gentlemen.'

When the little group of officers had thoroughly chewed over the news they had received and had then argued back and forth as to the best way of dealing with it and, in particular, the message that should be sent back to Moulay Ismail, the governor made his decision which was, his subordinate officers agreed, the only one possible in the circumstances. Then he dismissed them and sent for Captain Kilcummin and briefly sketched in the position to him.

'So, young man,' he concluded, 'I shall require your escort to Mrs Durliston's. She must be put in possession of the facts. Then I'm afraid I'm going to leave it to you and your wife, with whom Mrs Durliston seems to be on particularly good terms, to comfort her. She'll be both angry and heartbroken and I'm fully aware that mine is the easier task.'

'Yes, Colonel.'

By the time they reached Ferelith's lodgings she had heard of the messenger and of his special treatment, and was intelligent enough to have guessed its reason. 'Do you think he brings news of my father?' she asked Imelda.

Mrs Kilcummin considered the matter. 'I suppose it's possible,' she said at last. 'It doesn't seem very likely, though, does it? I mean, we know the man came from Moulay Ismail and he is in Meknes, they say, which by all accounts is a very long way from the sea.' Even as she spoke, she knew there was little logic in her reasoning but her prime consideration was to save Ferelith anguish. Moulay Ismail's reputation was not one of benignity.

When Colonel Kirke was shown into the saloon, Ferelith was conscious of a sense of irritation. Fending off the advances of an amorous governor was just about the last thing she wanted to do for the present. When she saw Captain Kilcummin behind him, she knew seduction was not in his mind.

'Colonel?'

'Sit down, Mrs Durliston, and forgive me if I do the same without invitation,' and he suited the action to the words. Ferelith followed his example. 'I have bad news for you, Mrs Durliston, so I shall come straight to the point. You've probably heard that a messenger from the Moorish King has arrived?'

Ferelith nodded.

'He brought us news of your father. No, he's not dead, so upon that score you may be at ease. However, that is the limit of the good news, I'm afraid. You may also be pleased to know that your father's mission was successful in that he reached Lisbon safely and in record time and was able to persuade Pedro to accede to our request for supplies. Unfortunately, they were intercepted on the return voyage by a veritable flotilla out of Sallé. The cargo was taken, the ship added to the Moorish fleet and all those on board taken captive, to be ransomed by their loving kinsmen and in the meantime set to work in the galleys. Except for Major Melverley.'

Ferelith blanched. 'Except for Papa?' She clutched at the arms of her chair. 'What are they doing with him?'

'He, too, is being held to ransom, though I understand he's being treated as an honoured guest for the time being,' he began.

Ferelith interrupted him before he could continue. 'But, Colonel, that's excellent news! We have only to raise the ransom and he will be free! How much is it? I'm sure we can find it: there's my portion which I'll gladly put up and I don't doubt my late husband's relatives will help. We must gather it as quickly as we can, the sooner to buy his release!'

The governor reached across and put a comforting hand over hers. 'Not so fast, Mrs Durliston. It's not quite as simple as that. Part of the ransom is demanded in money, of course, and is far from excessive for a man of the major's importance: a mere five thousand dollars in gold. However, Ismail is demanding more than that. He is insisting on the withdrawal of English troops from Tangier and the city's return to what he calls its rightful owners—by which he means the Moors, of course.'

Even Ferelith, prejudiced in her father's favour as she was, could see that this was a price beyond the governor's power to pay without reference to his own sovereign, but she had heard enough political debate in the drawing-rooms and round the supper-tables of the little colony to know that her father's fate was not necessarily sealed.

'Is that so impossible, Colonel?' she asked. 'Everyone knows the King would be glad of an excuse to be rid of the financial burden Tangier represents. Might this not be the excuse he needs?'

'There's speculation on the subject, certainly, fuelled by Parliament's dilatoriness in sending the garrison's pay and its insistence upon cutting the costs of the mole, but speculation isn't fact and frankly, my dear, even if the rumour were well-founded in this instance, can you im-agine the King of England giving way to the demands of some heathen tyrant, and all for the sake of one man? No, Mrs Durliston. I'm sorry to have to be so brutal, but Ismail's demand is impossible, a fact I'm sure he would be the first to acknowledge, if only to himself. He must know we can't accede to anything so outrageous.'

'The terms are surely negotiable?' she said. 'The Moors bargain over everything. Why should Papa's re-lease be any different?'

'I'm sure you're right: they can't possibly have any real expectation that we would meet these terms. We therefore have to assess what we think they *will* accept. A reduction in the garrison's strength? Cessation of work on the mole? A withdrawal from our outlying forts to the confines of the city? A removal of the right of citi-zens to go outside the walls? To maintain their plots out there? What limits do you think they would accept, Mrs

Durliston? More importantly, perhaps, what limits do you think we should be prepared to accept in order to free your father?'

Ferelith could see that the colony could concede nothing of this nature. 'Won't you even try to negotiate?' she demanded. 'You could at least offer a great deal more money.'

'As we intend to do, but I must warn you I'm not at all optimistic about the outcome. They must know all too clearly how much we had depended upon that cargo and therefore how straitened our circumstances are. They have the upper hand, though it would be bad tactics to admit it to them, and hope to starve us out without the trouble and expense of a conventional siege. Their hope is that we might give in more easily, given an adequate excuse. We shall, of course, offer a much higher ransom, but it will be rejected, no matter how high it is. That is the true position and you mustn't delude yourself that anything will alter it.'

Ferelith looked at him in despair. 'What will happen to Papa when they realise you are adamant?'

'He will probably be made to work like any other unransomed captive,' Kirke replied. This was a possibility but, although it was the usual practice where captives were concerned, his real expectation was that Melverley would be killed and his head returned to Tangier. It wouldn't be the first time the Moorish King had dealt with an enemy captive in that way. This was not the sort of thing to pass on to the man's daughter, however, and he hoped no one else in the colony would raise the possibility in her hearing.

'When will Moulay Ismail get your reply?' she asked.

'His messenger will be freed as soon as I return to the Upper Castle. I felt I had to explain the situation to you first.'

'How long will it be before we hear anything?'

'I don't know. It could be a matter of days. They will more probably wish to keep us on tenterhooks for a while. That's what I should do in Ismail's shoes. It could be several weeks. You must prepare yourself for a long wait.'

'And if, as you expect, it is all to no avail and Papa does not return, what then?'

'Your father left you in my care, Mrs Durliston—a responsibility I was happy to accept. In that event, I shall ensure that you're sent home on the first available vessel.'

'With Sally rovers intercepting our ships in both directions, my chances of getting back to England in the near future—or, indeed, at all—would appear to be slim,' she remarked drily.

'Quite so, Mrs Durliston.' He turned to Captain Kilcummin. 'You're relieved of duty for the rest of the day, Mr Kilcummin. Perhaps you and your wife would stay with Mrs Durliston.'

The very fact of Imelda's presence was a comfort to Ferelith, assuring her in a practical way that she was not completely alone, that there were friends, even in this benighted place, upon whom she might depend. Ferelith knew she must be a sore trial to her neighbours: the impotence of her position made her restless; it mattered not whether she sat down with a book or a tambour-frame—within five minutes she would be out of her seat again and pacing the room. The Kilcummins seemed to accept these aberrations with equanimity, maintaining a desultory conversation into which they sought to draw Ferelith, occasionally with success.

Ferelith was grateful to them, though she knew she was behaving abominably by the standards of good manners, but she resolutely resisted their offer to spend the night.

'You're very kind,' she said, 'but I have Latifa and the colonel has agreed to allow Amin to sleep here as well, so that there is a man in the house. I have to face the fact that I may soon find myself without my father, so I may as well get used to be being more or less on my own.'

The Kilcummins pressed their case but Ferelith was adamant and so after supper, with assurances that, should she need them, Ferelith would not hesitate to send for them, her neighbours returned to their own house and Ferelith retired to her room to attempt to sleep.

That she was finally successful was evidenced by the difficulty Latifa experienced in trying to wake her mistress up.

'Madam, madam,' she whispered urgently, shaking Ferelith and sending up a silent prayer to Allah that Mrs Durliston would not wake with any kind of cry that might alert the neighbours. 'Madam, wake up. Please wake up.'

Ferelith stirred and mumbled and then, seeing Latifa bending over her, she tried to focus on the maid's obvious urgency. 'Latifa? What is it? What time is it? Latifa—what's happened?'

Latifa put her finger to her lips. 'Ssh. Madam, you have a visitor. Very important, I think.'

Ferelith sat bolt upright in bed and threw the covers off. 'It's Papa! My father has come back! Oh, thank God!' She reached out for the wrap that lay across the foot of the bed.

Latifa helped her into it. 'No, madam. I regret, but it is not your father.'

Her hopes thus dashed, Ferelith stared at her maid in bewilderment. 'Then who...?'

'Downstairs, madam,' and then, as Ferelith reached out automatically for a tinder to light the bedside candle, Latifa caught her hand and stayed it. 'No, madam. No lights. Someone may notice. There is light enough from the moon.'

Ferelith hung back, suddenly suspicious. 'Are those your orders? No lights? Who goes visiting at this time of night? It's not—oh, Latifa, don't tell me it's Colonel Kirke?'

The maid giggled. 'No, madam, not on this occasion. Come, please.'

There was something in Latifa's giggle that allayed any darker suspicions Ferelith might have been harbouring and she followed the girl downstairs to the small parlour at the back of the house. The figure that stood there, enveloped in a hooded cloak, was neither as tall nor as broad as Major Melverley and Ferelith did not immediately recognise it. As soon as it turned, however, she realised that her visitor was the the one she had least expected—the Berber, Benani.

'You!' she exclaimed. 'What on earth are you doing here?'

Latifa, seeing that her mistress was neither upset nor alarmed by her visitor, quietly withdrew. The Berber had told her she was to do so but she had mentally resolved to ignore the command if Ferelith seemed unhappy at this turn of events.

He took her hands in an impulsive gesture. 'I have very little time,' he said. 'I am supposed to be on my way back to Moulay Ismail. If he suspects I have delayed, my life will be forfeit and I must be far from here before the first hint of dawn—your soldiers were kind enough to escort me well beyond the line of forts and I fancy Colonel Kirke would be none too pleased to learn that I had returned.'

'You were the envoy?'

He nodded. 'I hoped the errand would give me the opportunity for a few words with you. I asked the governor to be allowed to speak with you but he refused. What have they told you about your father?'

Briefly, Ferelith told him.

'Good. I was afraid they would tell you nothing at all; perhaps I was a little afraid they would tell you he was dead, thereby being able to do nothing to get him back while not letting you know that it might have been possible.'

'Have you seen Papa?'

'I have, and he is well. I spoke with him before I left and he sends his love and urges you not to worry.'

Ferelith laughed bitterly. 'I doubt he'd have sent any other message—or have been allowed to.' She looked up into the Berber's eyes. 'Tell me truthfully, Mr Benani— is he really all right?'

'By the soul of the Prophet, I swear it. When I left he was not, of course, happy, but he was fit and well, and I cannot imagine Moulay Ismail allowing anything to happen to him while we are negotiating with the garrison.'

Ferelith smiled tremulously and felt a tear of relief trickle down her cheek. 'Thank you for that assurance, Mr Benani,' she said. 'Can you also assure me that the situation won't change?'

'My name—to my friends—is Hassan,' he replied and added gently, 'No, I can offer no such guarantee. Only the King himself can do that. I cannot even offer to keep a watchful eye on the major: when I have delivered your governor's reply, I shall leave almost at once, Moulay Ismail permitting, for my home in the mountains. I do not serve the King exclusively.'

'So I shan't see you again?' Suddenly it was very important that that should not be the case, and Ferelith was not aware that in her concern her hands, which had been lying lightly in his clasp, were gripping his.

He raised each in turn to his lips, and then drew her gently closer. 'Sadly, I have to say that that is another matter for which I can offer no guarantee.' He kissed her then as gently and tenderly as he had done in the embassy garden but this time, instead of a surprised acceptance of the embrace, Ferelith's lips responded with the frightened urgency of one who, having found what she unknowingly sought, learned it is to be lost forthwith.

'If you took me with you now,' she said, 'I could rejoin Papa and you could hand me over to the care of your King until it is all finished.'

He kissed her again. 'Would that I could! Alas, I suspect that that would prove the least satisfactory of all solutions. No, my dear. It is best that you stay here. Who knows? If it is the will of Allah...'

The rest of the sentence was lost in the now mutual urgency of their embrace. Time had become of the essence and it was as if each of them vied with the other to crown a lifetime's expression of desire into a few brief moments. But time put more at stake than their mutual longing and it was Hassan who finally broke the spell.

'Enough,' he said. 'I must be gone. The only promise I can give you is that I will do what I can for your

father—but we must both resign ourselves to the fact
that that may not be very much.'

'And do we really have to leave it to the will of Allah
to decide whether we meet again?' Ferelith's voice was
full of impotent entreaty.

He kissed her again, briefly and with a distressing finality. 'Both whether and in what circumstances,' he
said.

He pulled the hood of his cloak so far forward over
his head that his face became a shadowy cavity, and then
he slipped through the smallest possible opening of the
casement window, over the sill and into the garden. The
garden walls were not too high for a man to scale with
ease, and there was no nightwatch protecting the backs
of houses. He was soon gone, leaving Ferelith with
nothing but memories and a casement window to secure.

The governor's guess that Moulay Ismail would keep
them waiting for his answer proved correct and it was
over three weeks of sleepless nights before an answer
was received. The King was happy to accept the increased offer of gold but much regretted his inability to
compromise on the matter of Tangier itself.

This reply, which was effectively an increase in the
price of the major's freedom, left the governor almost
speechless with fury.

'God's death, doesn't he appreciate the rudiments of
bargaining? He knows I meant him to come down in his
demands on the garrison! God damn me if I send him
a counter-offer!'

But he did, of course, and it was a most diplomatic-
ally worded one. What he did not do this time was to
discuss any aspect of it with Ferelith, nor did he send it
immediately. The messenger was kept under guard until
it suited Colonel Kirke's convenience to reply. Ideally
he would have liked to have been able to keep the
Moorish King waiting even longer than he had been
obliged to do but he was all too well aware that time
was not on his side. Food shortages were biting hard
and, if there was to be any chance of improving the situation, some kind of settlement had to be reached.

The fact that the governor didn't tell her about the new messenger did not mean Ferelith knew nothing of it. Now that merchants and traders no longer came to Tangier from outside, the arrival of anyone was an event, news of which sped through the city almost before the newcomer had reached his ultimate destination, and neighbours made sure Ferelith knew the good news.

She waited three days for the governor either to send for her or to visit and when he did neither she decided to force the issue. She knew the messenger was imprisoned in the castle and guessed that the governor would be in no more of a hurry than his adversary to send a reply. That didn't mean he hadn't decided what it should be, and Ferelith had every intention of finding out.

The adjutant on duty guessed her purpose exactly and regretted that he rather thought the colonel was busy.

Ferelith smiled with a calculated sweetness she was far from feeling. 'Then pray be so very kind as to tell him Mrs Durliston is here, that she has no intention of going away until she has seen him—and that in your opinion she means every word of it.'

'Yes, ma'am,' he said, taken aback. Who'd have thought the red-haired widow had such a sharp tone of voice when it suited her? Though they did say it went with the hair. He disappeared into the governor's office.

A raised voice was heard—not the adjutant's—and, although she couldn't make out the words, she was quite sure a desk was soundly thumped. Then there was relative silence. Eventually the door opened and the governor, smiling with carefully contrived benevolence, emerged.

'Mrs Durliston! I'm so sorry you found it necessary to come up here yourself,' he began. He gestured to the door which now stood open. 'Come in, my dear, and I shall explain everything—including the delay. Hunstanton,' he went on, addressing the adjutant, 'see to it we're not disturbed.' He ushered Ferelith into his office and closed the door.

Ferelith looked around her grimly. This was the room from which Hassan Benani had rescued her, and here she was walking voluntarily into it. How circumstances changed! 'Well, Colonel? I know there has been a messenger from the Moors here for some days. I presume it has to do with my father. What's happening?'

Kirke indicated a chair for her and handed her a glass of Madeira before attempting to answer her question. Then he briefly but comprehensively gave her the gist of Moulay Ismail's counter-offer.

'But that's preposterous!' she exclaimed. 'That's not bargaining!'

'My thoughts exactly,' he said.

Ferelith got to her feet impatiently. 'I don't understand,' she said. 'It's as if he doesn't want to negotiate. What are you going to reply?' He was silent and she stared at him in amazement. 'You are going to reply, I take it?'

'Of course. It's a matter of playing for time. Sooner or later supply ships will be here from England. Once that happens we know we've more time at our disposal.'

'Except that, if no messages to London have been able to leave Tangier, they won't realise there's any special urgency about it, will they? And that means it could be months before they arrive.'

The governor frowned. How he disliked the sort of woman who was able to assess a political situation as well as most men! It was understandable when a woman was plain and needed a means of drawing attention to herself. Ferelith Durliston had no need of such stratagems. All she needed to do was flutter those deliciously long eyelashes and most men would melt at her feet. He followed her over to the window where she stood looking out over the bailey, and patted her hand in what was intended to be a fatherly manner.

'Now, don't you worry about that. There are more ways to get a message back to London than by sending it through the usual channels.'

Ferelith looked at him scornfully. 'I suppose you could send it in a bottle and hope it washed up on the right beach,' she said. 'Or do you prefer to put your trust in the subject of another monarch? Will the French deliver a message? Or the Spanish?'

'You're forgetting the Portuguese already know the situation. Your father reached Lisbon safely.'

'They know what the situation was then,' she corrected him. 'They don't know what it is now—and they probably don't even know that the supplies they sent never arrived.'

Her assessment was too accurate for comfort. The governor slipped his hand round her waist. 'There's really no need to distress yourself, Mrs Durliston. I know it's easy to say, "Don't worry," but nevertheless that's my advice. Your father left you in my care. Why don't you be guided by him? Let me do the worrying while you...well, I suppose it's asking too much to suggest you enjoy yourself, but you know what I mean.' He gave her waist what he hoped would be interpreted as a friendly squeeze. 'Now you go home and be as easy in your mind as you can.'

Ferelith moved unobtrusively out of the encircling arm. 'What reply will you send Ismail?' she asked.

'My dear, I can't possibly tell you that,' he replied. 'These things must be kept very quiet indeed. There are plenty of people within the city whose allegiance is only partly to the English. We wouldn't want Ismail to know our terms before his messenger even leaves here, would we?'

Ferelith turned and looked him straight in the eye. 'Colonel, are you suggesting I might repeat what you tell me?'

'God damn me, Mrs Durliston, the thought never entered my head. It's just that, knowing, you might without realising it say something which would give a knowledgeable listener an indication of the way our minds were working.'

Ferelith supposed that was a reasonable argument, though she still wasn't happy about it. 'Colonel, may I make a suggestion of my own to get us out of this impasse?' she said.

He threw his hands out in an expansive gesture. 'Anything constructive is more than welcome, my dear. Speak out.'

Ferelith resumed her seat and his face fell, though she failed to notice it. He was rather afraid she would be here for some time.

'Are you going to send Moulay Ismail's own messenger back to him, or will you keep him and send one of your own?' she asked.

'I'll send the Moor back, of course,' he said, surprised. 'A messenger of our own is all too likely to join your father and we can ill spare anyone.' He was surprised so uncomfortably intelligent a woman hadn't thought of that for herself. The discovery almost restored his good humour.

'Yes, I realise that,' Ferelith said, unwittingly lowering his spirits again. 'But there are circumstances in which, if you used Moulay Ismail's messenger to accompany an envoy of your own—a non-combatant envoy, let us say, and therefore no loss to the garrison—that person might be able to negotiate far more effectively than a mere message-carrier.'

'True,' he said, treading carefully as if he knew a trap had been laid on the path ahead and was anxious not to be caught in it. He mentally reviewed his officers and was forced to admit that the only one of them possessed of the sorts of skills to which Ferelith was referring was Major Melverley. Then he recalled her reference to non-combatants. 'Whom had you in mind?' he asked cautiously.

'Me,' Ferelith told him.

'You,' he reiterated blankly.

'Who better? Who else has so strong an incentive to reach a satisfactory conclusion?'

'Perhaps too strong to allow for rational judgement,' Kirke suggested.

'That's a risk you'd have to take,' Ferelith told him. 'Surely it's worth taking if it secures the release of my father without costing Tangier its very existence?'

The governor shook his head. 'A brave idea, my dear, but quite out of the question. I very much doubt that you'd even live long enough to reach Ismail.'

'Not even with the protection of his own messenger?'

'Not as a woman. You wouldn't have travelled very far before you'd be completely behind the Moorish lines and abducted into someone's harem—in all probability, sold there by the very messenger who was supposed to be protecting you. As your father's son, it might be possible, though even then I doubt its wisdom. As his daughter it's out of the question.'

'Then I could dress as his son. In fact, now I come to think of it, that might be the very thing. An excellent suggestion, Colonel, for which I thank you.'

'No!' he said, alarmed. 'Certainly not, Mrs Durliston. I couldn't countenance such a hare-brained scheme! You go back to your lodgings and manage your household with the efficiency of which your father boasted. You must leave the diplomatic work to the men to whom it is second nature.' He put his hand under her elbow and guided her towards the door. 'When I hear such wild suggestions from your lips,' he told her, 'I give thanks to my Maker that I didn't tell you what my counter-offer would be. Had I done so, I should now almost be afraid you might do something foolish on your own account.'

Ferelith smiled up at him and fluttered her eyelashes. 'I don't think I've ever done anything really foolish,' she told him.

He seemed reassured. 'I'm glad of it—and not surprised. You've always struck me as a sensible little thing—just a bit wayward from time to time. Now, you go home like a good girl and in a day or two, when I shall perhaps have some news for you, I'll call in and let you know what's happening. How does that strike you?' She really was a very attractive young woman, he thought, and when she fluttered her eyelashes like that it confirmed his earlier judgement that she had only been playing the maid that said no but had it just the same.

'That would be very kind of you, Colonel,' Ferelith said. 'I shall look forward to seeing you.'

'And I, you, my dear,' he said sincerely. 'And I, you.'

If anyone was watching Ferelith when she left the governor's office, they would have seen that she made her way briskly towards the gate of the castle, as one would expect, but once there she stopped, apparently in thought, and then retraced her steps a few yards and turned the corner that led to the governor's house. Here she pulled the bell and requested the Turkish captive who answered it to advise Lady Mary of her visit. A few moments later, she was shown into the parlour where Lady Mary Kirke received visitors.

These did not normally include Mrs Durliston, though she had naturally paid courtesy calls on the governor's wife from time to time. Lady Mary found it hard to like the young widow. She had managed to convince herself that it was because the younger woman was 'more sprightly' than was suitable for her condition, but in truth she felt envious of her youth and her vitality. The climate seemed to suit her, she was rarely ill, and it was even rumoured that she had persuaded her two servants to teach her some Arabic. Only a few words or phrases, Lady Mary dared say, but even so a very eccentric thing to do.

The two women could not have presented a greater contrast to an observer. Ferelith's auburn ringlets and green eyes were complemented by the bronze slubbed silk of her morning-gown. A pale amber tourmaline ringed with freshwater pearls nestled in the lace that edged the bosom of her dress and drew discreet attention to her natural endowments. Lady Mary Kirke was far more magnificently dressed in rich crimson damask but her pallid, sickly complexion and the consequently lank hair of indeterminate colour, which her maid tried every day to coax into some sort of temporary life, were overpowered by the opulence of the fabric. Tangier did not suit the governor's wife and neither did her husband's behaviour, about which she had few illusions. The wager relating to Mrs Durliston had reached her ears but she was uncertain whether the widow had yet become one of her husband's conquests. Still, the courtesies must be observed.

'An unexpected pleasure, Mrs Durliston,' she said.

'You're very kind,' Ferelith replied. She was never sure whether to pity Lady Mary or to be irritated by her. If she treated her husband to these lacklustre airs, it was no wonder he found his pleasures elsewhere, and Ferelith knew that if she had found herself in similar shoes she would have fought back by more positive means than taking to her sick-bed on the slightest pretext. 'However, I feel bound to confess that this is more than a courtesy call and is very much on the spur of the moment. Lady Mary, I've just come from an interview with your husband and I need to enlist your help.'

Had it been possible for colour to drain any further from her ladyship's face, it would have done so. Good God, she thought, is the girl here to complain or to boast? And does she imagine I want to know about it either way? 'Of course—if I have the power to do so,' she said.

'Colonel Kirke and I have been discussing my father's unenviable position.' Ferelith hesitated. 'I don't know how much you know about it,' she went on with some diffidence.

'I believe it has been mentioned,' Lady Mary told her. In fact she knew far more than even her husband realised. He invariably talked his problems out at his wife and, because she seldom commented, assumed that what he told her went over her head. He was mistaken, and she was perfectly capable of drawing her own conclusions from the facts and opinions she was given. Her conclusions were not always the same as her husband's and she not infrequently had the satisfaction of being right. Naturally, she let no hint of this reach her husband.

'It seems they have reached some sort of impasse,' Ferelith went on, 'and I have suggested a way out of it but the governor doesn't seem inclined to adopt it.'

'I'm sure Colonel Kirke has a very good reason for rejecting your idea,' Lady Mary said. 'He has a great deal of experience in these matters.'

'Indeed, he has, and Papa always told me what an excellent commanding officer he is,' Ferelith assured her. 'But sometimes a fresh mind can suggest a solution whose very novelty ensures its success.'

Lady Mary considered. 'I'll agree that the outsider sometimes sees more of the game,' she said. 'What was your suggestion?'

Ferelith told her. 'Your husband insists that it's impossible,' she concluded. 'I don't think so and that's why I've come here: to persuade you to add your voice to mine.'

Lady Mary resolutely pushed from her mind the thought that, since Ferelith's plan would at the very least remove her from Piercey's roving eye, there was a lot to be said in its favour, and told herself that the girl's almost certain death—or worse, if what one heard about the Moors was true—would be a rather excessive price to pay for what was, after all, a weakness on Piercey's part rather than the girl's.

'I'm sorry to disappoint you, Mrs Durliston, but I'm afraid I agree with my husband. It would be most ill-advised.'

'But it could be successful,' Ferelith insisted.

'I suppose it might conceivably succeed, if you ever reached Moulay Ismail, but I doubt if you would get more than ten miles beyond Tangier. As for your success if you did reach the King—I should be disinclined to depend too much upon it. Doubtless you would have a certain curiosity value—for a while—but do you really want to put yourself in the hands of that man? I know you've not been here all that long but you must surely have heard the stories about him? He is not what one might call a *pleasant* man.'

If the stories about him were to be believed, that was an understatement of classical proportions. 'His people seem to be devoted to him,' Ferelith pointed out.

Lady Mary seemed genuinely surprised. 'What has that to say to anything? It's their duty to be devoted to their King as it is ours to be devoted to King Charles.'

'The English haven't always shown unquestioning devotion to their monarchs,' Ferelith pointed out sharply. 'Why should we necessarily assume the Moors would do so if the King was really as tyrannical as they say?'

'Because they are heathens without the benefit of the Bible,' Lady Mary told her.

Ferelith opened her mouth to tell her that, according to Amin, the Koran, despite what any Christian must regard as its scandalous licence in the field of marriage, held remarkably similar views about man's duty to his fellow men. Then she closed it again. She would probably not be believed, and if the governor's wife thought her visitor was in danger of turning renegade she would herself be duty-bound to tell her husband of that suspicion. Ferelith was in no danger of renouncing her faith and she had not the slightest desire to find herself in prison. She returned to the matter of her idea.

'Lady Mary, will you speak on my behalf?' she begged.

'No, Mrs Durliston, I will not. I should like to help you and if you can but devise a scheme less fraught with danger to yourself and more certain of success then I shall be happy to take your part, but this is a wild, harebrained idea, far too dangerous to be seriously contemplated.'

'Your husband said much the same thing,' Ferelith said wryly.

'There you are, then,' his wife said with finality. 'We can't both be wrong.'

Ferelith returned home unsure whether to be angry or dispirited. She certainly felt the frustration of impotence. She felt in her bones that if only she could get to see Moulay Ismail she would somehow be able to hit upon some proposal which would meet with his approval sufficiently to induce him to free her father. Of course there was an attendant risk, but then, didn't everything worthwhile carry one? She supposed the governor was right to try to dissuade her: her father had left her in his care and he would probably be failing in his duty if he didn't try to stop her entering into potentially dangerous undertakings. Similarly, she supposed

Lady Mary would have been less than a dutiful wife if she had not followed her husband's lead. Nevertheless, Ferelith thought they could both have given rather more serious consideration to her idea and it crossed her mind for one ignoble moment to wonder whether Colonel Kirke was actually quite glad to be left with an almost indefinite responsibility for her. She had little doubt that, as time went on, he would take increasing advantage of it—she had already been given a strong enough hint that she had not yet succeeded in depressing his interest in her. As she was a married woman with no kinship to the governor, he had no legal control over her at all, she knew. But she also knew that if she were to stand too heavily upon her right to her own independence, particularly in rejecting his advances, she would probably forfeit his very necessary assistance in returning to England to say nothing of her rightful share of any provisions that might reach the beleaguered city.

Perhaps if she could get in touch with Hassan he would be able to advise her as to the best course to pursue, she thought wistfully. She recalled how he had come, unbidden, to her aid on more than one occasion, to say nothing of the risk he had run to allay her anxiety over her father's fate.

His face came vividly to mind and so did his voice. She remembered, too, the feel of his arms around her and his lips on hers. In some ways she scarcely knew him yet she thought of him as an old and trusted friend, and nothing would have made her happier than to be able to pursue that friendship.

She knew enough about Tangier and the Moors now to know that Hassan Benani's role was not quite as it appeared. His presence in Lisbon, a footman at the embassy of his country's enemy, his appearance trading from a bum-boat, all these suggested that he was not so much an envoy of his ruler as a spy. That, Ferelith knew, ought to change her attitude to him, but it did not.

She wondered if a messenger could find him. Probably—but whom should she send? No Englishman would know where to look; a Moor or an Arab from the

city might know where to look but they could not
necessarily be trusted and, even if they could, might well
be stopped and searched by one of the garrison's military patrols. On balance Ferelith decided she had small
taste for the role of traitor and its consequent inevitable
punishment. Latifa or Amin would be the most likely
to be able to find him, but as runaway captives they
would automatically be killed if they were caught—and
their absence would soon be remarked upon.

Ferelith idled restlessly about the house for the next
two days trying to devise a solution to her dilemma, and
failing. No word came from the Upper Castle and she
knew the messenger had not yet been sent with the reply.
She wasted hours trying to conceive of a plan whereby
he might be induced to carry a message from her as well
as from the governor but she knew that was an impossibility. It would be easier to take it herself, as she had
originally suggested.

And why not? she thought suddenly. It would be by
far the most satisfactory way of dealing with Moulay
Ismail, and what was to stop her? Her father had asked
Colonel Kirke to keep an eye on her but he had imposed
upon her no duty of obedience. She was theoretically a
free agent and, had she been a son rather than a daughter,
no one would have thought any the worse of her for
what she was proposing to do.

She couldn't just walk out of the city, of course, and
head towards the enemy. If she was seen to be doing so,
she would be brought back forthwith, and she could
think of no means by which she might contrive to get
hold of a mount. She thought of Latifa. The girl would
surely like to be returned to her people? If she left Tangier
with Ferelith and they were caught, at least she could
not be charged with running away because she would be
with her mistress. It would be in her interest to keep
Ferelith safe until they fell in with some Moors, and then
Latifa's Arabic would be far more use than the few sentences Ferelith had learnt, sentences which had more to
do with running a household than with negotiating one's
father's freedom. Yes, Latifa was the answer to her

prayer. The only odd thing was that it had taken so long for her to realise it.

At first the maid was wary, suspecting a trap. Then, when she was finally convinced that her mistress was very much in earnest, she decided she was mad.

'Madam, it's impossible!' she exclaimed.

'Nonsense,' Ferelith told her. 'Difficult, maybe, but not impossible. All that's required is that we put our heads together. If I reach Moulay Ismail, you will be free. Isn't that sufficient incentive?'

'Indeed, madam—what greater incentive could there be? It's just that I don't see how it may be achieved. Meknes is a long way—many, many leagues. By the time we had walked so far, the messenger would have returned to Moulay Ismail and if the message he bore was unfavourable your father might well be dead.'

This was a possibility that hadn't occurred to Ferelith, but she did not allow it to be a stumbling-block for very long. 'Then we shall need horses,' she declared.

'Yes, madam, and how do we get them?'

'I've thought about that and the only thing I'm certain of is that we won't be able to get them from within the garrison. I could ask for two on the grounds that I want to go for a ride and I need you to chaperon me, but even if I was allowed to—which I doubt—they'd make sure a soldier accompanied us and he would be bound to insist we stay within the ring of forts.'

Latifa nodded and frowned, deep in thought. 'Does it have to be horses, madam?' she asked.

Ferelith shrugged. 'No, but what else is there? The garrison has nothing else.'

'No, not the garrison,' Latifa told her. 'The merchants have both asses and mules. Either would serve the purpose, though mules would be better.'

That made sense. 'Would it be any easier to get some?' Ferelith asked.

'Provided you're prepared to pay, madam, there'd be no problem. So far they still have no food value. Later it may be different.'

That made sense, too. 'We would still have the problem of getting out of the city, though.'

Latifa smiled. 'Only if you have it in mind to ride out of the Catherine Gate in broad daylight.'

Ferelith looked at her with renewed interest. Her maid had given the matter more thought than she had realised. 'Your alternative?' she asked.

'I suggest madam buys two mules—donkeys, if no mules are available—and arranges for them to be taken out of the city in the normal way: by the Old Gate in broad daylight. Their driver will have been told to head south with them to the Great Valley, then down the valley to the shore where he will wait in an out-of-the-way place among the rocks until after nightfall. Then you and I, madam, wearing dark-coloured clothes, will spend the early evening of the appointed day strolling on the shore beyond the Watergate, watching the fishermen mending their nets. As soon as it's dark, we make our way along the foot of the ramparts to the Eastern Tower. There we scramble over the rocks to the beach beyond. After that it's a mere quarter of a mile or so to the mules—and off we go.'

'Just like that?'

'Yes, madam. I don't see why not.'

'You seem to have given much thought to this, bearing in mind that I've only just broached the subject,' Ferelith commented.

'Every captive in every *bagno* in the world gives thought to his possible future escape,' Latifa replied. 'Why should I be any different? Since the bad news about your father was received, I've often wondered whether you might decide to do something about it yourself. I knew that if you did you would need help and that might be my opportunity, too.'

Ferelith looked at her curiously. 'Will you desert me as soon we're safely outside and with our mules?'

'No, madam. I'll go with you to the King. He's the one who has the power to restore me to my people and until we reach Meknes our interests are the same.'

'Good.' Ferelith was glad the girl had not trotted out protestations of loyalty to her mistress because she doubted whether she would have believed them in the circumstances. Latifa was a good servant but she was none the less a captive and Ferelith would be far happier about the possible success of the scheme if she knew that they both put their own interest first. That left no room for misunderstanding. 'I have some gold but the quantity is finite and must last us some time. What is the least amount you will need to secure some mounts?'

Latifa calculated quickly and named a figure which, she said, allowed for the possibility of having to make some disbursements along the way. Even so, it was less than Ferelith would have expected, so she nodded and gave the girl the relevant amount from the major's small treasure-chest.

'Let me know when it's all arranged,' she told her.

'I will—and you, madam, must make sure you have a plain dark gown ready. A cloak, too. A man's *burnous* would be better than a cloak of your own: the hood would be more enveloping and the cloth would be warmer at night. I'll get you one—it will cause less comment than if you do.'

Ferelith laughed ruefully. 'I can see I should have taken you into my confidence a long time ago,' she said. 'Very well—since you've already given much more thought to the scheme than I, I must be content to be guided by you. The plans are yours to make, Latifa. I shall but do as I'm told.'

CHAPTER SEVEN

FOR the next three or four days Ferelith, acting upon her maid's instructions, could be found at odd times strolling along the foreshore between the mole and the Eastern Tower, occasionally on her own, more often accompanied by the Sudanese maidservant. She explained this unexpected preference to a sentry with a sigh.

'One can no longer ride out or even walk with any safety beyond the walls and yet one needs both a change of scene and some fresh air and this little walk offers both and combines them with safety. At least,' she amended, 'it offers fresh air when the breeze is from the sea.'

The sentry laughed and said that was true enough. He decided privately that there was no 'side' to Mrs Durliston, who never stood upon being a major's daughter or a clergyman's widow, though there was many as would. What had happened to her father was a crying shame but, as he confided to a colleague that evening, if there was anyone who would come through the ordeal with colours flying, it was Mrs Durliston.

Thus, in a remarkably short space of time, there wasn't a soldier in the garrison who would have been surprised to encounter the auburn-haired widow anywhere in that locality. A couple of times she was spotted at a quite inadvisedly late hour, well wrapped up against the sudden chill of the night air to such effect that one man later said he hadn't been sure at first whether there was somebody there or not.

When Latifa finally brought news that all was arranged and they were to go that night, Ferelith felt she had adequately laid the groundwork for their undetected disappearance.

'I've managed to get hold of a horse and a mule,' Latifa told her mistress. 'The horse is likely to be a poor specimen and I suspect won't last us long, but while he does he will carry us faster than a donkey, and a mule will have no difficulty keeping up. I think I may also have secured a guide,' she added hesitantly because it had not been discussed.

'A guide!' Ferelith exclaimed. 'Is that a good idea? We already have whoever provided the animals knowing something is planned. Was it wise to bring in someone else?'

'I think it may prove so,' Latifa told her. 'All we know is that we should travel more or less due south but then we shall sooner or later be obliged to ask our way to Meknes and by that time we shall be well into what is for you enemy country. Much better—and probably quicker—to have a guide who can lead us directly to our destination.'

'I suppose so.' Ferelith sounded doubtful. 'I mean, it makes sense, but can we be sure this guide is to be trusted?'

'I hope so, madam. He was recommended by the man from whom I bought the animals and I've no reason to doubt his word. He says this guide owes him a favour.'

'Then we must hope he doesn't owe Ali Benabdala or even Moulay Ismail a bigger one,' Ferelith told her. 'I should like to appear at Ismail's court in a demonstrably voluntary capacity.'

Latifa had obtained a dark brown woollen *burnous* for each of them, on the pretext that Mrs Durliston wished them to be a surprise gift for Amin, thus accounting for the purchase of a man's garment. Ferelith put a quantity of her father's gold in a pouch hung round her neck and under her bodice so that its bulk was hidden by the curve of her bosom. She suspended two other pouches beneath her skirt and both women carried a further, larger pouch containing several round, flat loaves. These would be rock-hard within twenty-four hours, but none the less filling for that.

The first part of their design was easily accomplished because it had been practised so many times. Ferelith, her maid a few paces behind, left the house quite openly in the early evening light and they made their way down to the Watergate, where they stopped while Ferelith exchanged a few words with the sentry. They then walked down the sloping roadway that led to what had once been a well-maintained wharf and scrambled on to the stretch of sand where boats and nets were often drawn up to be mended. In one corner of this little beach head stood the Customs House, now in semi-ruin, a tribute to the life-expectancy credited to the port by its more recent governors. Ferelith's father had once shown her a map, the copy of one sent to the King, which depicted the whole harbour area as being as well-built and maintained as that of Lyme Regis or Portsmouth's Sally Port. The truth was sadly different and they had to scramble over fallen masonry as well as the natural rocks that littered this part of the shore. With the brief North African dusk soon to be upon them, there were few people about but Ferelith and her maid passed the occasional word with those that were, making sure that as darkness fell they were well to the south of the Customs House and were seen to turn back towards it by the soldiers on the ramparts above. Once they reached the Customs House, however, they slipped into the darker shadows cast by its corner tower and stayed there, their *burnous* hoods pulled well over their faces. They stayed there for a long time, waiting until the Watergate had been closed for the night behind the last straggling fisherman and then they waited for some time longer, having no wish to be spotted and taken for stragglers for whom the gate would have to be specially opened.

At last they decided they might safely continue with their plan. This time they moved furtively, keeping as much within the shadow of walls and rocks as they could and staying as close as possible to the city walls so that any sentry patrolling above would only see them if he came close to the edge and looked straight down. It took much longer to get back to the Eastern Tower than to come from it and then they had to be much more careful in scrambling over the rocks which were all that was left of the old mole. Here it was more difficult to keep close to the tower's walls and more difficult, too, to move silently. It would be all too easy to twist an ankle or break a leg among the debris of earlier attempts to create a safe harbour.

There was no particular need for speed at this stage, so the two women resisted their natural urge to hurry and finally found themselves on the smooth sand of the beach beyond the city. The bay here was a huge curve of level sand but the land rose from it quite sharply and too suddenly to allow for ease of ascent but not highly enough to rate as cliffs. Since this stretch was part of the English domain outside the city's perimeter, it was to be expected that the men of the Irish battery stationed here would be patrolling between the Eastern Tower and the river. Once past the river's mouth there was little danger of their being spotted even though they would still be on English land: York Fort was set too far back from the shore for any look-out to see them unless they actually took to the sea.

This final phase of their escape from the city went as smoothly as they had expected and Ferelith, at least, heaved a sigh of relief when they came upon the horses exactly where they had been told they would be, hidden within a natural encirclement of rock that was not quite a cave.

Ferelith's relief was somewhat tempered when their guide came forward. There was nothing untoward about the man himself but she was surprised to see that, while they had an elderly mule that had seen better days and a horse still too young to carry much weight and clearly malnourished since birth, his mount was a sharp little Barb, well-accoutred and well-fed. It seemed a remarkably good mount for such a man and she was quite sure the darkness was not enough to have affected her judgement. She glanced significantly from it to her own horse.

'Perhaps we could effect an exchange?' she suggested. Latifa translated the remark and her mistress wondered whether the translation had been entirely necessary.

'I am honoured, madam,' he replied through their interpreter, 'but sadly this is my father's horse and I am not at liberty to part with it.'

The answer came as no surprise and, as if to compensate them for having had to be so disobliging, the guide helped each of them into her own saddle. They were obliged to ride astride and the saddles were very different from those Ferelith was used to, but she dared say she would soon become accustomed to the difference.

Having seen his charges safely mounted, the guide led the way on to the soft sand, which deadened the thud of horses' hoofs and gave them an unobstructed route that rapidly led them past the last vestiges of the English presence and into the region that must have been controlled by the Alcaid.

There was no sign of the enemy or, indeed, of anyone at all. They might as well have had the bay to themselves. Even when Ferelith looked back over her shoulder towards Tangier, she could make out nothing, only the denser black that she knew must be the city's ramparts against the thinner black of the sky. No light pierced the night from the city, nor was any visible on the headland before them.

They had been riding for some time before their guide turned his horse inland, picking with the unerring accuracy of familiarity a spot where sand and low-growing, tough little ground-covering plants replaced the rock-strewn approaches to the land above. They followed him and were soon travelling inland and steadily southwards, their guide putting as much distance as possible between his party and the city before allowing them to rest. He insisted that the horses be walked about to cool off before being given the drink they so richly deserved and with which he had had the forethought to provide them. In answer to Ferelith's question, he assured them they would find water without too much difficulty between here and Meknes. It might not be lying obviously on the surface in rivers and lakes but he was of this country and he knew where it was to be found. Ferelith still felt uneasy about him but that, at least, was good news.

With occasional rests for the horses' sakes, they travelled through the rest of the night and well into the next day, eating when they stopped to rest the horses and drinking a small amount themselves. Ferelith found the hood of the *burnous*, heavy as it was, kept the sun from her head as effectively as any beaver but she was glad when, towards the end of the morning, their guide led them to a small grove of trees where he helped them to dismount, hobbled the horses and the mule and told them to get some sleep while he kept watch.

'Should we not take turns to watch?' she asked. 'You've been riding as long and as fast as we have. You, too, must be in need of rest.'

'I'm accustomed to it,' he told her, Latifa translating for them. 'Rest assured, lady, when I need to sleep I shall let you know.'

Ferelith was too tired to argue with him. She wrapped herself up in her *burnous*, settled her head upon her saddle and fell immediately into a deep sleep from which she woke refreshed several hours later to find the sun was well past its peak.

'We ride at night again?' she asked.

'We do, lady. Your woman tells me it's Moulay Ismail's harem you want to reach, not that of some insignificant local chieftain.' His grin and wink needed no translation.

'It's certainly Moulay Ismail I want to see,' Ferelith said repressively, 'though his harem was *not* in my mind. However, as I've no wish to fall into the hands of anyone less important than he, I bow to your judgement as to the best way of achieving that object.'

Although their guide both spoke and acted as if he had their best interests at heart, Ferelith could not be easy in her mind. Every time she looked at his rather splendid mount, she felt that same niggle of mistrust. Such an animal could not have been kept in Tangier in past weeks: its condition was too good. The guide must therefore have picked it up—whether from his father, as he claimed, or someone else—outside the city and that, by definition, meant beyond the English lines. The inference had to be that somewhere someone knew he had taken it. Perhaps he came and went on it quite frequently, in which case taking it on this occasion would provoke no comment, but presumably he must have told someone something to account for his going behind English lines at this time.

Perhaps he had just lied about it, she thought, but she knew she was not entirely convinced. She would have liked to have asked Latifa her opinion and had she been entirely sure that the man understood no English she would have done so. She was far from sure. Maybe it was nothing more ominous than that he was sufficiently intelligent not to need a whole sentence to be translated before he had guessed the end. Whatever the explanation, she had several times noticed that he was ready with his reply to something before Latifa had finished interpreting it and sometimes seemed almost impatient at having to wait till she was done. Latifa did not seem unduly concerned, though, and Ferelith knew it would be no more to the Sudanese girl's advantage to be taken by local tribesmen than it would be to her own so she decided to let herself be guided by her maid's judgement in the matter.

The doubts could not be entirely stilled, however. They were riding towards the mountains now and as the night wore on Ferelith had that uncomfortable feeling that they were not the only souls abroad. An hour ago they had struck the valley of a river their guide informed them was Oued Hajera. The name conveyed nothing to Ferelith and all Latifa could add was that she had heard of it. The feeling of being watched, perhaps followed, had become more persistent once they had begun to ascend this valley. It was probably nothing more than her imagination, to be accounted for by the presence of the brooding mountains on either side, not rising straight up from the Hajera floor but waiting behind the foothills, cutting off any prospect of what lay beyond. The air was clearer here and those dark sentinels could be easily distinguished against the lighter vault of the star-spattered sky.

'What are these mountains called?' she asked.

Latifa had no need to translate. She knew. 'The Rif, madam,' she said.

Ferelith's stomach moved uncomfortably. The Rif! A wild place, indeed, or so they said. The people of the Rif owed their allegiance to Moulay Ismail, like everyone else in al-Maghrib, but they only paid it when it suited them. They were proud, independent and ferocious warriors with their own customs and their own dress, stemming from the fact that they were said to be the original people of this country, known to be resentful of intruders. They were the Berbers, but Ferelith knew there was more than one kind of Berber and sometimes they spoke dialects which were incomprehensible even to Berbers from other villages. She remembered Hassan Benani. He was a Berber but, since he was the Alcaid's aide, it was to be assumed he had thrown in his lot completely with Moulay Ismail and was in all probability quite unconnected with the people from these mountains, as a Yorkshireman was unconnected with a Kentishman.

Despite the fact that nothing untoward occurred and neither of her companions seemed to be conscious of anything beyond the demands of their ride, Ferelith's unease remained and deepened still further when they dismounted to walk the horses or stopped altogether to give them a complete, if brief, rest.

At last, during one such rest, she took Latifa aside. 'Latifa, I've the uncomfortable feeling we're being watched, perhaps even followed. I've felt it for a long time. Haven't you?' She spoke in an undertone that was little more than a whisper.

She was sure her words were a complete surprise to the maid, whose eyes immediately roved fearfully round them and detected nothing. 'No, madam,' she said stoutly. 'Nor do I want to. The people of these mountains will have little time for such as me. Our fates would be the same, regardless of the side on which our fathers fought.' She shuddered as if that lent weight to her words and when the guide came over, understandably intrigued at the subject of a conversation from which he was so carefully excluded, she turned to him. 'Madam thinks we're being watched and followed,' she said.

He shrugged. 'Is that all? She may well be right—at least, so far as being watched is concerned. The Rifi will doubtless have been watching our progress and will continue to do so until we're out of their territory. There's nothing to worry about in that.'

The words were calming but Ferelith noticed that the one thing he didn't do, and which in the circumstances he might have been expected to, was to glance instinctively around—as Latifa had done—to see if there was anything to notice. It seemed to Ferelith that only a man who knew they were being followed, and by whom, would have no instinctive need to look about him. She made no comment: the less he thought she suspected, the better, but she wished she had said nothing to Latifa who would then have been unable to pass her suspicions on.

Dawn came suddenly and with it the opportunity to survey the surrounding landscape more thoroughly. Ferelith saw nothing. If they were being watched, the watchers were well hidden; if they were being followed, the followers had fallen back as the sun rose. She was still uneasy.

The guide noticed her surreptitious glances. 'Your mistress has been too long within the confines of Tangier,' he told Latifa. 'She's become afraid of the open country, afraid of her own shadow.'

Latifa faithfully translated his opinion. Ferelith snorted.

'Tell him I don't call this open country. In open country I could see further.'

'In open country there would be less shade, less water and the horses would travel more slowly,' he replied.

Which was, Ferelith thought, entirely beside the point, though undoubtedly true. Still, better to let him think he had stifled her female arguments. She did not reply and put up with the smug expression with which he resumed his duties.

It was much easier to find a secluded place in these hills in which to unsaddle the animals and sleep without fear of discovery, though the shady ravine they chose had little grazing for the hobbled horses. The guide told them that this time he would sleep for an hour and Latifa would keep watch and, so that she would know when to wake him, he drove a small stick into the ground and told her to wait until the shadow fell on it before disturbing him. He would wake her again in time to snatch another hour before they set out once more.

Ferelith protested. 'Why don't I follow Latifa?' she asked. 'That would give you two hours now and two later on. You had no sleep last night.'

'I needed none. No, lady. Your offer is very kind but you'll only drop off to sleep when you should be watching, and that's of no use to anyone. Better this way.'

Ferelith was offended at his assumption but she had an uncomfortable feeling he might prove all too correct so she accepted his opinion meekly and concentrated instead on trying to arrange her body in such a way that it didn't discover unsuspected lumps of rock just below the surface soil. Her sleep was as deep as it had been the previous day, and as dreamless.

It seemed no time at all before she was prodded awake. She opened her eyes and was surprised to see that the afternoon sun was still high in the sky. She was even more surprised to see that it wasn't the guide who had prodded her awake.

Several faces peered down at her. All had dark curly hair and all had hazel eyes. All were unknown to her. In all, they numbered eight, standing in a semicircle around her and the still-sleeping Latifa. Each man leant on his musket and Ferelith guessed that it had been with one of these weapons that she had been prodded. Their

guide was ranged with the newcomers, looking suddenly
very Arab with his dark eyes and straight hair, and almost
as much a foreigner as did she and Latifa. She reached
across and shook her maid until she, too, woke up.

'We have company,' she said.

Latifa sat up and stared wide-eyed at their visitors.
'You were right, madam,' she said. 'We were followed.'

'Or just watched,' Ferelith told her. She looked across
at the guide. 'Which was it?' she asked.

She had the satisfaction of seeing him open his mouth
to answer before he remembered that he didn't understand English. Then he shut it and looked blankly at her
before looking enquiringly at Latifa. 'Don't bother to
translate, Latifa,' she said. 'He understood perfectly well.
I thought he did—now I'm sure.'

Latifa's bewilderment turned to anger and she berated
the guide with a torrent of Arabic to which Ferelith could
only listen in admiration. She rather wished she could
understand what was being said, though there was no
mistaking its general drift. Then, when she saw the grins
on the surrounding faces, she decided it was probably a
good thing she couldn't.

Neither woman was prepared for what happened when
Latifa paused to draw breath. The man closest to
Ferelith, the eldest there and apparently the leader,
withdrew one hand from within his enveloping *djellabah* and produced two gold coins which he handed
over to the guide, who promptly bit them before
dropping them into his own pouch.

'*Shokran,*' he said.

The older man bowed. '*Mraba.*'

The guide turned, grinning, to the two women. '*Be-
slemeh,*' he said. He gathered up his reins and swung
himself into the saddle. 'A man has to live,' he explained and laughed. Then he turned his horse and
trotted him back the way they had come.

Latifa was appalled at the implications of that little
exchange. 'Oh, madam, and to think it was I who engaged him! What use is it to express my regrets? You
can hardly be expected to trust me again.'

'Since this little mistake leaves us both in the same plight, I'm inclined to trust you still but not your judgement,' Ferelith told her. 'You'd better explain where we're going.'

'I dare say they already know that,' Latifa objected.

'I dare say they do. It will do no harm to confirm it. The name of their King must carry some weight and there's always the possibility that dreadful man told them lies, anyway.'

Latifa spoke at some length and Ferelith studied the expressions on the listening faces in a fruitless effort to determine whether what they were told came as a surprise or not. When the maid had finished, the man they took to be the leader told them that the road they were on did not lead to Meknes, the King, or even Ali Benabdala.

'Then where does it go?' Ferelith demanded, using some of her recently acquired Arabic with more force than accuracy.

The fact that she used it at all clearly took them all by surprise and she saw several uneasy glances being exchanged.

'Into the Rif,' the leader said.

'I know *that*,' Ferelith told him scornfully, and still in Arabic. 'But where in the Rif exactly?'

She guessed from the apprehensive look on Latifa's face that this was either not the tone of voice expected of captives or else not the one expected of women—and quite possibly both. There was an old military saying her father had used on more than one occasion: 'Attack is the best form of defence'. There was a limit to the amount of attacking she could do in the present situation but Ferelith had no intention of making these brigands' lives—for as such she saw them—any easier. 'Well?' she demanded.

'Come with us,' the leader said and waved Ferelith's pathetically immature horse and Latifa's elderly mule forward.

The two women were assisted into their saddles and for a brief moment, when it became apparent that their escort was unmounted, Ferelith thought there was a chance they might whip up their mounts and dash off back the way they had come. Given the nature of the animals concerned, it was a faint hope at best and it faded away altogether when the reins were retained by their captors.

The journey was of necessity a slow one, geared as it was to the pace of the small band of Berbers. It slowed still further when they branched off the wide track that had not too inaccurately been called a road by their former guide, and into a narrow defile that obliged them to travel in single file. At first Ferelith asked questions, but they were ignored, the Berbers not indicating by so much as the flicker of an eyelid that they had heard her. Never one to pursue a futile activity, Ferelith herself relapsed into silence, despite an impulse to express her feelings to Latifa. It was an impulse she resisted because she was uncertain to what extent some of their escort would understand: if they had been following them for long, there was a very good chance that at least one of them spoke English while others were quite likely proficient in the other trading languages of Europe; whoever had organised this little party—and the paying off of the guide suggested that it was no spur-of-the-moment matter—would have taken care of that.

The defile turned a sharp bend and suddenly before them rose the clustered, flat-roofed houses and narrow, twisting streets of a small town, its minaret piercing the sky. It was much smaller even than Tangier but the amazing thing about this place was that there had been no sign of it at all on the approach, yet from here it seemed to command a view over the lower hills while at the same time clustering in the shelter of the higher ones.

Despite its small size, it was a warren of narrow lanes, some so steep that they broke into shallow steps up which the horse and the mule had to be forced. Eventually they were led into a small, muddy yard surrounded by what Ferelith would have described as cattle byres, and gestures indicated that they were to dismount. Their beasts were taken from them and they were told to follow their captors on foot.

They came to a halt before a heavy cedar door, the only opening in the blank, windowless wall of a house rather larger than its fellows. When the door was opened they were led through a small entrance hall into a courtyard that made Ferelith catch her breath with delight. A small and unexceptional fountain played in the middle, but the ground it stood on and the arched walls on either side were covered in a kaleidoscopic mosaic of ceramic tiles that turned an otherwise bare and functional courtyard into an oasis of opulent beauty.

All but a token guard from their escort disappeared into the house and Ferelith and Latifa were left to await news of their fate and wish they had somewhere to sit down.

It was impossible to estimate how long they stood in the courtyard for neither woman had any means of telling the time, but it was long enough for the beauty of the place to pall, especially when compared with the remembered delights of good food and comfortable beds. It was chilly, too, one of the functions of such inward-looking architecture being to provide a refuge from the sun and now the afternoon was heading rapidly towards its close which, combined with the effects of the altitude, made Ferelith very grateful for her *burnous*.

At last one of the doors opened and a man she recognised as having been one of her captors emerged and beckoned the women over. He led them into a surprisingly large room which must, Ferelith realised, be the *divan*, the Moorish equivalent of a salon. The walls were lined with simple, low, padded couches littered with brilliantly embroidered cushions, and two carpets covered the tesselations of the floor. Each was in the natural colours of the wool from which they were made and woven into each at the diagonally opposite side of the narrow ends was a pattern in black wool, as if a child had drawn geometric lines with thick charcoal. Later Ferelith would learn that these patterns were the symbols of the tribe concerned and that the same marks would be found tattooed on to the faces of the tribe's women. Softer, more colourful carpets were thrown over the sofas and hung on the walls above the ubiquitous tiles. The men who sat and lounged on these sofas were mainly, but not entirely, those who had brought the women here. Those Ferelith had not seen before were older and one, in particular, sitting in the central position along the wall facing her as they entered, appeared to be the most important in that it was soon apparent that he was treated with a degree more deference. He was quite old, certainly older than her own father, of only moderate height but with great dignity and with strikingly handsome features that time had done nothing to erode.

Subjected to the scrutiny of a roomful of men, Latifa cast down her eyes and covered the lower part of her face with the edge of her cloak. Ferelith tossed her hood back and met the old man's gaze squarely with one of her own.

'What are you doing here?' he asked in the careful Arabic of one to whom it was a second language.

'Ask your men,' Ferelith replied. 'They brought us.'

He frowned. 'I meant what were you doing travelling as you were so far from Tangier?'

'Your men paid my guide. Didn't they ask him?'

'We know what he said. I want to know what *you* say. The two may not be the same.'

'Don't you trust your spies?'

'Implicitly. Your guide was not of my tribe. I don't trust others.'

'Very wise. I wish I had been given that advice a few days ago,' Ferelith commented bitterly and was rewarded by a small smile. 'We were travelling to Meknes,' she told him.

'You were on the wrong road.'

'Perhaps, but that was where we wanted to be taken.'

'Do the menfolk of your people let their women travel alone in a strange land?'

'No, and if anyone had found out we should have been prevented from leaving, I'm sure. Besides, I wasn't alone. I had Latifa, and the guide.'

'You would have done better without a guide who takes you to Meknes on the wrong road.'

Ferelith smiled ruefully. 'We have no disagreement there,' she said.

'Why Meknes?'

Ferelith's Arabic was simply not good enough to enable her to give more than a very simple explanation and, when she turned to Latifa for help in explaining, she found the girl was so overpowered by their situation or, more probably, by being the cynosure of so many male eyes, that she was virtually dumb-struck and of no use at all.

When she had finished her inadequate and ungrammatical attempt at explanation, the men murmured among themselves and shook their heads.

'This,' said one of them, speaking very slowly and simply, as one did to a child, 'is a very strange thing for a woman to do.'

Ferelith tilted her chin defiantly. 'Would your daughter not try to save you?' she demanded.

He broke the gaze with which she had forced him to look at her and turned away, muttering something in which she thought she made out the words, 'not seemly'. She was unsure whether they referred to attempting to rescue one's father or to her manner towards her questioner.

'Your quest was doomed to failure,' the old man interjected. 'It will be doing you a kindness not to let you continue. You will remain here.'

'I most assuredly shall not!' Ferelith exclaimed, dismay at this arbitrary decision destroying any capacity for tact her limited Arabic might grant.

The man's eyes opened wide in utter amazement at being spoken to in such a tone—especially, Ferelith suspected, by a woman. Nevertheless, no matter how amazed or displeased he might be, it did not induce him to raise his voice. 'You will do precisely as you are told,' he said quietly. 'Your maid, as you call her, who was a captive and is a good Muslim, is now free and you are the one who will be ransomed. No doubt your father will be glad to buy your freedom.'

'My father is in the hands of Moulay Ismail,' Ferelith reminded him angrily. 'How may he buy my freedom when he hasn't the means to buy his own?'

The man shrugged. 'That is not a problem for me to solve. It is his duty as a father.'

Ferelith stared at him, aghast. 'This is madness,' she said in English, not because she wished to prevent his understanding her but because her Arabic was not capable of expressing her ideas. 'I don't believe you to be a foolish man, yet such an argument makes you appear one. Why, Papa is not even in a postion to write to other relatives and ask *them* to buy my freedom. All you're doing is condemning me to a life of slavery without yourself having any prospect of financial gain. Madness, sheer madness.'

Perhaps heartened by what the old man had in mind for her, Latifa found her voice. 'Ssh, madam, that's no way to speak. You should be more conciliatory.'

'Conciliatory! Perish the thought! Oh, Latifa, I'm glad enough for you, though I shall miss you, but the man is making things impossible for me. I can tell you this—and you're welcome to convey the information to him—I shall most certainly *not* be a willing captive.'

Latifa grinned. 'Few of us are,' she remarked drily. 'As for talk of madness, he knows perfectly well what he's saying. He has his own motives. Perhaps he wants you for his own harem,' she added helpfully.

'Latifa, you *must* make him understand. Tell him that if he will give me an escort to Meknes, and I can obtain my father's freedom, I shall ensure we pay him handsomely for his service. Can you explain that?'

Latifa looked doubtful. 'I'll try, madam, but we'll not talk of his service: he's the chief and serves no one, not even the King unless it suits him to do so.'

'The choice of words I leave to your own discretion,' Ferelith said impatiently. 'Just make him understand.'

Latifa spoke at some length and in a submissive and conciliatory tone that was listened to with obviously approving courtesy, and when she had finished the men spoke among themselves.

'What are they saying?' Ferelith asked.

Latifa shook her head. 'I've no idea, madam. They speak their own language and it means nothing to me.'

There was much nodding of heads and when every point of view had been expressed the chief turned again to Ferelith. 'We have heard of the freedom given to your women,' he said disapprovingly, 'and you are proof that it is so. Your maid has been more fittingly reared. We feel that you are probably going to be more trouble than you're worth. At the moment, we are unsure what we shall do with you: we may do as you suggest or we may offer you to the governor of Tangier who, in the absence of your father, is presumably responsible for you. Before we make up our minds, we need to consult someone better placed than ourselves. A messenger will go with the dawn light but it will be three or four days before he returns. During that time you will have your own secluded quarters in the women's part of the house, and you may have your Sudanese maid for company. The difference is that she will not be captive but you will. Is that understood?'

Ferelith assured him it was and sent up a small private prayer of gratitude that, not altogether as a result of good judgement, her own abrasive manner and Latifa's more submissively gentle explanation had achieved at least part of what she sought. It remained to be seen what the second opinion decided and Ferelith knew that much must depend upon the impression she made in that quarter.

She had hoped to be able to find out something about the person involved from the other women of the household but it was not to be. When the chief had said she would have her own secluded quarters, he had meant precisely that. She was secluded from all contact with the other women and was entirely dependent upon Latifa. Nor could the maid find anything out: the women of the household spoke only their own Berber dialect and Latifa could only communicate with them by signs

which were perfectly adequate for obtaining food,
blankets and suchlike, but hardly facilitated the
expression of more abstract requirements. The food was
simple but nourishing, tasty and plentiful, and the bed
was warm and comfortable so Ferelith did the only thing
possible, which was to make the most of the opportunity for a complete, if enforced, rest. At no time was
she called before the chief again, nor did she see anyone
except Latifa.

It was three days before Latifa brought her the news
that someone had arrived in some haste.

'I haven't seen him,' she said, 'but I think this must
be the person the chief sent for. The women seem to
think it will be tomorrow when they decide what will
happen. They indicated that he will need to sleep first.'

The newcomer might have slept that night. Ferelith
did not. Too much depended upon the outcome and
upon what the newcomer recommended. She suspected
that her only influence would be manifested by the
impression she made upon him and, without knowing
anything at all about his nature, it was impossible to
gauge whether it would be more productive to be as-
sertive or submissive. She tossed and turned for most of
the night and awoke heavy-eyed, but she made Latifa
brush down her travel-stained habit with greater
thoroughness than usual and took more precise pains
with the arrangement of her auburn curls then she had
been doing lately.

Eventually the summons came and Ferelith, with
Latifa close behind, was shown once more into the *divan*
where she found assembled most of the men who had
been meeting there when she first arrived. This time the
chief stood up. He bowed briefly in her direction.

'On this occasion,' he began in his careful Arabic, 'we
shall have the advantage of being able to understand each
other fully. This is my son, Hassan, who speaks your
language well.'

Ferelith turned expectantly to the figure indicated and
gasped as the figure, taller than that of his father, rose
from the sofa and bowed.

'Good morning, Mrs Durliston,' he said in slightly accented English. 'I hope you slept well.'

She was looking into the unmistakable eyes of Hassan Benani.

CHAPTER EIGHT

FERELITH heard Latifa's gasp of surprise behind her. She knew the colour had rushed to her cheeks and her impulse was to run forward to greet him. Something in his bearing, a certain unexpected reserve in his expression, made her hold back. Instead, she inclined her head.

'Mr Benani,' she said, 'I had not expected to encounter you here, but I must admit I'm glad to do so. You will be able to explain my case to your father far better than I.'

He, too, inclined his head as if in subservience to her wishes. 'The pleasure in this encounter is mutual. I have just come from Meknes. You will be relieved to learn that your father is well and that I'm fully aware of the terms upon which Moulay Ismail is ready to ransom him. The message I had from my father indicated that you seemed to think you could negotiate with the King to get him released. I own, I'm not sure how—Ismail is a tough man with whom to try to bargain—but if you will explain what you have in mind I can at least advise upon it. It will not be disinterested advice: I am Ismail's man, but if I can serve both your interests at the same time I shall be happy to do so.'

'I don't quite see how both our interests can be served,' Ferelith told him. 'After all, they represent opposing sides.'

'I don't make myself clear: I meant your personal interests—not the interests of the English. Both you and Ismail want to see your father ransomed. The reasons differ but the goal is the same. It is not necessarily the goal of Governor Kirke.'

He turned to his father then and spoke in the dialect incomprehensible to either woman. The elder Benani clapped his hands and gave an order to the boy who immediately appeared. The boy vanished, to reappear a few seconds later with an ornately carved cedarwood stool which he placed in the centre of the room.

'You will be more comfortable sitting down, Mrs Durliston,' Hassan said.

Ferelith accepted the seat with gratitude and began to outline her ideas relating to her father's freedom. Until she came to spell them out, she had not fully realised just how vague and uncertain they were. The scheme she had outlined to Colonel Kirke had contained no detail, no hint of what she thought she might offer Moulay Ismail as bargaining counters. Perhaps, if Kirke had thought her idea held any merit at all, he would have been the one to tell her the parameters of her negotiating licence. As it was, the politely blank faces of the men listening to Hassan's translation of her words told her that she was merely confirming their well-entrenched opinion of female intelligence.

'Do you think you could raise the necessary monies?' Hassan asked her.

'The figure is a high one but not impossibly so,' Ferelith told him. 'I could raise it against my own portion, I think. If not, I'm sure my parents-in-law would be willing to help.'

'But you don't have the power to offer any political compromise at all, do you?'

'No, none.'

'Since it is the political aspects of your father's position that most interest the King, how on earth do you expect him to take the slightest notice of your plea? He's unlikely even to grant you an audience.'

'To tell the truth, I'm not at all sure,' Ferelith said candidly. 'I only know that someone has to try and it's perfectly clear no one else is going to. If I had a brother, I should expect him to tackle it. I haven't, so the duty falls upon me.' She coloured. 'Forgive my blunt speaking but it has crossed my mind that since I am so very different in appearance from most women in this land, I might myself have a certain amount of curiosity value to the King. I thought he might be willing...' Her voice trailed off in the impossibility of putting into words what was in her mind.

'Correct me if I'm wrong, but you mean that you hope to offer yourself for the King's harem in exchange for your father's liberty?' he said, his voice harsh.

Ferelith smiled wanly. 'I don't think "hope" is quite the appropriate word, but yes, I suppose that sums it up rather well.'

He looked at her for several minutes before translating what she had said. Ferelith saw the expressions on the encircling faces change from polite boredom to a grudging respect that they were not the only people cognisant of the importance of duty and the honour that accrued by its fulfilment.

The men murmured among themselves and one of them asked, 'Do you realise that, if your father accepts this sacrifice on your part, he cannot in all honour seek to obtain your release at a later date?'

Ferelith hadn't thought that far ahead, but his point sounded logical so she nodded. 'Yes, of course,' she said.

Then the boy was summoned back to take her and Latifa to an adjacent room while the men continued their discussion. Since no matters of such importance were ever decided in a hurry, particularly not among people who enjoyed the debate and the necessary accompanying hospitality, they were brought a tray of coffee with a bowl of dates and another of almond-flavoured sweetmeats with which to while away the time. They had been there for nearly an hour when Latifa answered a tap at the door to find Hassan standing there.

Ferelith assumed he had come to call them back and got to her feet in readiness, trying to calm the suddenly accelerated beating of her heart.

As if he had read what was in her mind, he shook his head. 'Not yet,' he said. 'Latifa, wait outside. I would speak to your mistress alone.'

Latifa looked enquiringly at Ferelith who, after a moment's brief hesitation, nodded, and the maid slipped quietly out of the room.

Hassan Benani took both Ferelith's hands in a gesture that was more European than Moorish and led her to the couches that lined this room as they did the nearby *divan*.

'Sit down, my dearest. We must talk. I must tell you that, at the moment, the men are favourably disposed towards your cause, though I feel bound to say that I am not. However, there are matters of concern of which they feel you may not be aware and, as men of honour, they feel they cannot seriously consider letting you go through with this unless they can be sure you are under no illusions.'

Ferelith smiled a little shakily. 'Hassan, I am a widow, not a maid fresh from school. I do understand the implications of being a... a concubine.'

He smiled. 'I'm sure you do—or think you do, though you might find the demands of a Moorish King rather different from those of an English clergyman.'

Ferelith considered it. 'I don't see how,' she said. 'After all, all cats are grey at night and I can't really see that one man will differ so radically from another—the difference must lie in the degree to which one loves him— or not, as the case may be.'

'Either your husband was a very unusual Englishman or you are far more innocent than your widowed status makes you think,' he said gently.

Ferelith frowned, not sure what he meant. 'Well,' she said at last, 'I don't think Francis was terribly unusual, so that must make me rather innocent, I suppose. I think you're going to have to be a little more specific, Hassan.'

He sighed. 'For one thing, you wouldn't be a concubine. You'd be a slave and once the King had tired of you you might be given to a favoured courtier—if you were lucky. More probably you would be put to death to prevent anyone else claiming to have got his pleasure from the same source as the King.'

Ferelith paled. 'Surely not? That would be barbaric and I have always heard Moulay Ismail is an educated man.'

'He is—educated and discriminating, but you would be both a slave and an infidel and therefore of little importance on either count. I'm sure no one has ever depicted Ismail to you as a man of kind benevolence.'

'Well, no,' Ferelith admitted. 'Those are not characteristics attributed to him by the English in Tangier, but then,' she added shrewdly, 'I imagine one's enemy has to be painted blacker than he is in order to justify the battle.'

'Very true, but rumour doesn't entirely lie. To control al-Maghrib, a king needs to be ruthless and strong. Moulay Ismail is both and it binds his people to him, particularly against the infidel occupier of our land. He has done much good in the nine years of his rule. Public life and private property are now safer than they have ever been and highway robbery in his kingdom has been virtually eliminated. But never forget how he established himself in power and taught the people he was to be as much feared as respected. Did you know that, having defeated his nephew for the throne, he sent ten thousand heads of men, women and children killed in his nephew's camp to adorn the walls of Fez and Marrakesh, and then made a bridge for his victorious army with the bodies of prisoners interwoven with rushes? Is that the man who will be kind to an infidel female slave?'

Ferelith went pale and shuddered. 'No,' she whispered. She looked into his eyes, appeal in her own. 'You said you were the King's man. How can you ally yourself with such as he?'

'Because he represents the best chance we have had of expelling the infidel from this land—and a king needs to be strong if he is to rule. Look what happened to your King's father when he was weaker than his advisers.'

'Is it so important to drive out the infidel?' she asked.

'When they own our cities and control our people, yes.' He smiled. 'If more of them were like you, I fancy the need would be less pressing.' He raised her hand to his lips and kissed it and then, suddenly and without warning, he swept her into his arms, kissing her with a force and vigour that took her breath away, a far cry from Francis's gentle, tender embrace. But when her breath returned she found herself responding with all the urgency he could have desired, her mouth fighting to express the unimagined desire she had felt for him since that first stolen kiss in Lisbon.

His fingers undid the buttons of her jacket and slid it from her shoulders and he sunk his lips on to the thrusting curve of her breast, now entirely revealed beneath the linen shift. Suddenly Ferelith knew she wanted more than she had ever dreamed of before, and knew with unerring certainty that in Hassan Benani she had met a man with whom there would be no equivocating, no false modesty and no holding back. He would not be shocked and would not expect the woman with whom he eventually shared his life to be shocked in her turn.

Ferelith knew with desperate, impotent certainty that she needed to be that woman—and that the very circumstances in which she found herself precluded it. She was here to save her father—and Hassan's opinion of the infidel had just been very clearly expressed.

She pulled away, forcing herself to ignore the surprise and hurt in his hazel eyes, and pulled the drawstring at the shift's neck up in an unambiguous gesture. Hassan silently handed her her dark green jacket and held it while she shrugged her shoulders into it.

'My apologies, Mrs Durliston,' he said. 'It had not been my intention to offend you.'

Ferelith shook her head, saddened by the formal address. 'It wasn't...you didn't,' she whispered. 'It was as much myself.' She hesitated, uncertain how to continue yet feeling something more was needed. 'I'm here for other reasons. I dare not lose sight of them for how then could I live with myself?'

The harsh lines of his face softened. 'Let me at least persuade you to return to Tangier. You shall have my escort and can be reasonably sure I shan't sell you to local tribesmen on the way. I can guarantee you safe conduct and the governor will be pleased enough to have you back, I don't doubt. You'll be with your own kind again. We shall drive you out but at least you won't be with strangers when you go.'

Her heart cried out that it wasn't with her own people she wanted to be, but she knew that what she did want was impossible, so instead she just shook her head. 'No. Take me to Moulay Ismail. Let me plead for my father. Who knows?' she went on with forced lightness. 'Perhaps I shall have the good fortune to tackle him on one of his more benign days.'

There was nothing light about Hassan's reply. 'That would be good fortune, indeed. Can I really not persuade you to return? I'm sure my father and his friends would be happy for you to do so.'

'No. Persuade them to let me go to Meknes,' she said. 'Then I shall be content.' That last sentence was, she thought, probably the biggest lie she had ever told.

'What did he want, madam?' Latifa asked when she slipped back into the room. She might no longer be technically a captive but she had no desire to be left in a place where she could not converse with the other women, nor had she any wish to set out on her own to find the Sudanese mercenaries with whom her father had fought.

'To persuade me to return to Tangier,' Ferelith said, taking comfort in the fact that it was at least half true.

'And shall you?'

'I hope not. I've asked to be allowed to continue to Meknes.'

'It was good advice, madam,' Latifa pointed out.

'I know it, but my duty takes precedence. If they agree to let me go, will you accompany me to Meknes?'

'Nothing would please me more,' the maid said warmly. 'That's where I should find my own people. I don't want to stay here, among strangers, but I must be frank with you, madam: if they decide you're to return to Tangier, I'll not go with you. I'd far rather stay here among strangers but as a free woman than return to captivity in Tangier.'

'Then we must both hope our hosts make the right decision,' Ferelith told her.

It was some hours before she was sent for, and as she entered the *divan* her eyes sought out Hassan Benani. He was there, but he avoided her glance, a fact which hurt her as much as if he had slapped her face.

'We have consulted together,' his father said. 'We feel that the best advice we can give you is to urge you to return to Tangier, but we understand your reasons for wanting to go to Meknes and if you are still of the same mind in the morning then we shall ensure you reach there safely.'

'Thank you,' Ferelith said. 'Latifa would like to accompany me to Meknes where she will find Ismail's Sudanese regiment.'

He nodded acquiescence. 'And if you decide to return to Tangier?'

'No. She would prefer to stay here.'

He smiled and Ferelith suddenly saw the likeness to his son. 'Whichever decision you make, you leave with the dawn.'

Ferelith spent a second sleepless night, and the fact that she knew the journey before her necessitated as much sleep as she could get before they set out did nothing to make it easier. Not for one moment did she contemplate returning to Tangier; the choice of Tangier or Meknes was no choice at all and it was not that decision which kept her awake. That feat was accomplished by thoughts of Hassan Benani, a man who had aroused a mixture of emotions among which desire and guilt predominated.

She had been drawn to him from the beginning. She had known it in Lisbon even though she had perhaps not recognised it for what it was. He had thrice come to her rescue in very different circumstances and had left her each time wishing to know him better. She had to admit that she had thought beyond the prospect of merely pursuing a pleasant acquaintance and the fact that he was a foreigner, a heathen and an enemy made little difference. He had given her every indication that he was similarly drawn to her but none of how serious his interest might be and now he seemed perfectly willing for her to distance herself from him. It was disconcerting and she could think of no way of ascertaining his true feelings.

She had loved—still loved—Francis dearly; he had been a kind man, tender and gentle in the marriage-bed in a way that she suspected Hassan Benani would not necessarily be. For two years she had mourned and not thought it possible that she would ever dream that another man could take his place to the slightest degree. She knew that it was not a case of replacing Francis: no one could do that. It was more a matter of another man carving out his own niche in her heart while leaving Francis's intact, yet at the same time acknowledging that the new love would take overwhelming precedence over the old.

It was that knowledge which made her feel guilty because it seemed to represent a disloyalty to the man who had filled her waking hours for the whole of their brief marriage. Moreover, this new love—for she had no doubt that that was what she felt for Hassan—was of a very different sort. They had only kissed but she knew already that it was of a strength and violence unimagined in the placid calm of an English vicarage. Yet even if she discounted her duty to her father and her loyalty to her late husband's memory, what prospect could it hold? Marriage was out of the question: not only was he of a different faith but he viewed with equanimity the prospect of having more than one wife.

This was not a prospect which filled Ferelith with the disgust that any modest and right-thinking Christian should feel—on the contrary, there were aspects to it which were extremely practical, particularly if one discovered that one did not actually love one's husband. If one felt for him what she knew she felt for Hassan, the thought of sharing—worse, of being superseded in his affections at a later date—with another woman was intolerable to her in her present frame of mind. Nor could she contemplate with equanimity the prospect of becoming his concubine, to be cast away, ruined and in a strange country when his passion waned. Yet even as that conviction took emphatic form in her mind, she knew that, if he came to her now, she would give herself to him without hesitation.

Or would she? Had she not already withdrawn from his embrace? Perhaps her lifetime's training was not so easily set aside. At all events, he had taken her decision without question. She would attempt to do what she saw to be her duty to her father and would never see Hassan Benani again. Perhaps it was as well. When she had been a child, Annie had had an irritating habit of saying, whenever a set-back occurred, 'Ah, well, no doubt it'll all turn out for the best. You'll see.' She hoped that this would prove to be an occasion when it did.

Annie's maxim was not to be put to the test just yet. Ferelith had given no thought at all as to the constituents of the party that would escort her to either Tangier or Meknes and, even though she knew Hassan had come from Ismail's court there and would presumably return, she was genuinely surprised to discover that he would be leading them. She made no comment, however: some awkwardness seemed to attach to their meeting, a certain formality that had not been present even when they were barely acquainted. She longed to say something, to break the film of ice that lay between them, but she was unsure how to phrase it and dreaded the possibility of its receiving a bitterly cold reception, so she refrained, telling herself it was inappropriate when there was so large an audience.

Her previous mount had been replaced by an inelegant but sturdy little mountain pony and there was a second one for Latifa, who declared it a great improvement on the mule. Their total escort numbered some half-dozen men, all well-mounted and armed with muskets as well as their traditional sabres and knives. Nor were the women permitted to travel in the clothes in which they had arrived. Both were given instead the traditional clothes of Berber women—the red-and-white striped *fouta*, or skirt, over white robes and a white woollen shirt covered by a white shawl topped with a conical straw hat with coloured woollen pom-poms appropriate to that village. The women of the Benani household dressed them and roared with laughter at the finished result, the full glory of which Ferelith and Latifa could only see by peering into the disturbed waters into which the fountain's spray dropped. One of the older women made it clear by signals that they ought to wait until their chins had been appropriately tattooed, and Ferelith's horrified denial needed no interpreter but sent them off into repeated peals of laughter. When they appeared to set off on their journey, even the men were unable to repress smiles.

Hassan helped Ferelith on to her pony and patted the saddle-roll strapped over the croup. 'Your European clothes are there,' he told her. 'Dressed like this, you will occasion less comment, especially from afar. It becomes you,' he added.

Ferelith snorted, temporarily forgetting their previous encounter. 'Beauty lies in the eye of the beholder, they say,' she commented.

'Then no one in these mountains who beholds you will be disappointed,' he replied.

It was an answer that bewildered Ferelith. Had it been accompanied by a warm smile, perhaps a lingering touch of fingers, she would have known it to be the compliment it appeared. She was unsure how to interpret it when the accompanying face was as expressionless as the voice and when, far from there being a warm smile, there was not even an exchange of glances.

The women soon learned that they were less than a third of the way to Meknes. A succession of frequently changed and very fast horses could cover the remaining distance in as little as three days, provided the rider knew the route, which was mountainous and therefore by definition treacherous. They could expect to take at least twice as long.

'And that,' one of the men confided to Latifa, 'will be faster than you would have been able to make with those beasts you rode in on.'

Latifa conceded that they hadn't been the fastest in al-Maghrib.

The man hooted with laughter. 'Not the fastest? Why, they'd have died before you got halfway. The mule will pick up with rest and good grass and he'll have a couple of years' work left in him, but the horse...' He shrugged his shoulders and threw out his hands. 'Maybe three years on good lowland grass would do the trick, but who's got the time to wait that long before putting him to work? No Berber, I can tell you, and his basic quality's not good enough to make it worth the wait even if you've got the grazing.'

The journey soon proved the superiority of these Rifi tribesmen over their previous guide. For one thing, they knew the terrain as thoroughly as Ferelith knew the convolutions of the little knot-garden at home. It was a familiarity apparent in their every move. They had brought food with them, but they also knew how to live off the land and stale, dry bread did not figure in their diet. When their original guide had spent much of the time looking over his shoulder at the surrounding landscape, Ferelith had assumed it to be a sensible precaution, evidence of his reliability. These men felt no need of such deliberate caution either because they knew it to be unnecessary or because their eyes were so accustomed to the region that they would spot anything untoward without any special effort.

It was easier to sleep at night, too. There were enough men to provide an adequate guard while everyone had sufficient sleep. A fire kept them warm and each person's *burnous* became a blanket. The midday heat—less oppressive at these altitudes—was the excuse for nothing more than a prolonged rest, welcomed by both men and beasts. All in all, both Ferelith and Latifa felt safer and more comfortable on this journey than they would have believed possible a few days ago.

The mountain ponies were particularly sure-footed and Ferelith, unaccustomed both to riding astride and to riding without stirrups on a saddle whose design owed much to the rudimentary cross-tree that formed the basis of the camel-saddle, slipped into the habit of giving hers a greater length of rein than she might otherwise have done. He picked his way with unerring accuracy and was perfectly content to follow the horse in front, trotting when he did and dropping back to walk when he did, too.

It was on the third day out that fate intervened. Ferelith was fourth in line on a particularly bad stretch of road which reduced her pony's pace to a slower walk than usual. When a bend in the road hid his leaders from him, he roused himself to a brisk trot to close the gap, thereby throwing his rider temporarily off balance. As he rounded the bend, loose rocks, their stability undermined by the reverberations of clattering hoofs, tumbled down, bouncing off their more stable fellows and crashing on to the path either to lie there or to continue their descent on the other side. The rockfall was unexpected and noisy, and Ferelith's pony, deprived of the security that was conveyed to an animal through the tension of the reins, did what he would have done had he been alone, unaccoutred and unridden. He bolted.

Ears back and head outstretched, he left the path with such impulsion that Ferelith, taken completely by surprise, was jerked backwards in the saddle and found her precarious balance with great difficulty. She tried to shorten the reins but by this time the animal had the bit firmly between his teeth and was responding to nothing. He sped along the valley floor faster than she had thought him capable and out of the corner of her eye Ferelith noted the boulders strewn in the path of the stream alongside which they were now charging. She must keep her seat at all costs. There was no moss-softened landing here. She thought she heard the comforting clatter of hoofs in pursuit but dared not turn round and her dismay was complete when the pony veered off into a side-ravine where the ground was considerably worse. She survived the sharp, unanticipated turn and could only pray that the deteriorating terrain would slow the animal down. She was hauling at his mouth now, desperately trying to bring him to hand, but he seemed oblivious. Suddenly the ravine in front of them was barred by a hedge of cactus. Deliberately planted, it marked the boundary of a small farm and must have had an opening. Ferelith's pony was in no state to consider such refinements. He slid to an immediate stop, his head down and his hindquarters tucked under his outstretched forelegs and Ferelith, with no stirrups to help her stay in place, was precipitated forward on to his neck from whence she slid ignominiously down to the ground, avoiding the cactus by inches.

She was entirely unaware of this sole piece of good fortune because in missing the cactus her head had instead struck a half-concealed rock and she was unconscious from the moment it did so. Thus it was beside an inert figure that Hassan Benani drew rein and hurriedly dismounted. He knelt down and loosened the shawl to feel the pulse in her neck and sigh with relief that it was beating. Then he stood up and surveyed the place to which events had brought them. He knew it, though it was a long time since he had been here. Beyond the hedge would be the remains of a small farm, deserted by its owners some years ago and probably not kindly treated by the passing winters, though the prickly pears seemed to have flourished against the odds. As a hedge, it simply fenced off the blind end of the ravine, giving the previous owners a barrier against marauding predators and keeping their few goats and sheep in at night.

He lifted Ferelith's unconscious body and carried it over to what remained of the entrance to the enclosure, now itself largely overgrown with cactus. His own horse followed its master. The pony was unconcernedly grazing. He could attend to that later.

The primitive, one-roomed farmhouse still stood, but the flat thatched roof had caved in although the walls of sun-baked mud bricks still stood, perhaps because the builder had used the rich harvest of rocks offered by the land to supplement and strengthen the less permanent material.

Hassan cleared a space in the lee of the wall that offered the most protection from the prevailing wind and laid Ferelith down until he had shifted the worst of the roof's debris. He looked up at the sky. They would have to remain here until the morrow. Rain was unlikely but the night would be bitterly cold and a fire would be essential. Still, there was time enough to see to that. In the meantime it was more important to attend to Ferelith.

He had covered her with his *burnous* and now he undid the stopper of his leather water-bottle, moistened the end of her shawl and pressed it to her head. As she began to stir, he put the bottle to her lips, coaxing them apart so that drop by drop the revivifying liquid could be given her with the minimum of wastage—he had observed no water supply at this end of the ravine.

Ferelith's head moved involuntarily from side to side. Her eyelids fluttered and opened and when she found herself looking into Hassan's eyes she did not immediately recognise him. She frowned.

'I think I know you,' she whispered. 'I'm not sure. Where...?' Her voice tailed off.

'Ssh, no need to speak. Yes, you know me. Hassan Benani. You were on your way to Meknes and your pony bolted. Do you remember that?'

Ferelith nodded.

'Good, that means you'll soon be back to normal. You fell. I didn't see it but at a guess I'd say you came off when he slid to a halt. You were lucky, believe it or not. A few inches further over and you've have been impaled on a fence of prickly pear.'

'Up here?' Ferelith asked.

'You'd be surprised what grows in some of these sheltered valleys. Now—I need to fetch your pony in from the open ravine and then I must gather materials for a fire. Tonight will be cold. Will you be all right while I do that?'

Ferelith started to nod but it hurt so, instead, she said, 'Yes, I think I'll do.'

'Good girl. I shan't be long.'

Ferelith had no idea whether he kept that promise or not because once her head was no longer supported on his arm she somehow drifted into sleep, to be woken later on by the gentle crackle of burning fronds. She turned her head towards the fire and watched it in silence, unobserved by the man who tended it, noticing the way the flames cast a sharp edge of warm light that threw his profile into relief against the darker background of the walls.

Satisfied the fire had taken, he turned towards her and smiled to see she was awake. 'How do you feel?' he asked.

'A bit shaky but the fire somehow makes everything seem better.'

'There's no food beyond some cheese and some dates in my saddlebag,' he warned her.

Ferelith smiled weakly. 'It sounds a veritable feast.'

'We'll catch the others up tomorrow and we'll not die of starvation in the meantime.'

Ferelith looked puzzled. 'Shouldn't we rejoin them before nightfall?' she asked.

'Even if you were fit to ride as you are, we should travel too slowly to reach the main trail before dark. It gets dark faster up here than anything you're used to. The men know where they're going. I know where they'll spend the night, and they'll not leave in too much of a hurry tomorrow. We should be with them by midday.'

'Will Latifa be safe?'

'If she's not, someone will answer to me.'

They were reassuring words and Ferelith almost immediately slipped back into sleep. When she next woke, the fire had burnt down to warmly glowing embers. She stirred, and saw that Hassan was sitting beside her, tailor-fashion, dozing in the residual warmth, a warmth of which he must have had much need since it now transpired he had covered her with his own *burnous* as well as the one she had been wearing.

As soon as she moved, he knew and was fully awake. 'How do you feel?' he asked.

'Hungry and somewhat stiff,' she told him. 'Otherwise I think I'm all right. I'll know when I stand up.'

She moved as she spoke and he put his hand on her shoulder to prevent her getting up. 'Stay where you are. Time enough to test your head when dawn comes. The hunger we can deal with now.'

He unwrapped the broad leaves in which the soft sheep's cheese had been packed and laid it on the ground between them. Then he did the same thing with the dates. He slid his arm round Ferelith's shoulders and raised her to a sitting position. 'Eat,' he commanded.

Ferelith's left hand was nearest the food, so that was the one she stretched out towards it. Immediately he caught it. 'No,' he said. 'Use your right hand. Do you want to be taken for a barbarian as well as an infidel? Eat like this,' and he demonstrated with his right hand how to detach a small piece of cheese and roll it into a ball with the fingers of one hand before popping it in his mouth to be followed almost at once by a date.

It was trickier for Ferelith to master the technique because she had to reach across herself to the food, and when she succeeded it was with much giggling.

'My father would have said I look like a cow handling a musket,' she told Hassan.

'Very elegant,' he commented ironically.

'That would have been the point. I think. Hassan, this must be some of the most delicious food I've ever eaten.'

She used his name without thinking, almost without realising she had done so, and was quite unconscious of the quick look he cast her.

'Any food is delicious to the starving man,' he said.

They ate in silence for a few moments, making every mouthful last a long time so that the effect of having had a full meal might be more easily achieved.

'Do you know,' Ferelith said, 'I'm beginning to get quite good at this? Look,' and she deftly rolled up a small ball of cheese and held it out for inspection.

He smiled. 'We'll make a Moor of you yet,' he said.

Ferelith chuckled. 'Not a Berber?' she asked and on some impulse which she could never explain she popped the titbit into his mouth instead of her own.

Hassan looked taken aback but not displeased, and in return he removed the stone from a date with a deft flick of his dagger and held it to his companion's lips.

'No, not all at once,' he told her. 'Take a small bite at a time. See how long it can last.'

Ferelith did as she was told, realising as she came to the end of the date that the air was suddenly and unexpectedly charged with an almost unbearable tension. As she swallowed the last remnant of fruit, her eyes met his and were held in a gaze of frightening intensity. It seemed an age, an eternity, before his arm slipped round her waist to draw her to him. Her own arm rose, tentatively at first and then more certainly, to rest round his neck so that the drawing of each to the other became mutual and their lips met with an urgency that seemed to reach to the very depths of their being, to be effortlessly sustained while two brief movements discarded both the *burnous* that covered her, blanket-like, and the one she wore. Her Berber garments gave Ferelith her first experience of the prolonged and sensual delights of being gradually disrobed, garment by garment, the intervals filled with an increasingly intimate embrace that heightened perception and sensuality alike until her whole body pleaded with him to take her.

His kisses explored her naked body, rousing her desire for him till she groaned in anticipation and yearning and when he entered her it was suddenly and with a thrusting force that made her cry out at its power. As his manhood plunged deeper within her and her own body responded to the pulsating rhythm with which they became one, Ferelith rejoiced in the sensation of being so completely possessed and she gave herself without reservation to the acceleration of their mutual climax and its final, triumphant plunge.

'Don't withdraw,' she whispered urgently. 'Please don't withdraw.' She had made that plea to Francis once and he had been shocked. Now, somehow, it mattered more than ever.

'I shan't,' Hassan replied. He kissed her lightly and reached out to draw a *burnous* over them. Ferelith sighed with pleasure as the action caused him to move within her once more. She knew now that her instincts had been right: this was a man who would not be easily shocked, a man with whom there would be no need to pretend, within the walls of the bedchamber, to a modesty she did not feel. It was a realisation that gave her a contentment hitherto undreamed of and all the more potent because not for one moment did it occur to her that he might not see it in quite such simple terms, much less that he might not feel as she did.

When he finally, gently, withdrew that too was as it should be and she felt no sense of the deprivation she had become accustomed to when dear, tender Francis had done so. She had assumed that, because her husband withdrew as soon as he had reached his climax, had then kissed her once and gone to sleep, all men were the same and that it was she, with her sense of loss, who was unusual. Now she knew it was not so, that her instincts were right. She did not love Francis any the less, but there was no denying her comfort, her sense of fulfilment, had suddenly become infinitely greater.

She lay in Hassan's arms for a long time, the warmth of her content emanating as much from her sense of well-being as from the covering *burnous*. It was he who nudged her back into the real world.

'You must dress,' he said gently. 'We both must. The temperature will plummet in an hour or two and I've no wish that either of us freeze to death.'

His aid was needed since Ferelith had little recollection of how the various layers went together and the end result was accomplished with much laughter from them both.

'A man of considerable experience, I conclude,' Ferelith said teasingly as, her robing completed, he attended to his own.

He looked round at her, surprised. 'Of course. Would you want it any other way?'

It was somehow not the reply she had expected and it flustered her. 'No, I suppose not,' she said.

Ferelith woke with the dawn to find Hassan was already saddling the horses. He told her to drink some water and together they finished the cheese and dates setting out after their companions.

Hassan seemed more reserved this morning than Ferelith had expected him to be after the intimacies of the night and she found it distinctly disconcerting. She wondered what was to happen about their journey to Meknes. Clearly they must catch up with the others but were they to continue? It seemed the only thing to do: Hassan would presumably be expected back there and it was also where Latifa wanted to be, but Ferelith was unsure what was to happen to her scheme for releasing her father. Hassan had not wanted her to become part of Moulay Ismail's harem before. He would most certainly oppose it now, and what that left Ferelith to bargain with, she had no idea.

She turned such thoughts over and over, and longed to be able to discuss them with Hassan, but the trail necessitated their riding in single file, not a procedure that led to conversation, much less discussion, and when they caught up with the others who, as Hassan had predicted, were not hastening unduly, there seemed to be even less opportunity for private converse. In fact, Ferelith thought she could have been forgiven for thinking Hassan was almost glad there was no chance to be alone together.

The situation did not improve when they stopped for the night. As before, the two women curled up separately, a little apart from those men who were not on guard. Ferelith reminded herself that this was the Moorish way and, in any case, the passions that had erupted between Hassan and herself were illicit in both their societies. In appearing to ignore her, he was merely behaving as man of honour should.

She told herself that, but she failed to convince herself. No matter how hard she tried to treat him with outward indifference, she found her eyes continually seeking him out, watching the curve of his head, the angle of his chin, the grace of his hand on the rein. Not once did she catch him glancing at her, or even in the act of glancing away as if she had been under covert scrutiny until there had been a risk of their eyes meeting in common attraction. It was almost as if she no longer existed. Indeed, only their continued progress towards Meknes proved that she did.

As the third dawn broke with still no word, no sign, no acknowledgement of any bond, however fragile—and it was beginning to seem increasingly fragile—between them, Ferelith knew she must bring the matter up herself. Hassan was obviously not going to, and with Meknes no more than a day's ride away her need to clarify her position was becoming desperate. When he took two horses down to the stream to water them, she followed.

He glanced up when he heard the footstep behind him. 'Go back,' he said. 'You shouldn't be here alone.'

She looked around her, misunderstanding him. 'I'm safe enough, surely? If you're not adequate protection from bandits, we're well within sight of the others.'

'You shouldn't be alone with a man who is not a member of your family,' he said harshly.

She laughed a little shakily. 'When only a few days ago we were completely alone all night? Aren't you being a little nice?'

'That was different. It was unavoidable.'

'It was certainly different. As to its avoidability, my recollection is that neither of us tried to avoid it.'

'That's true enough, though it's not what I meant. We were wrong. *I* was wrong,' he amended. 'As a man of honour, I should not have acted as I did. I undertook to bring you safely to Meknes. I have reneged on that undertaking.'

Ferelith felt her heart growing cold as she thought she perceived his line of thought.

'Nonsense,' she protested. 'I've been perfectly safe and I'm sure I shall remain so until we arrive.'

'Oh, you won't be found with your throat slit,' he told her scornfully. 'You won't arrive in the condition in which you set out, either, and that is entirely due to me.'

'You make me sound like a consignment of olives,' Ferelith said bitterly. 'Did nothing that happened between us mean anything to you at all?'

He heard the entreaty in her voice and his heart cried out to her in the distress he knew she was suffering.

Nevertheless, he steeled himself to sustain the indifference he had assumed these last days because he knew that in the long run it would be better for both of them.

'An unfair question,' he said. 'You have your duty to your father and I have my duty to my King. Anything that might conflict with that must be set aside. At least Ismail will know you're a widow,' he added.

'Indeed,' Ferelith said with enthusiastic sarcasm. 'How dreadful it would be if he thought me to be a virgin and then discovered otherwise.'

Hassan smiled sardonically. 'Dreadful for us both, I assure you.'

Ferelith backed away, her eyes full to overflowing with the dismay his callousness provoked. 'You really don't care at all, do you?' she demanded. 'It means nothing at all to you.'

He longed to take her in his arms, to kiss the tears and unhappiness away. The knowledge that he could not lent a hard edge to his voice. 'It means a great deal to me to stay alive,' he said. 'My life matters to me, as it does to my father.'

Ferelith turned from such brutal frankness and ran, stumbling, back to Latifa, who observed, but said nothing.

CHAPTER NINE

FERELITH knew nothing of Meknes save that Moulay Ismail had made it his capital. She was therefore entirely unprepared for the discovery that he had set to work with his own hands, to say nothing of those of every captive Christian, local tribesman, slave and servant he could impress into his service, to build a palace to rival that of the hated Sun King at Versailles. The style was different: this was no pale imitation of the sort that many European monarchs were said to be building. This was Moorish from its foundations to its roof; its arches, like pointed horseshoes, glowing with the predominantly blue and green tiles that covered every surface not encrusted with intricate carving.

'Is it not magnificent?' Latifa breathed. 'They say the *haras* alone houses more than twelve thousand horses.'

'Then our two should not place an undue burden on the King's resources,' Ferelith told her sharply. In fact, the sheer vastness of the place had taken her aback. She was not quite sure what she had expected. After all, Moulay Ismail was a king, so something a little grander than the castle at Tangier was to be assumed. At the other extreme, Hampton Court was said to be the largest of King Charles's palaces and no one would imagine that some Moorish heathen would exceed the King of England in splendour. Tangier, a city of entirely Portuguese construction and style, had not prepared Ferelith for the glorious architecture of the country to which she had come, any more than had the distant scattered homesteads she had glimpsed from the ramparts.

From Hassan Benani's example, to say nothing of the courtesy of his father and the women of the Benani household, she had learnt that 'heathen' was not necessarily synonymous with 'savage', and she began to wonder whether the usual opprobrious epithet so freely employed by the English should be regarded with suspicion. After all, the word 'infidel' meant much the same and that alone suggested that each religion viewed the other in a similar light. As courtyard led into courtyard and tiled room into carved antechamber and, thence into another courtyard, each courtyard and many a room with its own fountain, Ferelith began to wonder whether it was altogether wise to disregard, much less to mock, a faith whose believers could produce such breathtaking artistry. She wanted to say as much to Hassan, who led them through the labyrinthine palace, but for all he was three steps in front of her he had withdrawn so far in spirit that he had become a stranger with whom she dared not speak.

They stopped at last as court officials filtered the applicants for audience with the King. Hassan Benani, like every citizen, had right of access to his monarch, but there were always matters which could be more easily dealt with by lesser officials and many who came with small concerns were content to have their cause attended to by these lesser mortals. Neither Ferelith nor Latifa, being both women and foreign, had any rights at all.

The glances cast in their direction as Hassan spoke to one official after another told them he was explaining Ferelith's errand and at last they were ushered into the presence of Moulay Ismail, the man whom none at the garrison had ever seen yet who controlled their daily lives like a puppet-master.

Ferelith had expected a dais and a throne from which the King could look down upon his subjects, the status awarded him by birth and custom symbolised by his physical elevation.

She saw nothing of the sort. The audience-chamber was a huge, ornately decorated and richly carpeted *majelus*. The Sultan himself sat among the cushions of cloth of gold in company with men who might have been his ministers or his friends or simply supplicants from distant regions of his realm. All wore white. Some wore the red hat that indicated education at the University of

Fez the oldest place of learning in the world. All of them studied Ferelith with great interest.

Hassan bowed. 'Mrs Durliston, the daughter of Major Melverley,' he said and turned to Ferelith, looking her straight in the eye for the first time since that unhappy interview by the river. 'Speak English,' he told her. 'The King will have a good interpreter.'

Ferelith rightly construed this as an instruction to disguise, at least for the present, the fact that she had acquired a smattering of Arabic. She recalled how well Hassan had hidden his own expertise in English. It was often useful to be able to understand when others thought you couldn't. She was less happy about the other implication.

'But you speak English,' she protested. 'Can't you...?'

'No,' he said shortly. 'The King will require an independent translator in order to verify what his secretary has reported from me.'

He stepped back and took a seat among the cushions that lined almost the whole perimeter of the *majelus*.

Moulay Ismail beckoned a man forward and, after a cursory glance at Latifa, stared at Ferelith in silence. Ferelith quailed inwardly but she tilted her chin defiantly and stared back. He was not a tall man nor— somewhat unexpectedly in view of his reputation—was he old. He might have been forty, he might have been much less. He was certainly no more. He had the look of a man who lived well, with jaded, cynical eyes and a discontented downward turn to his mouth. He looked as if nothing would surprise him and few things give him pleasure.

'At least you don't despise the clothes of my people,' he said at last, through the man whom he had beckoned towards him. 'Do you not have European clothes with you?'

'I do, Your Majesty,' Ferelith told him. 'They're in my saddle-roll—and somewhat the worse for wear,' she added honestly.

His expression remained unchanged and he gestured towards the door. 'Put them on,' he said. 'We shall speak later.'

One of his guards moved forward to escort her from the room but Ferelith stood firm. 'And my maid?' she asked.

Mild surprise replaced boredom. '*My* maid,' he corrected her. 'You will have no further need of her. She will enjoy my protection for the time being.'

She was clearly dismissed, his tone brooking no argument and, since it was hardly in Ferelith's interest to antagonise him, she bit back a retort and one or two questions relating to Latifa's well-being that she might otherwise have asked.

As she left the room with her armed escort, they passed Hassan Benani. Ferelith could see him out of the corner of her eye but she steadfastly ignored him, though the effort cost her dear. She was led through a maze of rooms and corridors until any sense of direction she started out with had been completely baffled. They finally came to a halt before a pair of heavily carved doors upon which her escort beat his fist. The doors were thrown open almost at once, as if their arrival had been expected, and a man who was very fat, very black and very magnificently robed stood aside for her to enter.

He beckoned Ferelith to follow him and she realised from the giggles emanating from behind carved lattices that she was in the harem, the women's quarters from which all men except the master—in this case the King— were prohibited. Her guide must therefore be a eunuch. The Benani harem was modest in both size and decoration compared with this, which, Ferelith soon realised, was a palace in its own right. They eventually stopped before another smaller but equally intricately carved door and her guide knocked imperiously on it with his staff. Since it proved to need no unlocking by the bowing slave-girl who opened it, Ferelith decided it must have been beneath the dignity of her companion to have opened it himself. She was ushered in and the door closed behind

her, leaving her alone in the room with the slave and
another, rather older, woman.

This one introduced herself as Farah and spoke
French, which was probably why she had been selected
to look after the new arrival and, mindful of Hassan's
advice, Ferelith resisted any temptation to let them know
she understood some Arabic. Farah already had
Ferelith's dark green habit and was shaking her head
over its condition and, looking at it against the background of a room which, while simple in comparison
with others in the palace, was still the height of opulence
compared with almost any room in Tangier, Ferelith
could only concur with her opinion.

A sunken bath in an adjacent room was being filled
with hot water from a conduit, a luxurious device which
Ferelith had never seen before. When it was ready, Farah
and her assistant divested Ferelith of her Berber robes
and she stepped gratefully into the unadulterated pleasure
of a bath that was not only precisely the right temperature but big enough to stretch out in. The slave-girl
scrubbed her with perfumed soap, towelled her dry with
soft, absorbent towels of a very different fabric from
the stiff linen ones she was accustomed to, and then
smoothed her skin with perfumed oils before wrapping
her in a silken robe of peacock-blue. Then she was led
back into the room lined with mattressed couches along
three walls and Farah sat her down on one of these and
pulled up a low table upon which were set out a pot of
chocolate, bowls from which to drink it and a plate of
sweetmeats. Ferelith sank back against the cushions and
sighed sybaritically. There might be restrictions—even
quite unacceptable restrictions—to life in a harem, but
there were undoubtedly considerable compensations, too.

Having seen her charge happily sampling the gazelles'
horns, the stuffed dates and the macaroons, Farah produced a sheaf of papers which she handed to the younger
woman.

Ferelith dipped her fingers in the bowl of rose-water
and wiped them dry on the napkin the slave held out to
her, and took them. To her surprise each sheet carried

a drawing of European women's clothes. They were not all the product of one hand: the style varied and so did the artists' proficiency. Nor did they necessarily depict the most recent fashions and some seemed to be of German origin, while others were French and some were English.

'Where did these come from?' she asked.

'They've been collected over the years,' Farah told her. 'Some were drawn by former captives ransomed from the French and English, some by infidel captives like yourself. Some have been described to our own women who have then drawn them. Those are the least satisfactory, I think: such work is not part of a Moorish girl's education.'

'Why were they assembled?'

'Feminine curiosity mostly, though the King has occasionally sent for them. The clothes you brought with you are quite different: all these are most immodest and show a great deal of bosom; yours, on the other hand, covers everything and is most discreet.'

Ferelith smiled. 'That's because it's a riding-habit. It would be most indelicate to ride *décolletée*.'

'The King is anxious to see you in the sort of clothes you usually wear,' Farah went on. She glanced doubtfully at the habit, 'I don't think that would please him. You see, we have had many European captives here but never one of so exalted a rank as the daughter of Major Melverley. Perhaps we should make you something more fitting. Our women have nimble fingers. If you would oversee the work, I'm sure something appropriate can be made.'

Ferelith suppressed a smile at the thought of her supposed 'exalted rank'. 'I'm sure that could be done,' she said, 'but not in time for my audience with your King. I imagine he will be sending for me soon.'

'What makes you think so?' Farah seemed surprised.

Ferelith tried to remember his precise words. 'He told me to put my normal clothes on and that he would see me later,' she said.

Farah smiled. 'He won't have meant today, and quite possibly not tomorrow, either. "Later" means exactly that. Some time in the future, when the whim takes him.'

'But I need to see him soon,' Ferelith protested, horrified. 'I've come to plead on my father's behalf. I can't wait forever!'

'You have no choice but to await the King's pleasure. He knows what business brought you here. All the more reason to demonstrate that you are his to command, not the other way around. We have time to make you something new. Will you guide us?'

Ferelith smiled wryly. 'It will give me something to occupy my time, I suppose, and it looks as if there will be plenty to occupy. Yes, of course, I will.'

The choice of fabrics brought to her was breathtaking and none was of wool, not even of the finest weave. There were silks and sarcenets, satins, damasks and brocades. Some were heavy and lustrous, others were interwoven with gold or silver thread, while yet others had been embroidered with coloured silks or with gold or silver thread but in patterns which were exotically different from the motifs used by English embroidresses. It was, Ferelith thought guiltily, like being let loose in a silk warehouse without the inconvenience of considering the cost. The fabrics spread out for her inspection were worth...'a king's ransom' was the phrase that came to mind. At any rate, far, far more than Moulay Ismail had asked for Major Melverley. In a strange way, the sheer incalculable costliness of these materials brought home to her with far greater clarity than the magnificence of the palace had done the futility of her errand. She had always known that the monetary ransom demanded had been small, given the circumstances. Now she realised that to Moulay Ismail it was insignificant. Tangier was the realistic price and Ferelith herself a very inadequate substitute.

'These are superb,' she told Farah, picking up and unrolling a bolt of pale sea-green satin embroidered with minutely precise birds and flowers at regular and close intervals across its entire surface. 'Where do they come from?'

'That one from China, others from India but much is from the merchant ships of the Italian kingdoms and from France.'

So this display represented some of the King's one-eighth share of his corsairs' booty. Ferelith felt far less guilty about making her choice.

Looking-glasses were brought so that she could hold fabrics up against herself and judge their effect and she spent a long and enjoyable time becoming so absorbed in the task that more serious considerations were put temporarily out of her mind.

In the end, however, she returned to the heavy sea-green satin that had first appealed to her and then, having asked Farah to fetch her paper and pencil, she sketched what she had in mind, not forgetting the essential smock—the undergarment whose gathered sleeves and lace-embellished neck would add decorative emphasis to what Ferelith was determined should be the most magnificent gown she had ever worn.

The women were fascinated by the task before them and worked willingly and well, sometimes dissolving into hysterical laughter at certain aspects of the dress they were making. They were particularly entertained by the boning in the stiff bodice which, Ferelith insisted, had to be inserted in such a way that her breasts were pushed together and upwards. One of the women, roughly comparable to Ferelith in size, tried it on to the ribald amusement of the others.

'How do you breathe?' she demanded through Farah. 'How do you make love? All I can do in this is stand up very straight.'

'You could sit down very straight,' Ferelith pointed out, 'and you'd soon get used to breathing. As to making love—well, one takes it off before one goes to bed, of course.'

The women exchanged glances.

'But what if your husband suddenly wants to make love then and there, perhaps in the middle of the day?'

Ferelith was taken aback. Francis had never made such a request and it had never occurred to Ferelith that there might be men who did, though, now she thought about it, she supposed there must be.

'In the middle of the day one would be wearing something less formal,' she told them. 'All the same, I think one would still adjourn to the bedchamber.'

The women exchanged glances again but said nothing more.

Ferelith had every reason to be pleased with the finished gown and the women every reason to be proud. The long, stiff, pointed bodice with its low-cut bosom swelled over the hips into a generously cut skirt of softly folding gathers, which was looped up at the front to reveal a petticoat of the same material. The sleeves covered only the upper arms and were cut in small, square panes joined at the corners by some of the largest pearls Ferelith had ever seen. The sleeves of the smock peeped through the intervening spaces and then billowed out at the elbow, exuberantly trimmed with lace. Delicately wrought lace also edged the neck of this undergarment and protruded sufficiently to hide the first indications of her nipples. A scarf of finest gauze was further draped round the neck of the dress, to be fastened with a brooch of pearl at the point of cleavage, thereby both holding the scarf of modesty in place and drawing attention to what it sought to conceal. A rope of pearls round her neck and two suspended from her ears completed the ensemble, and Ferelith had no cause to be dissatisfied with the result.

It took the women of the harem two days to make the dress and during that time Ferelith saw no sign of Latifa, whom she more than half expected to be sent to the women's quarters, too, though in what capacity she was unsure. In the end she asked Farah to find out what had happened to her. This the older woman was able to do through the eunuch who had charge of the harem and eventually brought the news that Latifa, having been questioned very closely on all matters pertaining to Tangier, had been returned to her people with instructions that she was to be treated as a daughter by one of the commanding officers until such time as she could be married or taken back to relatives in the Sudan.

Another worry during those two days of concentrated sewing was the possibility of Moulay Ismail's sending for her before the gown was completed. It was a needless worry. So far as Ferelith could ascertain there was not so much as an enquiry as to whether she was ready. Not, she reflected, that Moulay Ismail seemed to be a man given to considering the convenience of others. A further three days passed without a word and now that Ferelith had time on her hands she also had leisure in which to wonder what Hassan Benani was doing, what he was thinking and, more importantly, whether she had completely misread his character. She had been so sure that his feeling for her had been more than the adulterous lust that moved Piercey Kirke. She was still convinced of it, even if his feeling had proved to be short-lived. Harder to accept was the ease with which he had put her from him and had then delivered her to his King as if nothing untoward had ever happened between them. He had done so with no sign of affection, no tender farewell, no begging for her understanding. She was too unhappy to consider that any of these displays of affection would have made the parting even more difficult to bear. To Ferelith, the absence of their declaration meant the absence of their existence. Perhaps she should have realised that a man who could contemplate with equanimity the possibility of four concurrent wives was unlikely to be capable of feeling deeply about any of them. She found little comfort in such reflections.

She was able during the three days of inactivity to satisfy some part of her curiosity, thereby causing further innocent merriment to the other women. She asked Farah whether she minded being one wife among many.

Farah smiled indulgently. 'I'm no one's wife, nor likely to be,' she said. 'Whom did you take to be my husband? Ali?' Ali was the chief eunuch.

Ferelith laughed. 'No, but I thought Moulay Ismail. He does have wives, I presume?'

'Indeed he does, as many as the faith permits, but I'm not one of them. I am—or was—a concubine. He grew tired of me, as was to be expected, but had enough affection not to turn me off.'

'But you're obviously the most senior woman here,' Ferelith said, puzzled. 'Where are his wives? Surely they live in the harem, too?'

'Of course, but each has her own entirely separate quarters, her own slaves, her own eunuchs. Sometimes they visit among themselves, occasionally they visit here. Should they do so while you're here, you must treat them with great respect.'

'Of course,' Ferelith assured her.

At last the summons came. The Englishwoman was to be presented to Moulay Ismail as soon as he returned from his ride.

The women raced to get Ferelith ready. The ride would probably last several hours but the King had been known to become suddenly bored and return within the hour. Whichever happened today, Ferelith must be ready and waiting. Better she should kick her heels under guard in an ante-room than that Ismail should be kept waiting.

Her heels had plenty of practice. The room in which she was left alone, a guard on the door, was lined with the customary low, wide couches on three sides and on a shelf in a niche stood its only other movable article, a small French clock with an ornately chased face and filigree hands. Three tedious hours dragged by before she was sent for. Three tedious hours during which she found it was easier to stand than to sit for the stiffly boned bodice of English fashions was made for stiffly carved upright chairs, not for the low, wide, softly cushioned seats for which the loose garments of the Moors, both men and women, were ideally suited.

The door was eventually opened and an imposingly caftanned official beckoned her to follow him. A short corridor brought them to the door of the great *majelus*, and, as before, Moulay Ismail, robed in yellow, sat in the centre of the couch facing the door, his courtiers on either side while lesser members of his entourage sat at the extremities of the room.

Ferelith glanced rapidly along their ranks, seeking the one familiar face, both hoping and dreading to find it, and when she did, being still unsure which emotion predominated, she glanced away quickly. Her heart might be broken but she had too much pride to let anyone guess it had even been touched. She walked across the heavily patterned tiled floor until she stood immediately before the King. Then she dropped him a curtsy of precisely the depth she would have accorded King Charles. The ghost of a smile with which it was received told her she had done the right thing. The interpreter moved unobtrusively to his place by the King.

'You are sent to us by our friend Benani,' Ismail stated.

Ferelith chose to interpret it as a question. 'No, Majesty. I arrived here safely through the good offices of Benani and his son, but I came here of my own volition and set out from Tangier without reference to them.'

'Nevertheless, had it not been for them, you would not now be standing here.'

'That is correct, sir.'

'Are you here with the blessing of Colonel Kirke?'

'No, sir. When I suggested to him that I should come, he said it would be a waste of time.'

'But you thought differently?'

'Not exactly. I thought he might possibly be proved right, but I also thought there was a chance he was wrong and it wasn't a chance I wished to forgo.'

'Upon what basis did you assume there was a chance?'

Ferelith hesitated, sensing that much might depend upon the answer. 'Sir, my acquaintance with monarchs is limited but it seems to me that any ruler who has gained the respect of his subjects is probably a just man.'

'A clever answer. Do you equate respect with fear?'

'No, sir, I do not.'

'Would you deny that I am feared?'

'No, for if I did you would know I lied. You are greatly feared. You are also greatly respected and it's my hope that my quest will appeal to that part of your nature which has earned the respect of your people.'

Moulay Ismail leant back against his cushions. 'Now we come to the interesting part,' he said. 'We presume you have come to plead for your father's liberty.'

'I should prefer to say that I've come to see whether we can come to some sort of arrangement which would result in that.'

'Semantics,' he said dismissively. 'Now, if Kirke didn't send you, you have no power to negotiate on a political level. You cannot, for instance, offer me Tangier.'

'That is so.'

'Tangier would be a considerable ransom. What can you offer that may compare?'

Again Ferelith hesitated. 'There are sometimes things between which comparison is not entirely possible: *harira* and gazelles' horns, for example. Whether one preferred soup or sweetmeats would depend partly upon how hungry one was and partly upon one's particular preference.'

He nodded. 'Very true. You intrigue me—go on.'

'Sir, may I with respect ask after my father? Is he well? Shall I be allowed to see him?'

Ismail's face clouded at the change of subject. 'You have our word that Major Melverley is alive and well. As to whether you will be allowed to see him, that will depend very much upon what you propose to offer.'

Ferelith realised she had placed one false step and must retrieve her position. She inclined her head deferentially. 'Thank you for your assurance, Majesty; my mind is at rest. Sir, I offer you the only thing I have to offer for my father's freedom. Myself.'

She was aware of heightened interest from those present, not least Moulay Ismail.

'Are you aware that we already have all the wives our faith permits?'

'Yes, sir.'

'Were you assuming we should put one of them aside?'

'No, sir.'

He leant forward and looked at her through narrowed eyes. 'Are you a virgin?'

Ferelith flushed and looked him straight in the eye. 'No, sir. A widow.'

'With children?'

'No, sir. My husband died before that was possible.'

'You realise that you would never see your home and family again?'

'I accept that that is all too probable.'

'Yet it is a price you will pay?'

'If it will save my father—yes.'

'You have a very pronounced sense of duty. Your father has been told nothing of your arrival here. What do you imagine will be his reaction when he learns of it?'

'I should think he'll be very angry indeed,' Ferelith said truthfully.

Ismail beckoned. 'Come over here.'

Ferelith advanced until she was standing immediately in front of him.

'Turn round. Slowly.'

She did as she was told, taking good care to avoid catching Hassan's eye. She felt like a beast in a cattle sale and, while it might mean nothing to him to see her being coldly assessed by a roomful of men, it mattered to her knowing, as she did, that Hassan Benani was the only man to whom she would willingly grant this particular privilege.

When she was facing Ismail once more, he stood up and flicked the gauze scarf with his fingers.

'Remove it,' he said.

She unfastened the brooch and did as he bade her. She caught the short, swift intake of breath as he realised how much was revealed beneath its concealing folds. His fingers reached out again and this time stroked the upthrust sphere of her breasts, playing briefly with the nipple imperfectly hidden by the lace that edged the smock. She saw him smile; saw, too, the hungry eyes of the men still sitting on the couch behind. They might not be able to see what their King could see, but they had their imaginations and Ferelith knew that if Ismail rejected her any one of these would be all too willing to take his place.

Ismail nodded. 'Replace it,' he commanded, his eyes indicating the scarf, and Ferelith obeyed with alacrity. He returned to his seat. 'You may see your father,' he went on and paused to consider. 'Tomorrow. Yes, he can be brought up tomorrow. There will be one condition.'

'Sir?' Ferelith hoped he couldn't see her crossed fingers hidden in the folds of her skirt. Pray God he's not going to forbid us to speak, she thought.

'You may see him and you may tell him you've come here to plead for his freedom—to appeal to our better nature. What you may *not* tell him is the price you have offered to pay.'

'May I be told whether it is a price your Majesty is willing to accept?' Ferelith asked.

'No, you may not. That is something upon which it pleases us to leave you uncertain.'

'Then at least accept my thanks for letting me speak with Papa,' she said.

He inclined his head in acknowledgement and gestured to the guard to remove her. Her instinct was to get out of the room as fast as she could but she held it in check long enough to drop Ismail another low, straight-backed curtsy before she went.

If she was not to mention to Major Melverley the offer she had put to his captor, it would better if he saw her in the old, familiar green habit rather than either a sumptuous gown he had never seen before or clothes from the harem. The habit would suggest she had only very recently arrived. Her father was no fool and by this time presumably had the measure of the man who ruled this country. Better by far to open the way to as few questions as possible. It was therefore thus attired that she left her own room and followed her usual escort through the passages of the palace—all of them as unfamiliar as those of the previous day—to a room not dissimilar to the one in which she had spent so many tedious hours the day before. The floor tiles were plain and a thick, heavily patterned woollen carpet had been thrown over them. There was also a low table and, as she arrived at the door, so did a slave bearing a tray with a beaked brass coffee-pot, some drinking-bowls and the ubiquitous basket of dates.

As the door opened, Major Melverley glanced up and the surprise on his face when he saw his daughter, surprise which almost immediately changed to concern, was proof, had she needed it, that no word of her presence here had reached him. Recalling the speed with which similar news would have sped through Tangier, Ferelith could only reflect upon the efficiency with which fear of the King's wrath had stilled tattling tongues. She held out her hands.

'Papa,' she said.

He came towards her and they hugged each other with the fervour of kinsfolk who had never expected to see one another again. When the major released her, Ferelith glanced around. They were alone. There was nothing to prevent her telling her father the deal she had offered Ismail. Nothing except her word—and a suspicion that they might be alone but were not necessarily unobserved. She was never sure which reason was the one that made her stay silent.

The major's appearance shocked her. Ismail had told her he was alive and well, and she had believed him. The first was true enough but the second was certainly not, a fact which made her feel very angry. He was much thinner than she remembered and his face was drawn and aged, with the pallor of one who stayed—or had been kept—indoors.

'Papa, you're far from well. I asked Ismail how you were and he gave me his word you were well. He lied!'

'I doubt it. He hasn't seen me since I arrived. He only knows what he's told and I don't suppose anyone has the courage to tell him I'm ailing. Besides, it's a temporary matter. Once I get back to good, sound English food I shall be all right.'

Ferelith, who for some weeks now had eaten nothing resembling 'good, sound English food' with no ill effects at all, forbore to say so though she conceded that the food served to captives, no matter how eminent, might be less satisfactory than that eaten in Berber villages or Kings' harems.

She put a hand on her father's head. 'You've a fever, Papa. What other symptoms are there?'

He shrugged. 'A recurring flux that's sometimes bloody. That's all. They tell me it frequently affects foreigners but they soon get over it.'

It crossed her mind that a man who had been a captive for several months might be expected to have recovered from an indisposition if he was going to do so at all but she kept the reflection to herself. 'I will ask the King to send his own physician,' she said. 'He told me you were well and I'm sure will see it as his duty to restore your health.'

'You've a touching faith in his benignity which few others would share,' the major said drily. 'Now, my dear, pour me some coffee—a luxury I've not sampled for longer than I care to remember—and tell me exactly what you're doing here. You appear to be well enough but I own I'd be happier if I thought you were safely back in Tangier.'

'I'm very well, Papa,' she told him. 'You've no cause to worry on that score. As to my purpose—why, it's simple enough. I came to seek out Moulay Ismail and plead for your release.'

His cup stopped halfway to his mouth and he stared at her. 'Frithy, you're mad.'

'Nonsense,' she said briskly. 'The King must have realised when he made his demand that there was no question of Tangier being given up to ransom one officer, not even a senior one. Why, then, shouldn't he find the pleading of a tearful daughter just the excuse he needed to give way and demonstrate his generosity of spirit and simultaneously divest himself of an embarrassment?'

'A very strange reading of his character. Tell me, how did you persuade Kirke to let you do it? More to the point, perhaps, how many men did he have to release from garrison duty to accompany you? Are they as safe as you seem to be?'

Ferelith coloured. 'Colonel Kirke didn't exactly let me—and he didn't exactly send an escort. Latifa hired a guide and horses and arranged everything on the understanding that I would set her free once we had slipped away. It all worked very well except that our guide sold us to some Berbers—but don't worry, Papa. It all turned out for the best. I don't know what *might* have happened, of course, but their chief turned out to be the father of that man Benani—do you remember him, Papa? He came to Tangier with the Alcaid Ali Benabdala and was at the governor's ball. The older Benani sent us on our way with an escort which included his son, so we couldn't have been safer.'

Major Melverley was too ill to notice the somewhat self-conscious manner in which she brought Hassan into the story. His only sensation was one of gratitude that she was alive to tell the tale. He closed his eyes in horror at the thought of what might have happened. 'It was a madcap thing to do, Frithy, the very height of folly. I'm glad you care so much for your father to contemplate such a scheme, but I wish you hadn't carried it out. And you've seen Ismail, you say?'

'Yes, Papa.' She nearly added, 'Twice,' but remembered just in time that she didn't want him to know how long she had been in Meknes.

'How did he seem?'

Rightly construing this not to be an enquiry as to the King's health, she said, 'I can't say I warmed to him and of course he asked a lot of questions, but that was only to be expected. I answered truthfully and I think he recognised that. That's all there is to report, really.'

The major frowned. 'Did he give you any indication that he might fall in with your plan?'

'No, Papa, none. Nor that he wouldn't.'

'Pity. It would be nice to know where one stood.'

'Papa, forgive me, but even if he agrees would you be well enough to travel? Tangier is a long way.'

'Perhaps not, but if the chance is offered me you'll not find me rejecting it. A few days in my daughter's company would probably be all the tonic I would need to set me up again and, if it didn't, then at least I'd die happy.'

Looking at him, Ferelith suspected that this was nearer the truth than she liked to contemplate. She tried to think of a way of telling him that, if he was to be freed, his daughter would not be going with him. None came to mind, partly because she knew that any excuse she gave, including the forbidden truth, would simply have the effect of making him refuse to leave at all, thereby defeating the whole object of the exercise.

She forced herself to smile. 'We'll have to see what can be done, Papa,' she said. 'Now, Papa, have you learnt any Arabic in captivity?'

He stared at her in surprise. 'Of course I have. It's been essential.'

'Good. I'm going to open the door and ask the guard who's probably standing there to come in. You will then translate for me.'

'Translate for you?' the major said, bewildered, knowing full well that Latifa had taught his daughter more than a smattering. 'But I thought——'

'Just do as I say,' Ferelith interrupted him before he could finish the sentence. The door had been locked but she had only to tap and the guard opened it.

'I want you to go and find—or send someone, if you're not allowed to leave your post—an official at this court who speaks English or French and who has nothing—absolutely nothing, you understand?—to do with infidel captives. When he's been found, I want him brought here without delay, and if you get orders before he arrives to move either of us back to our quarters I shall personally complain to Moulay Ismail.'

The major translated the instruction with a few diplomatic modifications and they awaited events. What neither of them knew, but the guard did, was that after his interview with Ferelith Moulay Ismail had immediately returned to his private quarters and changed his robes before continuing his audience. The significance of this would have been apparent to the major, who in several months had heard most of the stories, both true and false, about the King's strange moods. One of the most soundly based, of which Ferelith was happily totally ignorant, was that yellow was the colour Moulay Ismail wore when death—neither his own death nor death in the abstract but the very concrete death of someone else—was on his mind. The fact he had changed the colour of his caftan after his interview with Ferelith told his courtiers that she was in favour. That state might prove temporary; indeed, it probably would, but while it lasted it would be no more advisable to disregard her wishes than it would be to disregard those of the King himself.

Ferelith's message was sent and its carrier returned with Hassan Benani, much to her discomfiture. It had never crossed her mind that anyone other than a complete stranger would arrive. She would have been happier had that been the case because she was very conscious of the embarrassment Hassan's presence caused her. He appeared unaffected, as distant in his manner as at any time since that night in the ravine. She reminded herself that on this occasion he had had the long walk from the *majelus* to school his demeanour into the appropriate level of disinterest, but she found it galling that he seemed to have no difficulty doing so.

'You remember my father,' she said without preamble. 'You recall how he looked in Tangier. Look at him now. He's a sick man, yet the King told me he was well. You heard him. Papa says that will be what he's been told by those who do not wish to be seen to have been neglectful.'

'Major Melverley is probably right. Moulay Ismail has a way of dealing with those who fail in their duty. People therefore have a tendency to tell him what he wants to hear.'

'How soon will he recover?'

Hassan shrugged. 'I'm no physician, but not quickly, I think.'

'My opinion precisely,' Ferelith said triumphantly. 'I want you to go back to Moulay Ismail and tell him how ill Papa is and ask him on my behalf—*very* humbly, you understand—to send his own physician to him so that he can be upon the road to recovery before he takes the road to Tangier.'

'I admire your certainty that he intends to free your father,' Hassan said with cold politeness, guessing that perhaps she had already received a private message confirming what everyone at the *majelus* had expected.

'There is no certainty,' Ferelith snapped. 'You heard Ismail. None at all, but Papa's freedom is the reason I came here and I have to remain optimistic about my chances of success.' She hesitated and looked at him tentatively. 'I think I made quite a good impression, don't you?'

'Quite remarkably so, I'd say.' He turned to her father. 'I take it you'll be happy to have a Moorish doctor examine you?'

'I'd be a fool not to,' Major Melverley said. 'If there's a chance of my being released, though, I'd rather leave as soon as possible and take my chances of recovering along the way.'

Hassan looked at him and privately calculated that his chances would not be great. 'You would be better advised to recover here, under expert care, if the King agrees to it,' he said.

'And risk Ismail changing his mind on a sudden whim? No, thank you. I may not have a choice, but if I do it will be to go.'

'Very well, but you will not object to the King's being asked to provide a physician in the meantime?'

Major Melverley shook his head wearily. 'No, of course not.'

Hassan turned to go and Ferelith caught his arm. 'You will put it very tactfully, won't you?' she begged.

He looked down at her and smiled sardonically. 'That, Mrs Durliston, is the one thing you may be very sure of.'

Ferelith and her father were left together for some time after Hassan's departure and then each was taken away in a different direction. Ferelith expected to be returned to the women's quarters and was somewhat taken aback to find herself ushered into a room which, as near as she could judge, was the King's private sitting-room. It was neither small nor intimate and was, if anything, even more opulently furnished than any other apartment she had yet seen, but there were no courtiers beyond two men she had seen before and who had seemed to be ministers of some sort. Apart from them, there was an amanuensis and the interpreter. The King was sitting cross-legged among his cushions, smoking a hookah. He looked her up and down in a manner which, in a man of lesser standing, she would have described as insolent.

'You have seen your father.'

'I have, Your Majesty, and thank you for the opportunity.'

'You told him nothing untoward?'

'I kept my word,' she replied, biting back the urge to add, 'As you very well know.'

'I understand you are not happy about his state of health.'

'No, sir. He's a very sick man. I hope Your Majesty will feel able to send a physician to attend him.'

'You may depend upon it. I had been told he was well and if my doctor's opinion concurs with yours someone will answer for it.'

This was not quite what Ferelith had had in mind but she must choose her words with care. 'And will your doctor be authorised to offer treatment, should his opinion echo mine?' she asked.

Ismail looked mildly surprised. 'Of course, and for as long as he is here.'

Ferelith's face was wreathed in smiles, her worries over. 'Your Majesty is most generous,' she said. 'I'm sure his recovery will be rapid.' She paused, unsure how far to venture. 'I've no wish to appear presumptuous, sir, but may I enquire whether a decision has been made concerning Papa? Will he be released?'

Ismail frowned. 'You are importunate, madam, but, yes, a decision has been made.' He leant back, watching her through narrowed eyes and Ferelith forced herself to wait to be told—or not—rightly guessing that a further question would be unwise.

Ismail was in no hurry to satisfy her curiosity. He puffed at his hookah and ate some almonds from a silver dish beside his couch. 'You intrigue me, Mrs Durliston,' he said at last. 'You are a very striking woman. Not beautiful—not by the standards we apply, though I accept it may be otherwise in England—but certainly striking and with a temperament that is also quite different from those to which I am accustomed. Your forthrightness may well pall, but for the time being it intrigues me enough to persuade me to take advantage of the bargain you were prepared to strike. You shall stay here and we shall see for how long you can hold our interest. Your father will be sent back to Tangier.'

Ferelith swept him a curtsy, her head low in obeisance this time. 'Your Majesty is indeed kind,' she said warmly, deliberately suppressing her more personal qualms as to what the future might hold. 'We must hope his recovery won't be long delayed, so that he may the sooner reach his regiment.'

'His recovery will be in the hands of Allah,' Ismail told her sternly. 'Your father will leave tomorrow with an escort. Hassan Benani will be entrusted with the task of returning him to Tangier.'

'Tomorrow! But he is far too ill! Sir, you cannot have thought—give him at least a few days of good food and proper medical care so that he may have a good chance of safely completing the journey.'

'Do you suggest that a doctor has more influence than Allah?'

'No, of course not, but we find that sometimes God needs some help.'

'Indeed? A sure indication of his inferiority. They leave tomorrow. If it is the will of Allah, he will live. Besides,' he added, spoiling the effect somewhat, 'it suits our convenience to have him gone.'

'In what way?'

'We consider it probable that if he were here for several days he might learn the precise nature of our bargain, and that would be a pity because I suspect he would forbid you to continue with it.'

That was undoubtedly so, but Ferelith denied it stoutly. 'He is a man of honour, sir, as you are yourself. He would realise I had given my word.'

'Were you a son, that would be conclusive, but the word of a daughter, though sincerely given, can always be overruled. There is another reason for his early departure.' He paused expectantly, inviting the inevitable question.

'Which is?'

'I cannot in honour take advantage of your part of the bargain until I have fulfilled my part of it. The sooner your father gets back to Tangier, the sooner my jaded palate can sample the exotic spices of an English-woman's skills.'

CHAPTER TEN

FERELITH had no opportunity to speak to her father again before he left. She sent a message to Moulay Ismail begging to be allowed to bid him farewell but if it reached him the King chose to ignore it. Ferelith was not altogether surprised, guessing that he would be unwilling to risk her giving some hint of the bargain they had struck, to say nothing of the probability of Major Melverley's having to be taken forcibly to Tangier once he realised that his daughter was staying behind. He would soon realise she wasn't in the party, of course, but Ferelith had no doubt some plausible excuse would be offered together with assurances that she would follow later, and the King's representative could hardly claim her indisposition, for instance, if she were to be seen very obviously fit and well.

Farah took pity on her and arranged for her to be taken through the women's quarters to a heavily latticed oriel set over the main doorway to the palace. Its normal function was to allow selected members of the harem to watch the arrival and departure of important visitors without themselves being seen from below. Ferelith was grateful for this concession and pressed her face to the heavily carved cedarwood screen. She thought the major looked rather better than he had the previous day, the effect, no doubt, of good food and a proper bed, to say nothing of the ministrations of the doctor. She fancied he walked with a firmer step, too, and she felt less pessimistic about his chances of reaching Tangier, but her eyes filled at the realisation that this would almost certainly be the last time she would see him.

She was unlikely ever to see Hassan Benani again, but perhaps that was all for the best. Seeing him now, helping her father into the saddle, organising the rest of the escort into some sort of order, left her with an ache that burned deep inside her with an intensity that frightened her. She loved him and she had demonstrated it to him in the most unambiguous way it was possible for a woman to do. She had believed he felt similarly yet he had turned away from her with heartbreaking coldness after willingly accepting her gift. He had watched with apparent equanimity her meeting with Moulay Ismail and, although the prospect of giving the Moor that which she desired to give only to the Berber was one which tore her apart, he seemed unmoved by it. It was true that in her calmer moments she could appreciate that there was very little he could do about it, but her calmer moments were few and the pain with which she had seen his indifference and with which she now watched his preparations to leave was well-nigh unbearable.

Hassan, who had a closer view of Major Melverley, did not share Ferelith's relative optimism. True, the older man had improved dramatically during the night, but it was an improvement that needed consolidation, and that would not be acquired on this journey. Hassan knew better than to waste time and invoke the wrath of his sovereign by suggesting they should delay their departure for a few days. Major Melverley, only a month or two ago, had been a soldier fit to go into battle. Now he had to be helped into a saddle he would then have swung himself into without a second thought. Hassan's concern, though genuine, was not entirely unselfish. If the major died before reaching Tangier, there was a very strong chance that the man charged with his safe delivery would also die when word of the failure reached the King. This was something against which precautions could be taken and accordingly, when they were well out of sight of the city walls, he dispatched one of his fellow Berbers to his father with a carefully worded message.

In the palace, Farah had news for her charge that ought to have gone some way towards dispelling her very natural gloom at being parted from her father. Moulay Ismail had given instructions that she was to be equipped with an extensive wardrobe in both the English and

Moorish styles. Furthermore, a lavish apartment was being fitted out for her exclusive use though Ferelith observed it was being done without reference to her taste or preferences. She was to have her own slaves, but first there was the matter of clothes.

The lustrous fabrics of India and China had lost their power to absorb her. Ferelith tried to throw herself into the preparation of a wardrobe the like of which she had never been offered before, but it was impossible. Her concern for her father, her despair over Hassan, her dread of her own future, all conspired to put her thoughts elsewhere.

'How far is it to Tangier?' she asked Farah once.

Farah was vague. 'About five days' journey, I think.'

That seemed excessive. 'So long?' Ferelith insisted.

Farah considered. 'In a litter, yes. Less on horseback, I suppose.'

Quite a lot less, Ferelith guessed. Perhaps just three days, especially if her father's health stood up to it well. Moulay Ismail had said that honour precluded his taking advantage of her offer until her father was back in Tangier. It was desperately important to her that her calculations should be correct. If it took three days for them to reach Tangier, it would take another three for the escort to return to Meknes with the news. That meant that she had six days—more, if she was lucky, less if she wasn't—before the King could expect her to keep her side of the bargain. Six days to get used to the idea of becoming the plaything of a reputedly licentious monarch until he tired of her, and then to a life of idleness and gossip among the women of the harem.

On the second day, she received a summons, but not from Moulay Ismail. Farah led her through the labyrinth of rooms and passages that constituted the harem, a palace within a palace, until they crossed a small courtyard and stood outside the most imposing doors Ferelith had yet seen, covered as they were with beaten brass that caught the sun and gleamed like solid gold. Here Farah left her and, as her back turned, the doors swung open and Ferelith was admitted.

She guessed at once, from the grandeur of her surroundings, that she stood within the entirely self-contained quarters, of one of Ismail's wives.

A slave-girl, more splendidly dressed than any Ferelith had so far seen, greeted her and led her through several more rooms until they came to a *majelus*, smaller—as was to be expected—than that of the King and furnished in prettier colours but no less a formal audience-chamber. Five women lolled among the satin cushions, one of them very much more senior than the others. With a start, Ferelith realised that this must be the Queen Mother. For some foolish reason, it had never crossed her mind that the harem would house the older ladies of the court as well as the younger. Ferelith dropped her a deep curtsy.

'I understand you speak French,' the woman said.

'A little. Competently but not fluently,' Ferelith told her.

'That will be sufficient. You are the Englishwoman who has offered herself to my son in place of her father?'

'Yes, *madame*.' Ferelith was quite pleased to find her guess proved accurate.

'Do you intend to turn renegade?'

Ferelith hesitated. It was not a matter to which she had given any thought. Many captives in Moorish hands went through a ceremony in which they renounced their Christian faith and adopted that of Islam. Such men— few women felt the need thus to recant—were then accepted as good Muslims and treated as equal to any others, with equal opportunity to advance themselves through trade, learning, the civil administration or sheer hard work, whichever way their talents lay. The word 'renegade' had been coined by their compatriots to describe them. To most people in Christian Europe, it was an incomprehensible thing to do. To anyone labouring in the galleys with no hope of ransom, either through poverty or lack of concerned kinsmen, it was the answer to a prayer.

'I've given it no thought,' Ferelith told her.

'It has not been suggested to you?'

'No, *madame*.'

The Queen Mother looked at her in silence for a few minutes, giving Ferelith the impression that she was undecided whether to believe her.

'When you made your offer to my son, was it in your mind that you would become Queen?'

Ferelith smiled. 'No, *madame*. That eventuality seemed so remote that I don't think it even crossed my mind.'

'So in what capacity did you think you were offering yourself?'

'I knew that concubine was the best I could hope for.'

'A high price to pay for your father's freedom.'

'Very high.' Ferelith hesitated. 'I suppose, if I'm completely truthful, I would have to admit that I half hoped—more than half hoped, I suppose—that Moulay Ismail would be sufficiently impressed by my willingness to sacrifice myself that he would free Papa without accepting me.'

Moulay Ismail's mother was clearly no more impressed than her son had been. 'If that is what you hoped for, you displayed a lamentable ignorance of my son's nature.'

'So it would appear.'

'And you are a widow? Without issue?'

'Yes, *madame*.'

'Turn around.'

Ferelith rotated for the Queen Mother much as she had done for her son and with exactly the same feeling that she was a cow at auction. This time, though, there were five people scrutinising her and by their manner she suspected that none was charitably disposed towards her.

'That will do.' Ferelith stood still again and wondered what verdict would be pronounced. The Queen Mother turned to her daughters-in-law and Ferelith, with several days' practice of listening to the slaves talking, had little difficulty following. 'I don't think we have anything to worry about, my dears. She is unusual. She will absorb his time, perhaps for some weeks, but it will be the attraction of novelty. They say European women are not taught how to keep a man's interest and I'm sure she has not. For all she's a widow, there's much of the innocent about her. The novelty will pall. She will soon be discarded.' She turned back to Ferelith and reverted to French. 'You may go back to your quarters. I doubt if we shall meet again.'

Ferelith curtsyed. 'Thank you, *madame*,' she said, and followed a slave-girl back through the multiplicity of rooms to the brass-bound doors. Here a eunuch led her back to her own quarters and left her with much to think about.

She was unsure whether to be pleased with what she had overheard or not. Her feminine pride was not at all happy at the suggestion that her attraction was only the attraction of novelty, nor that she lacked the skill to keep a man's interest. She had experienced no problems keeping Francis's. Even the Queen Mother's final conclusion, that she would soon be discarded, was one she received with mixed feelings. Nothing would give her greater pleasure than for the King to tire of her but she was uncertain what was implied by 'discarded'. Did it mean he would simply not seek her company and she would be left entirely to the amusements of the harem? That might be tedious but it would be comfortable. It might mean that when he had tired of her she would be sent to rejoin her father. On the whole, Ferelith thought that was rather unlikely and, if it happened, she would be obliged to lead a very secluded life in England because the scandal would be considerable. Even so, it was the more attractive prospect of the two. The final possibility was so awful she would have preferred not to contemplate it at all. 'Discarded' might all too easily mean exactly that: either turned out, penniless, into the Meknes streets to fend for herself, or to be killed by whatever means a Moorish king customarily used to rid himself of a fallen favourite.

In the end, she asked Farah what might happen to her if Moulay Ismail lost interest in her.

Farah shrugged. 'Who knows? The best advice I can give you is to keep his interest alive as long as you can, and certainly to intrigue him to such an extent that he retains an affection that will ensure your future comfort even when his desire for you has waned.'

'You don't think he might send me back to my father?'

'No.'

This was said so positively that Ferelith knew it would quite simply never happen. 'But you don't think he would...' she hesitated, reluctant to put it into words '...have me killed?'

'It has happened but it isn't usual. If you somehow managed to strike up a liaison with one of his subjects and Ismail found out, that would warrant the death sentence. It would be treason, you see. Nor would it be a good idea to anger him by arguing with him or by refusing to gratify his whims.' She looked at Ferelith with some pity. 'You've not chosen an easy path, you know.'

'I'm beginning to see that with rather greater clarity than when I thought up this scheme,' Ferelith admitted. 'Tell me, Farah, why should the Queen Mother have asked me whether I intended to turn renegade—and whether anyone had suggested it to me?'

Farah hesitated. 'I can't be sure, but I imagine it was an attempt to discover what the King has in mind for you. You see, he has the four wives the Koran permits but he may easily put one aside. He won't do so, however, unless the new wife is also a believer. His present wives were chosen by his mother. She'd have no hesitation in having him set one of them aside if she thought it advisable for him to take someone else in their place, but she would not welcome a wife who did not owe her situation to her mother-in-law. It goes without saying that no existing wife wants to be put aside—in their shoes, would you?'

Ferelith admitted she would not. She now had a clearer idea why the Queen Mother had sent for her. Had there not been a suspicion—albeit only in the older woman's own mind—that matrimony might be among her son's intentions, she would not have bothered with anything so unimportant as a new concubine. She deduced from the part of the conversation that she was not supposed

to have been able to understand that the Queen Mother
considered that threat could be discounted. Ferelith had
not the slightest desire to become Ismail's wife, but the
fact that it had been considered a serious possibility was
interesting and might perhaps prove to be useful, not as
something to be brought about but as something to be
hinted at in order to exert some pressure. It could be
achieved indirectly, by a simple indication that she was
considering changing her faith. At least she felt less impotent to control her life. The feeling might be an il-
lusion but it raised her spirits. She wouldn't be at all
sorry to learn that the party on its way to Tangier—to
say nothing of those who would return with the news
that their mission had been accomplished—had been delayed. She had no hope of keeping Moulay Ismail from
her bed indefinitely, but the longer it was before she had
to face him the better she would be pleased.

Unfortunately, Ferelith had assumed, despite
considerable evidence to the contrary, that Moulay
Ismail's mind worked along the same straightforward
lines as her own. She was therefore entirely unprepared
for the message which arrived in the course of the third
day to say that she was to be brought to his bedchamber
that evening wearing the sea-green gown he had previously admired.

When the eunuch, Ali, brought the message, she stared
at him aghast.

'But it can't be. Not yet. He promised me I should
not have to keep my part of the bargain until Papa had
reached Tangier. After only three days, we can't possibly know.'

'Three days is the length of time it takes a messenger
to get there,' Ali replied. 'His Majesty naturally assumes
that if three days have elapsed without word to the contrary then they must have arrived.'

'But surely he will wait until he knows for sure?'

'Why? He's shown considerable forbearance already.'

Ferelith could see the logic behind the argument but
she regarded it as perfidious. Ismail must have known
how she would have interpreted his words. However,

since there was absolutely nothing she could do about it and since a few days more or less could make no difference at all to the final outcome, she swallowed her indignation and her sense of having been in some way cheated, and forced a smile.

'I take your point. Will you see that he is told it will be my pleasure?'

Ali smiled and bowed, but Ferelith knew he was not deceived.

Nor was Moulay Ismail.

'I understand I have sent for you a little sooner than you would have liked,' he said through his interpreter, after surveying her in silence for several minutes.

'Sooner than I had expected,' Ferelith corrected him by a small emphasis on the last word.

'A subtle but important distinction. It seems to have lost something in the translation.'

'A risk that must always be considered when translation is necessary,' she reminded him.

'Very true, and a good reason for eliminating the possibility of misunderstanding.' He turned to his interpreter. 'Go,' he said.

The man bowed and went, leaving Ferelith wondering how they should manage without him unless she revealed that she understood a certain amount of Arabic. She was on dangerous ground. If he knew—or suspected—that she understood, he would know that she was more aware of what was said in her presence than they had assumed and that, coupled with her secrecy on the subject, would not be likely to dispose him well towards her. If, on the other hand, he was unaware of her admittedly limited ability in that field, she would have to be very careful indeed not be betray it. She remembered the guide who had sold them to the Berbers and the certainty she had felt from time to time that he understood perfectly. Furthermore, it wouldn't be easy to prevent so shrewd a man as Moulay Ismail from discovering her secret and he was unlikely to be charitable about it when he did. It seemed that the path ahead was likely to be more than a little fraught.

He gestured to the couch beside him and, correctly interpreting this as an invitation to sit down, she did so, accepting gracefully a date stuffed with marchpane which he almost immediately popped in her mouth. There were pots of coffee and chocolate on the low table before them and Ferelith, in response to a gestured enquiry from her host, indicated that she would prefer the latter. He poured it into a drinking-bowl of delicate Chinese porcelain and handed it to her, a gesture which Ferelith recognised as being of the utmost condescension. She thanked him—in English—and sipped it gratefully.

He tapped her on the arm to attract her attention. *'Shokran,'* he said. *'Merci—shokran.'*

Ferelith smiled, nodded and repeated the word. Now she would have the added difficulty of remembering which words she was supposed to know and which she wasn't. Still, it was reasonable for him to expect her to learn some of the language which now surrounded her, and the little courtesies of life would do no harm. He fed her another date and then dipped his fingers in the bowl of rose-scented water and wiped them fastidiously. His eye went to the gauze modesty-scarf and he flicked it carelessly with his fingers, his eyes looking pointedly at the pearl brooch.

Ferelith put down her chocolate and unfastened the jewel and then, in response to his gaze, she started to remove the scarf.

He caught her hand and stayed it. *'Lentement,'* he said.

Ferelith's eyes flew to his face. 'You speak French?' she said.

He smiled, but his eyes were still on the scarf. 'A little.'

Ferelith guessed this was an understatement and before long realised that his knowledge of that language, while not perfect, was more than adequate.

She did as she was bid and removed the scarf as slowly as she could.

Ismail's arm replaced it round her shoulders, the fingers playing with the round white globes of her breasts and the line of her neck and throat. His other hand removed the baroque pearl from her ear so that his teeth could nibble the lobe before his lips kissed and caressed her neck, her throat, and sought the darker tips of her breasts, still partly concealed by the gown's stiff bodice. His fingers forced them still upwards till they rested on the bodice's frame and then he kissed them, gently and persuasively at first. Then, suddenly and unexpectedly, his mouth closed round the nipple and he bit, causing her to cry out in a pain that overcame the control she had hitherto been able to exert to disguise her distaste at what he was doing. It was a distaste more for the man than the deed but none the less deep for that.

Her cry seemed to please him. 'So,' he said, 'you're not so incapable of being roused, after all.' As he spoke, the arm round her shoulder tightened its grip, holding her where she was. He thrust its fellow beneath her voluminous skirts, not with seductive intent but to determine the degree and nature of the barriers European women employed against their violation.

Ferelith stiffened against his touch, thereby unwittingly conveying a challenge. He stroked the mound of Venus and smiled as she squirmed. 'The stories are true, then,' he said, withdrawing his hand. 'You women make it easy for your men. Stand up.'

Ferelith did so.

'Turn around.'

She obeyed.

'Now—undress for my pleasure. Slowly.'

Ferelith hesitated. 'I cannot, Your Majesty,' she said.

His face darkened with anger and for a moment she thought he would strike her. 'Do you refuse to do as you are bid?' he demanded.

I wish I dared, she thought. Aloud, she said, 'No, sir. I cannot. The lacing is at the back and cannot be undone by the wearer. It needs a maid.'

The scowl lifted and he got to his feet. 'Then you shall have one. You will have the distinction of being the only woman in the world to reduce Moulay Ismail to servant status.'

'Then I am much honoured,' she murmured as she felt his fingers first unlace her bodice and then, as it became progressively less taut, slide beneath it to the softer body under the smock. She could not deny that the action aroused sensations that were not entirely unpleasant and, had the man been someone else, how differently she would have felt, how gladly she would have succumbed to a sensuous touch.

He watched with evident pleasure as she stepped out of the gown, a pleasure enhanced by the fact that he now knew there was nothing save her smock between them. The neck, no longer supported by the bodice, revealed her breasts in their entirety and the fabric, full as it was, clung to her shape so that every move both revealed and concealed.

Ferelith guessed that he derived some perverse pleasure in thus prolonging her apprehension. She could therefore scarcely believe her good fortune when his attention was halted by a loud rap on the door.

It was clearly both unexpected and unwelcome. The sheer fury on Ismail's face told her that. He had dismissed his attendants and it looked at first as if he would ignore the interruption. Any such intention was thwarted by a further loud tattoo.

The King glowered but his attention was now completely diverted. The tone of his shouted command to enter bore witness to his fury.

Ferelith pulled her smock around her as the eunuch entered. He gave no sign of having noticed her at all but bowed deeply to his sovereign.

Ferelith's Arabic was just able to follow the ornately formal phrases with which he proferred his apologies for interrupting his master. She had no doubt of the sincerity of his protestations and suspected it must have taken considerable courage to knock on the door. He brought word of a messenger returned from the north, and the news this man carried was of such importance that the King's advisers felt His Majesty should be advised of it immediately.

Ismail directed a suspicious glance at Ferelith and was satisfied to see on her face the expression of total boredom characteristic of those who were audience to an incomprehensible conversation.

'Is it Tangier?' he asked. Ferelith found it difficult to maintain her blank façade.

'No, Majesty. I believe not. It seems more serious than that. There is much activity between the Berber villages, but I have no details.'

'I will speak with the messenger. Send for Benani. We shall need his good offices.'

'With respect, Majesty, Benani should be at Tangier by now.'

Ismail said something which Ferelith did not understand at all but which she guessed to be a pungent oath and swept out of the room, leaving her unsure what she was supposed to do now. Eventually she dressed herself as well as she could unaided and a short while after that the eunuch who had brought her there returned and escorted her back to her quarters, where the other women commiserated with her on her misfortune. Ferelith's view of it was somewhat different.

Hassan Benani watched his charge unobtrusively but with considerable concern. Major Melverley's health had seemed distinctly improved when they had set out compared with the previous day, but that was not saying very much. He had still been an obviously sick man. Hassan had looked up at the latticed grille in the women's quarters and had seen the slight movement behind it that told of spectators. He guessed one of them would be Ferelith and hoped that from that distance, and through the impediment of the heavy carving, she would be able to make out no more than that her father was more upright in his posture than when she had last seen him. That would give her the encouragement of believing that her sacrifice was not in vain and might even, by the grace of Allah, give her the courage to bear the indignities the King was likely to exact, indignities of which Hassan suspected she had no idea. He saw his task as a simple one: to get the major to Tangier alive and with his health in a state from which he might at least have a chance to recover. This was what Moulay Ismail expected of him but his sovereign's wishes were not paramount in Hassan's thoughts just now. It was what he owed Ferelith. Once in a king's harem—any king's—she would not leave it alive and, while the life it offered would be luxurious to a barely conceivable degree, he didn't think it would appeal to the young English widow. Ferelith displayed a far greater independence of spirit than any other woman he had ever met and certainly had been accustomed to a far greater independence of action. Whether this was necessarily a good thing, he doubted. It had, after all, resulted in her present plight, which would have been unthinkable for any good Berber girl save, perhaps, in the realms of myth and legend.

In short, it behoved him to ensure that her magnificent gesture should not be wasted, but he was becoming increasingly convinced that it would be. The strain of the journey was quite simply too much for Major Melverley and by the end of the first day he had lost all the advantage gained by a night's good sleep, a doctor's care and some nourishing food. The effects of the medicine he had received wore off during the first night and the flux returned with renewed vigour. In the morning, he was so weak that mere assistance to mount his horse was insufficient. He had to be lifted into the saddle and it was very soon evident that there would be no question of making the sort of speed Moulay Ismail had had in mind. Hassan dared not put the horses out of a walk and even that pace was frequently interrupted by the major's need to dismount in order to make himself comfortable again. The fever returned during the day and the escort party took it in turns to hold him on his horse during his intermittent bouts of violent shivering.

When they stopped for the second night, Hassan did what he could to make the major comfortable, placing him as close to the blazing fire as he dared and giving up his own blanket and those of some of his men to supplement that warmth during the increasingly prolonged shivering fits. When the shivering changed to sweating, he made sure there was someone to wipe his face and adjust his covers. Hassan himself crouched by the fire, dozing for brief periods in between which he took note of the deteriorating condition of his charge.

In the course of the night, Major Melverley beckoned him over. Hassan gently placed the hand back beneath the blanket. 'What is it, Major?' he asked.

'How far to Tangier?' he asked weakly.

Hassan shrugged. 'I don't know. It will depend upon the time we make. At our present rate, I'd guess another two days.'

'I thought as much. I'll never arrive.'

'You're a sick man but not so sick that you need give up yet. Two days—maybe even a little less if we're lucky. Then you'll have all the care you need. Keep your determination a little bit longer.'

Major Melverley shook his head feebly. 'It will take more than determination now, and we both know it.' He managed another weak smile. 'A miracle might do it and, to tell the truth, I don't much mind whether it comes from your Allah or my God, I'll willingly give thanks to either.'

'Come, Major, you'll be telling me next you're prepared to turn renegade,' Hassan jested, knowing that few things were less likely.

'I'll not go as far as that, but I'll gladly give credit for a miracle to any who could have brought it about. But I've no time to waste in idle banter.' He was forced to stop then, while the ague racked his frame.

Hassan waited patiently until the tremors eased. 'There was something you wanted to say?'

'My daughter. Benani, has she offered herself in my place?'

Hassan picked his words with care. 'It looks as if she may have done,' he said.

'If only I'd known! I'd never have allowed it. Poor girl, what must she be suffering!'

'You were not to know and you may rest assured that she will be fed, clothed and housed in the height of luxury,' Hassan told him in an attempt at reassurance.

'If I die, it will have been in vain,' the major persisted. 'Benani—if I die before we reach Tangier, will you free my daughter?'

'Major, I had already determined to try everything in my power.'

'Get her back to Tangier, but, if that isn't possible, make what arrangements you can for her welfare. I'm sure a merchant-ship may be found which would carry her back to England.'

'Rest assured, Major, I shall do all I can to free your daughter, and when that has been achieved I shall make whatever arrangements she desires for her future well-being.'

The major nodded and closed his eyes. Hassan returned to his place by the fire, leaving the Englishman to get what sleep he could in the expectation that this might prove to be his last slumber during which, by the grace of Allah, perhaps he would slip quietly away.

But Major Melverley's hold on life was more tenacious than his Berber escort had anticipated and when morning broke he was still alive. He was no better than he had been the day before, but neither was he noticeably worse. Hassan told him they would stay where they were for that day, at least. The major became quite agitated at the suggestion. 'No, no, let us continue,' he urged. 'If I can reach Tangier, I must do so.'

'You stand a better chance if you have a day's complete rest,' Hassan told him.

'Another day with Ferelith in the hands of that monster?' the major replied. 'No. The sooner I get back and alert the garrison, the better.'

'The regiment at Tangier would have no hope of marching on Meknes to free Mrs Durliston,' Hassan said gently. 'They'd be cut to pieces before they even spied the city walls. Colonel Kirke knows that and won't even make the attempt. Even if he were willing to, one day here or there will make no difference.'

'All the same, I want to be on the move. I insist we keep travelling.'

Hassan decided that the degree of agitation exhibited by his ward was such that it would render a day of rest futile, so he reluctantly agreed that the journey should continue.

Major Melverley made a titanic effort to demonstrate that he was still more than capable of achieving his destination and Hassan's heart sank, knowing the power to do even the little of which he was capable was due to the sudden desperate surge of energy that death sometimes brought to the dying before it took them.

The major kept going until midday and then was seen quite suddenly to flag in the saddle. His escort hurriedly lifted him down, but by the time they laid him on the ground he was dead. They dug a grave in the light soil at the side of the road, far enough back to be out of the way of passing traffic. Then they wrapped him in his blanket and buried him, marking the place with a border of stones and small stone cairn so that passers-by would know this was a hallowed spot.

Then Hassan gathered the small group of men around him. 'Now Moulay Ismail must be told it was not possible to keep his promise,' he said.

One man snorted. 'Rather you than me,' he commented.

Hassan smiled grimly. 'Not one of the advantages of leadership, I agree,' he said. He turned to one of them. 'You, Omar, are to ride to my father immediately and as fast as you can. Tell him what has happened. He'll know what to do. The rest of you must come with me. When you are asked what happened, you will tell the truth. We have nothing to hide.'

'Wouldn't it be better to say we were attacked by bandits and a stray bullet hit our friend?' one of them suggested.

'And all of us hang for not fighting hard enough as well as for not taking sufficient care of that poor soul? Is that what you'd prefer?'

Omar hastily disclaimed a preference to hang and, since no one else had any better suggestions to offer, they made their way back to Meknes without delay.

Hassan had been attached to Moulay Ismail's entourage long enough to know exactly how his master's mind worked. He knew, from the look in the King's eye, that he would not have waited for word of Melverley's safe arrival in Tangier before benefiting from his side of the bargain. He would allow a reasonable interval to elapse before convincing himself that by now they must have arrived and that would be his justification. It was just possible that Ismail might err on the side of generosity and allow four days, but three was much more likely—and not only was it already the third day, but that day was more than half over. Hassan and his companions could make better time returning than they had on the outward journey simply because they would not be held back by a sick man, but even if they pushed their horses to the limit and rode through most of the night they could not reach Meknes before nightfall next day and to achieve even that goal would be a major undertaking; the following morning was a more realistic one if their horses were not to drop under them.

Hassan's main source of worry was, incongruously, Ismail's sense of honour. It was that which would ensure Ferelith's safety for at least three days, and when the King received word that a royal promise had not been kept through death's intervention his anger would know no bounds. If, by some happy chance, he had not yet taken Ferelith fully into his harem when the news arrived, he would have the option of releasing her and that would mean that someone—and Hassan hoped it could be he—would return her to Tangier. Ismail would also consider the alternative option of declaring her to be an orphan left in his care. In that event she would not return to Tangier but she would be safe from the King's advances and he would probably seek to find her a husband. Ferelith might not be as grateful for that kindness as a Moorish girl would be in similar circumstances but she was sufficiently intelligent to realise that it was the best that could be expected.

If, on the other hand, Ismail had already sought his reward, there was almost no way he could emerge with honour from the situation. He could—and almost certainly would—attempt to do so by executing the man through whose incompetence the promise had not been kept. It was precisely to pre-empt that solution that Hassan had sent messengers to his father. There would still remain the problem of Ferelith's presence, a continuing reminder of his dishonour. Only if Ferelith ceased to be there could he begin to pretend that nothing had happened and few things were easier than for a female to sicken, waste away and die in a very short space of time. It happened in harems all over the world when some unfortunate female had displeased her master. There was another solution but Hassan dismissed it from his mind: Ferelith was an infidel and Ismail was Allah's representative on earth.

Hassan had no idea what he was going to do when he reached Meknes. His duty was clear: he must give the news to the King. After that it would be a matter of anticipating and countering every move Ismail made—if he could.

They made excellent time and Hassan had every expectation of arriving at the palace only three or four hours after dark but he had already set other plans in motion and these now began to have their own effect. The short, dramatic dusk had barely given way to night when a large, well-armed troop of horsemen emerged from the shadows of the rocks ahead and barred the way.

The older Benani shook his head. 'Such haste,' he said. 'Is that any way to treat a good horse?'

'Let me go on, Father,' Hassan requested. 'I've important business with the King.'

'Not so important that it can't wait a few hours. Oh, I know what's in your mind but your own safety is at least as important to me. The outcome of recent events is in the hands of Allah. You have done what you can to influence them but now we must talk while the horses have a rest.'

Hassan hovered on the brink of disobedience, but to what end? He knew what he wanted to achieve and he longed to engage in the action that would achieve it, but action without a prior plan was futile. His father was right. He shrugged.

'Lead on,' he said.

The morning was well advanced before Hassan Benani and the small party of men with whom he had left Meknes a few days before galloped back into the main courtyard of the palace. He threw his reins to one of his companions and strode through the main doors in the direction of the *majelus*, where Moulay Ismail might be expected to be at this time.

The King looked up at the bustle of his entry and his eyes narrowed.

'You made good time, Benani,' he said, suspiciously.

Hassan bowed deeply. 'We returned with all due haste, Majesty. I bring unwelcome news.'

Ismail waved away the advisers who stood near him and beckoned Hassan closer. 'Unwelcome news?' he echoed.

'Sir, the Englishman died before we reached Tangier.'

An ominous and unbroken silence fell upon the room. Glances were exchanged and, that done, all eyes focused on the King. His reaction was not hard to anticipate but it was as well to be sure.

'His health had improved before he left here.'

'It had, sir, most noticeably. Unfortunately it deteriorated rapidly under the pressure of the journey. The first day was accomplished with reasonable speed but he was so much worse by the evening of the second day that, in truth, I didn't expect him to last the night. He did, however, and became so agitated at my suggestion that we should rest the whole day that I deemed it better to accede to his insistence that we should continue. He died when the sun was reaching its zenith and is buried with all due decency beside the road. The grave is marked.'

The King's face grew thunderous and Hassan awaited the expected outburst. Instead, he beckoned a servant forward and whispered in his ear. Then he called for his scribe and dictated to him a letter addressed to Colonel Piercey Kirke, Governor of Tangier, informing him of

Moulay Ismail's deep regret that his servant, Major Hugh Melverley, had died of an ague as he was being returned to Tangier. The governor would be comforted to know that the major had been decently buried and would be gratified to learn that the person to whom the major had been entrusted would pay the penalty for his carelessness. When the scribe had gone to copy up the letter in a fair script, Ismail turned back to Hassan.

'In a few moments you will be taken from here,' he said menacingly. 'Before that, however, you will explain to Mrs Durliston exactly what came to pass. It is important that she knows the circumstances of her father's death. We have no wish that she should have the slightest suspicion we might have connived at it.'

Hassan bowed. 'I shall be happy to absolve Your Majesty of any hint of responsibility.' He hesitated. What he needed to say next had to be said before he was taken off to the palace dungeons because, once there, he had no guarantee that any message would reach the King. It must also be worded in such a way as to be quite unambiguous and yet not as an overt threat. 'I understand, Majesty, that my father and his Rifi tribesmen are on their way to Meknes. My father is an old man and concerned at my continued absence in your service, honoured though he is that I was chosen. He seeks to beg Your Majesty to release me from it, so that I may begin to take my rightful place as his successor. We both implore you to consider earnestly the wishes of an old man.'

Hassan knew that Moulay Ismail's army of efficient spies would already have brought him word of the unusually large contingent of Rifi Berbers converging on the capital. The King's army was more than capable of wiping them out with cannon-fire from the ramparts but both he and the King knew equally well that, if he did so, all the Berber tribes in al-Maghrib would unite against any king who was so foolish. The tribes might fight among themselves, sometimes with unbounded ferocity, but if they felt themselves threatened they would unite against any later comers to this land, no matter how powerful they might be. The Berbers had been here first. It was their land and they were proud of that fact. Others ruled only with their co-operation—and Moulay Ismail was already fighting the infidel. How could he fight a war on two fronts? Everyone in the room knew all these facts as well as the two protagonists themselves. Hassan's skill had been in offering his monarch a way out of a possible impasse with honour. If Hassan died, the Berbers would, at the very least, cease fighting on the King's behalf. More probably they would also harry his troops from their mountain fastnesses, and the King would be twice a loser. But if he decided he had no further use for this young incompetent who had caused him to appear to have acted with dishonour, his magnanimity could restore him to his father, thus removing the son from his presence while ensuring the continued—and quite possibly strengthened—support of the Berbers for their King.

He ordered the scribe to be sent for and when the man appeared he was instructed to read over again the contents of the King's letter to Tangier. That done, Ismail flicked his hand in dismissal and turned to Hassan.

'It will receive consideration,' he said.

By this time Ferelith had arrived. Hassan turned as she entered and was moved to pity. It was impossible to tell whether Ismail had been over-hasty in exacting his side of the bargain or whether Ferelith had been worn down by apprehension at what lay in store for her. She still moved with her head high but he sensed that it was an act, that her usual proud self-assurance was lacking. Her face was pale and drawn as if sleep had been a stranger to her for many nights.

When Ferelith had learned that the King had summoned her, she had assumed it was to resume his interrupted enjoyment and it was only when she realised they were not in the private part of the vast palace that she began to wonder what it might betoken.

The last person she expected to see was Hassan Benani and she was not at all sure she particularly wanted to see him. She knew she looked at best tired and anxious.

Farah had commented that she would not hold Ismail's interest if she looked like that and it followed that Hassan, too, might lose such interest as he had had—though that, she supposed, might not necessarily be a bad thing.

Hassan, she noticed with an aching heart, either observed nothing or was unmoved. She transferred her gaze to the King and curtsyed.

'You sent for me.' It was a bald statement of fact, her tone as flat as her spirit.

'You will recall that Benani here was to accompany your father to Tangier.'

Her brain sharpened then, assisted by having something to fasten on to. 'Yes, of course. Are you back already?'

Hassan inclined his head. 'Mrs Durliston, I bring bad news. Major Melverley didn't reach Tangier. He died on the way.'

'You were attacked? By whom?'

'No, madam, there was no attack. The illness from which he was suffering when he left here killed him.'

Ferelith remembered the departure she had watched through the grille. 'But he was much better the day you left!' she exclaimed.

'Yes, he was, but the strain of the journey was too much for him. Once the medicine had worn off, his condition worsened rapidly. I tried to persuade him to rest for at least a day, but he refused. He has been buried with decency and the grave is marked. His Majesty has been generous enough to inform Colonel Kirke of these facts.'

Ferelith's lacklustre eyes travelled from him to Ismail and back again. 'So it was all for nothing,' she whispered. 'It has all been in vain.'

Hassan longed to take her in his arms, to comfort her, to offer her a sounding-board for her grief, but he dared not show less than total indifference for both their sakes. Her words, too, were all too easy to misconstrue.

'The King could not have done more,' he said. 'He is as dismayed as you that his efforts on your father's behalf have come to nothing.'

Ferelith frowned, bemused. This was not quite what she had meant yet she couldn't place the flaw she knew was there. She shook her head as if that gesture would clarify everything and, when it failed, she turned to the King.

'With your permission, sir, may I retire?'

He waved her away testily. She was proving an embarrassment and he was beginning to regret the impulse that had led him to accept her offer. Something would have to be done about her but just at the moment he didn't much mind if he never saw her again. He watched her go and then turned his attention to the Berber. Difficult people, these Berbers, and none so difficult as the Rifi. Benani had always seemed different from the rest, had always put his King's interest first. Now he was reverting to type. Still, at least he had the intelligence to do it with tact and, as the future leader of his tribe, it would be useful to have him under some sort of obligation.

'Take him away,' Ismail said. 'Your fate is something I'll not want to decide in a hurry.' It would do the arrogant youngster no harm to moulder for a few days. His ultimate gratitude would be all the greater.

CHAPTER ELEVEN

FERELITH'S grief over her father's death was made worse to start with by the dread that Moulay Ismail would send for her. She reasoned that there would now be no restraints at all upon his demands for the very simple reason that there was now no one to take up the cudgels on her behalf as she was sure her father would have done had he lived. She felt herself overwhelmed by her tribulations and, had Farah not insisted on staying with her, would have found some means of putting an end to an existence to which there seemed no further point.

Farah sensed this and was determined to give her charge no opportunity to take her own life. She was only partly moved by compassion for Ferelith's position. It was equally important in her eyes that the King should not be further embarrassed by the suicide of the daughter of a man who had died while under the King's protection.

As the days passed and she was not summoned, Ferelith's spirits rose infinitesimally. Perhaps, she thought naïvely, Ismail was allowing her a period of mourning; it was not the sort of consideration she would have expected from him but it was none the less welcome for that, and when Farah brought her the gossip that Hassan Benani was expected to be released despite his negligence, she managed a smile.

'I'm glad, for it was no fault of his that Papa died. I wish him well.' She sighed. It was probably all for the best that she would never see Hassan again, especially since the pain of his indifference would be well-nigh unbearable. She would have to content herself with clinging to the memory of the all too brief happiness they had shared.

Farah sat beside her and put her arm round Ferelith's shoulders.

'You need a friend in whom you can confide,' she said, thinking that if some of the other rumours she had heard were true Ferelith's need might be considerable. 'Oh, not me—I'm part of the old order here and, while you can safely put your trust in me, you should only do so up to a point: I will always put my duty to the King first.'

'As should all his subjects, no doubt,' Ferelith commented.

'Quite, but some—yourself, for instance—have less strong bonds of allegiance than others.'

'Like Latifa, you mean?' Ferelith asked. 'You remember—the Sudanese girl who was my maid when I came here. She had been a captive in Tangier.' She nearly added the information that Latifa had helped her escape that city but the germ of an idea was forming in her mind and she did not. Perhaps word of Latifa's part in Ferelith's arrival here had not slipped out or had at least not reached the women's quarters. It probably had, since gossip sped through these corridors even faster than it raced through Tangier, but there was no point in being too specific, just in case it hadn't.

'Yes, like her.' Farah hesitated. 'I don't know what became of her but, if she's still in Meknes and is willing to serve you, would you like me to see if she can be fetched?'

Ferelith looked doubtful. 'Would she come as a servant or as a slave?' she asked. 'It would be a cruel turn to bring her here and free her, only to take her into another form of captivity.'

Farah thought privately that a Sudanese orphan might welcome such luxurious captivity as the palace offered but she wisely kept this consideration to herself. 'There are free servants here,' she said. 'I can but ask.'

'Then would you do so? Only she must come of her own volition. I don't want any pressure exerted to make her come.'

Ferelith gave little thought to the matter of the source from which Farah would seek permission. Had she pondered the matter, she would probably have assumed it

would be Ali, the eunuch who managed the business affairs of the harem and, as a consequence, was rumoured
to be one of the wealthiest men at court. Instead, Farah
sought private audience with Moulay Ismail and was
granted it two days later.

The former concubine rarely sought such an audience
and when she did it was always to good purpose, so her
request was never refused. She was, in Moulay Ismail's
opinion, the ideal concubine: she had been inventive and
co-operative while she enjoyed his favour and since his
interest had waned, many years ago, she had never
slipped into bitterness or jealousy. He therefore held her
in some affection, and that was a state of affairs she
took very good care not to jeopardise. She wasted no
time on preliminaries—the King became easily bored.

'I wish to speak of the Englishwoman, Majesty,' she
began and noted that the sudden brief frown advised her
to be careful. 'There are rumours about your plans for
her. So far as I know, no hint of them has reached her
ears and I'm not here to enquire into their truth. She
has been very much pulled down by her father's death
and, if there is any basis for the rumours at all, you will
not wish her to appear in her present state.'

That was very true. The Englishwoman had lost her
bloom very quickly and, now that Farah mentioned it,
it probably was due to worry over her father. It sounded
as if his death had brought her even lower. 'Go on,' he
said.

'Sir, when she arrived here she was accompanied by
a Sudanese girl, Latifa. She misses her and I know would
welcome her back in her service, but as a free woman.
I think it would enable her to get over her loss much
more quickly if it can be arranged but the decision, of
course, must be yours.'

'I seem to recall having the girl placed with a Sudanese
commanding officer's family until she could be returned
to the Sudan, though that may be years away. I suppose
she could be traced. Someone must know where she
went.'

'May I make a further suggestion, Majesty?' Farah ventured.

'You may, but it must be your last—you grow importunate.'

'Rumour—a stronger rumour—also has it that you will release the Berber, Benani, as a sign of your munificence. He knows the girl and she has every reason to trust him. If he is sent to seek her out, the gesture will be such as to increase his sense of obligation to Your Majesty because the honour will be apparent to all.'

The King considered the matter, watching Farah through narrowed eyes. He knew her well. There was no indication she was dissembling, no hint of guilt or anxiety, and he could conceive of no possible ulterior motive for either her request or her suggestion. He was not by nature a trusting man—no king who wished to remain on the throne could afford to be—but he could spot no trap here.

'I shall consider both ideas,' he told her, 'but at my leisure.'

'I can ask no more,' Farah replied. 'I thank Your Majesty for so graciously consenting to hear me.'

Hassan was not altogether surprised to be released but he had not expected it to be effected in front of the whole *divan* and to be accompanied by an errand which, while it could perfectly well have been carried out by any minion, nevertheless represented his restoration to favour. The purpose of his errand puzzled him. He was to offer Latifa service with Ferelith. No doubt Mrs Durliston would be glad to have her former companion restored to her, but Hassan remembered how she had looked when he last saw her and it seemed to him odd that a man who could reduce a woman to that in no more than—what? Forty-eight hours?—should now be seeking to please her with a serving-girl. Then he heard other rumours, and began to understand.

He found Latifa without much difficulty but persuading her was another matter.

'I'd be happy to serve Mrs Durliston,' she told him. 'She's a good mistress and would treat me well, but what value does being free have if one is working in the palace? What need has the King of a servant-girl who is free? How long should I remain so?'

'I can't answer those questions,' Hassan told her. 'All I know is that the matter of your freedom was given great emphasis, so I think you may depend upon it, and that means you will be able to come and go as you wish. Ismail's motives are a mystery to everyone, though I suspect he may have his own reasons for wanting to ensure Mrs Durliston's happiness. I imagine your freedom will remain until you find a husband—which you are far more likely to do in the palace than anywhere else.'

'And you, sir—what happens to you? Do you now return to the Rif?'

'No,' Hassan said thoughtfully. 'No, I don't think so. I've a feeling I may be needed here. Latifa, take this position the King offers. Whichever way you look at it, you'll be better off than you are now, and who knows? It may not be for long. There is a Rifi in the *souk* who mends slippers. You will be free to leave the palace. If ever you need help, let him know. He'll be able to find me.'

Latifa looked at him shrewdly. 'And not only if the help is for me, I think,' she commented.

Hassan smiled. 'I leave you to judge that. Will you serve?'

She stood up. 'The food will be good,' she said. 'That is lure enough.'

Ferelith was delighted to see her former slave again and greeted her with the warmth of one meeting an old friend after a long absence. Latifa made no comment on her mistress's changed appearance. She wondered how much the Berber, Benani, knew, and how much he perhaps guessed at. It seemed, however, that he was at least prepared to help her mistress and Latifa decided that frequent visits to the *souk* for this and that would do no harm. At the very least it would accustom the palace staff to seeing her come and go.

She soon found out that it was not quite as she had imagined it would be. She was certainly free to come and go—'Madam wants me to find so-and-so,' 'Madam has expressed a wish for this'—such phrases opened the door but she was never allowed to go alone. An Arab boy—rescued from a French privateer when he had been still too young to tell his rescuers anything except that his name was Zaid—was detailed to accompany her. He thought he was thirteen, though at first sight he seemed older because he was unusually tall for that age, being nearly as tall as Latifa herself. She wasn't quite sure whether he was sent with her for her protection or to carry back to the palace a report of where she went and what she did. She suspected that the latter was the more probable but pretended it was the former and when she took a pair of Ferelith's favourite *babouches* to the little Berber in the market to be repaired—even though they could perfectly well have been done within the palace— she drew his attention in the course of conversation to what she described as her 'little protector, who comes with me everywhere'.

The old Berber was politely uninterested. 'You're fortunate to have an employer who takes such care,' he said, giving Zaid no more than a cursory glance. By nightfall, Hassan knew that Latifa could never be contacted secretly.

Ferelith's spirits continued to improve once she had Latifa to look after her, and the ministrations both of the Sudanese and Farah brought the colour back to her cheeks if not yet the sparkle to her eyes.

Then a summons came from the King.

When the message was brought to her, Ferelith paled and caught at a pillar to support herself.

'No,' she whispered. 'Farah, can't you say I'm ill?'

'No, my dear, because I couldn't prove it and then we'd both be in trouble. You are to wear a caftan and *d'vit*—and a veil. I think therefore you may not be seeing His Majesty alone.'

Ferelith had already become accustomed to the greater comfort of Moorish costume and was quickly dressed in a particularly splendid caftan, a long-sleeved straight dress of emerald-green silk embroidered heavily with gold round the neck and hem with a broader panel of the same down the centre. Over this went the *d'vit*, equally long but with a wider sleeve and open down its entire length. This one matched the caftan exactly and was worn with gold-encrusted backless slippers, a matching scarf of silk gauze over her head and a veil, small and triangular, over the lower part of her face.

Thus attired, she followed her escort through the now-familiar passages to the public rooms of the palace, relieved that Farah was being proved right. She was safe enough in the presence of the King's advisers.

She tried not to be unnerved by the silence that fell as she entered the *majelus* and, since it was impossible to curtsy gracefully in the narrow skirt of a caftan, she bowed as Farah had taught her. The King looked at her with mixed feelings. There was displeasure because she was, in his estimation, the ultimate source of his present embarrassment. Mingled with that was the undeniable fact that there was something very stimulating about that creamy skin and extraordinary hair. If only she could be persuaded to be more responsive...

'We have given much consideration to the question of atoning for the fact that your father died in our care, after we had given word he would be safe. Had we known he was so ill, certain events would not have taken place. It has exercised our mind how best to make what amends we can.'

He paused and Ferelith looked at him hopefully, but puzzled. Did he mean he had made up his mind what he was going to do, or was he asking for suggestions?

'If Your Majesty wishes to send me back to Tangier, I shall not object,' she said.

Moulay Ismail frowned. Did European women never know when to hold their tongues? 'That won't be necessary,' he said icily. 'Our intentions are rather more generous than *that*. We have decided that the only fitting restitution we can make is by marrying you.' He finished his declaration with a triumphant inflexion that was quite lost on an appalled Ferelith.

'But you have a wife!' she protested. 'In fact, you've got four and that's all the Koran allows you,' she amended, wondering by what aberration he had overlooked this fortunate state of affairs.

Since the response he had expected was abject gratitude, he was both disconcerted and annoyed, and found himself explaining matters to her in a way that was really most inappropriate for a ruler.

'I also have the power to put a wife aside and take another,' he said, irritated at appearing on the defensive. 'That is a relatively simple matter. The more serious impediment is the question of your religion. You will, of course, be obliged to convert to Islam.'

Ferelith clutched at the straw he seemed to be offering, without paying heed to the possible consequences, though she retained the sense to pick her words with a degree of care.

'Then sadly, sir, your most generous scheme becomes impossible. I cannot turn renegade, even if I would.'

'Nonsense. Anyone can and many do—even men, and it's a great deal more unpleasant for them, I can tell you.'

'Sir, there are two reasons why it cannot be done. For one thing, it would deeply offend my father, were he still alive, and I do not believe a parent's death absolves the child from respecting their wishes. For another, there is the question of my late husband. He was a clergyman— a *mullah*,' she added, just in case there was any misapprehension. 'How may the widow of a clergyman possibly recant?'

In fact, there was absolutely nothing to stop such a widow doing precisely that, if she felt strongly enough about it, but Ferelith could tell by the consternation on the faces before her that they were quite unprepared for that particular argument. Doubtless they would look into it, but at least she would have bought herself some time.

'This is a matter which must be investigated,' Moulay Ismail said. He was obviously furious at the turn events had taken and his anger was not improved by the knowledge that there was nothing he could do until the learned men reported back to him. 'In the meantime,' he went on, 'you will receive instruction in the faith. Or do you object to that, too?'

'Not at all, Majesty,' Ferelith said with absolute sincerity. 'Knowledge increases understanding. I've already learned that Islam has much to teach me. I welcome the opportunity to learn more.'

It seemed as if this speech, which was very obviously sincere, had gone far towards mollifying the King and he dismissed her in a much more benevolent frame of mind than would have been possible a short while before.

Once out of the audience-chamber, Ferelith's impulse was to rush as fast as she could back to her quarters to talk to Latifa. She had had the glimmer of an idea when she had suggested the Sudanese should enter her service and she had been guilty of wasting time until now. Yet now, when time was of the essence if it ever had been, she was obliged to patter sedately along these interminable corridors at the quite unnecessarily dignified speed her escort deemed appropriate.

She burst into her own apartments to be brought up short by the presence of Farah as well as Latifa. Nothing untoward in that, of course, but she remembered what Farah had said about trusting her. Now was the time to pretend. She couldn't pretend to exult: that would conflict too sharply with what Farah knew to be her feelings about the King but, even knowing Ferelith's repugnance and fear, there was one pretence she would believe. Ferelith only hoped it wouldn't deceive Latifa, too.

She held her arms out sideways and circled gracefully on one spot. 'You are looking,' she said, adopting what she hoped was a grand manner, 'at the next wife of Moulay Ismail.'

'So it is true,' Farah said. 'He has told you? It's definite?'

'So it would seem. There remains the problem of religion, of course, but I shall be given instruction.' She deliberately left it to sound as if the outcome of the instruction was inevitable.

Farah thought of the other three wives and of the one who was about to be discarded—admittedly into a life of considerable luxury, but none the less discarded for that—and decided that the preparation of Ferelith's food had henceforth better be carried out exclusively by her and by Latifa. It was no bad thing the girl was always dashing off to the market for one thing or another.

She smiled. 'Well, my dear, if you're happy about it, what more can be said? Latifa and I will have to take very good care of you from now on. Latifa, look after your mistress. I've things to attend to.'

Once Farah had gone, Ferelith let her mask of satisfaction drop. 'Latifa, come here. We must speak.'

Latifa, who knew better than her mistress that walls had ears and harem walls more than most, shook her head. 'Madam, there is something I've been meaning to ask you and, frankly, your present good humour is as good a time as any. I have need of new *babouches* and I've seen the very ones in the *souk*. I didn't have enough money with me this morning. May I go back for them now?'

Ferelith stared at her. 'Don't be ridiculous. It can wait until the morning. We've more important things to talk about now.'

'No, madam, I'd really rather not wait. My old ones are almost falling apart.'

'Then use a pair of mine for the time being. Keep them, if it comes to that. I don't imagine I shall want for slippers in the future, do you?'

Latifa shook her head. 'No, madam, that's no good. I'm taller than you are and your slippers pinch my feet.'

Since *babouches* were so designed as to fit almost any foot, this argument made so little sense that Ferelith suddenly realised her maid was simply requesting an excuse to go out again and, since she had a high opinion of Latifa's intelligence, she guessed that it might have something to do with her recent announcement.

'Very well,' she said, 'but can you wait long enough for me to discuss something with you?'

Latifa caught her mistress's hands and pressed them. 'Madam, I really don't think it's necessary. I can see how thrilled you are. In any case, the King will probably decide your bridal clothes without reference to you—it's quite customary, you know. All the more *pressing* matters you may safely leave to me, I promise you. Now, madam, will you send for Zaid?'

Ferelith was baffled. She had no doubt at all that Latifa had some scheme in mind, though she had no idea what it could be. She was desperate to discuss with her maid some way of getting out of the palace. Once outside, she would just have to put her trust in God— or Allah, perhaps—and hope to escape altogether, a goal which would be more easily achieved with Latifa's help than without it since its success would depend in part on her acquiring the clothes of a peasant woman before she stepped on to the streets, and who but Latifa might be willing to get them for her? Still, it could probably wait an hour or two.

She sighed. 'Very well, but don't waste time—I really do want to talk to you.'

Latifa was soon making her way to the cobbler's tiny shop bordering the *souk*.

'I need some really good slippers urgently,' she said. 'Have you heard the good news? My mistress is to marry Moulay Ismail. We have to wait for instruction in the faith, of course, but then it goes ahead.'

The shoemaker seemed only marginally interested. 'What brought that about, then?' he asked, bringing several pairs of *babouches* out for her inspection.

'A matter of honour, I gather: her father died while in his care, leaving her with no male protector. There's nothing here that appeals to me. Can you make me some? Red, I think, and with far more gold thread than any of these.'

'I could have them for you tomorrow. Lucky woman, your mistress.'

'Isn't she? I think the thing that excites her most is the prospect of all those new clothes. She can't manage on what she's got, so I suppose it will be up to me to find something suitable.'

'I dare say you'll manage—you strike me as a resourceful young woman. Anything you want in the shoe line, I'll be happy to oblige. Tomorrow morning?'

'I suppose it'll have to be, but I don't want to come all this way and find you've let me down.'

'No fear of that, I'll have something for you, all right.'

Zaid grumbled all the way back to the palace. 'All you ever do is come here, to the *souk*, and then as often as not to that little Berber. What's so special about his shoes that you can't get made at the palace, that's what I'd like to know?'

'If you had an ounce of imagination, young man, you'd see that the quality of his workmanship is every bit as good as the palace shoemaker's, he's a great deal more obliging and doesn't foist you off with some apprentice, and he thinks up *much* more original decorative ideas. Now, that may not matter much to you, but it does to me—and to Mrs Durliston. She's a woman of considerable taste. Of course, if you don't want to come with me, I'm sure Ali can find someone else who'll be delighted.'

Since this was undoubtedly true, as Zaid knew from the comments of his fellows, he changed his tack slightly. 'It's all very well to say that, but I don't get any opportunity to do anything on my own account. I have to stick with you and it's never crossed your mind to ask me whether *I* want to get something,' he complained, aggrieved.

'No, it hasn't,' Latifa replied, surprised. 'Why didn't you say anything? I tell you what: tomorrow, while I'm collecting the slippers—which will take a good ten minutes, maybe longer—you can go off on your own business, just so long as you're back when I want to return.'

'But my orders are to stay with you—for your protection,' he said doubtfully.

'Well, I won't say anything if you don't,' Latifa suggested. 'Mind you, if you're not back, I shan't wait. I shall go home on my own and tell them you just disappeared.'

Zaid blanched at the thought of the possible consequences. 'Oh, I'll be back. No need to worry about that. Do you mean it? Really?'

Latifa smiled tolerantly. If only he knew how she had been racking her brains to think of a way of getting rid of him for a few minutes! 'Yes, really,' she assured him. 'But only ten minutes, mind.'

Back at the palace, Ferelith was even more bemused by Latifa's insistence on returning for the slippers next day, and her general humour was not improved by the fact that, during the maid's absence, Farah had taken her, heavily veiled, to receive her first instruction. This had not gone well. The *mullah* had assumed that he would simply instruct her in the requirements, both of belief and of practice, set out in the Koran. He had imagined that the only complications would be those caused by the language. He was totally unprepared for a questioning Protestant mind that demanded to know the whys and wherefores of every statement save those that were matters of simple history. Tempers had frayed on both sides and they had not parted on amicable terms, the *mullah* having interpreted Ferelith's frequent 'But I only want to *understand*,' as an oblique way of saying he was wrong. On her way back to her own apartments, Farah—who had been more than a little shocked at Ferelith's boldness in questioning what she was told—advised her that if it was intended as a delaying tactic it would only be partially successful.

'Moulay Ismail won't wait forever,' she warned. 'Be sensible, agree with everything and get the marriage concluded as quickly as possible.'

Since Farah continued to hover after Latifa's return, Ferelith pleaded a headache, drank the infusion the older woman prepared, and went to bed, knowing that Farah would soon go, leaving her in Latifa's competent hands.

As soon as she heard the door close behind Farah, Ferelith sought out Latifa.

'We *must* talk,' she insisted.

Latifa led her back to her bed. 'Lie down, madam, and keep your voice low. If you let it get excited, your headache will worsen.' She dropped her own voice before she continued. 'Now, madam, you're going to need some new clothes. Some clothes that are quite different from what you've been wearing, isn't that right?'

'Yes, indeed,' Ferelith said, though she was not quite sure whether they were both talking about the same thing.

'Very well. I think I may have found just the thing and as soon as I have you must try them on. I shall go out again tomorrow with Zaid, who has some business of his own to attend to—and I said he might do so while I was busy at the shoemaker's. When we get back I hope to have some good news for you.'

'Latifa, I'm not sure if I understand you—but I know I *must* make you understand me. There's something I have to make clear——'

Latifa put a cautionary hand on her mistress's mouth. 'Madam, I *do* understand you, but, you see, there's nothing you can do from *inside*. It must all come from *without*, if you follow me.'

At last Ferelith was sure that she did. She relaxed and smiled. 'We seem to be of a mind, Latifa,' she said. 'I don't quite see how you will be able to arrange anything beyond the change of clothes, but I leave it to you.'

'Very wise, madam, if I may say so. Besides, it's always far better if these things retain the element of surprise for as long as possible—and for as many people as possible. Now get some sleep. If you haven't already got a headache, you ought to have.'

Zaid was no longer the sullen boy who normally accompanied Latifa. She thought it was really almost pitiful, the pleasure with which he was looking forward to just ten minutes of real freedom. She fished in her purse and brought out a small coin.

'Have this,' she said. 'Madam won't miss it—but only ten minutes, mind.'

His face lit up, revealing the youth his height belied, and he had soon disappeared into the crowds, leaving Latifa with the shoemaker who had produced a pair of red *babouches* that she said were almost what she had been looking for.

'This, too,' the man suggested. He reached behind him and brought forth a small parcel which at first sight appeared to consist of a fabric of particularly rich ornamentation. 'They tell me your mistress is shorter than you.'

'A little. I'm not sure that this will appeal to her at all,' she went on.

'About the height of that boy who just went skipping off, I gather.'

'Almost exactly. A different build, though.'

'Naturally. Colouring, too.'

Latifa pursed her lips as if debating the merit of the fabric. 'That shouldn't pose a problem.'

'As long as you don't overdo the walnuts.'

'Perhaps I'll take it, but it'll come back if it's not what she had in mind.'

'Fair enough. I'll tell you what. If your lady wants to get rid of it, I'll save you the trouble of coming all the way back here. You'll have tomorrow or the next day. Early. If you come out of the Bab el Nouara and head straight across from the gate to the banks of the Oued Boufekrane, you'll find a friend of mine among the trees. He'll relieve you of it and that'll save you the long walk here.'

'That's very kind of you, but it will have to be after daybreak: there's a limit to how early people like me, to say nothing of young Zaid there, are allowed out.'

'Don't worry. My friend will wait.'

Hiding the parcel from Farah's sharp eyes was Latifa's immediate problem. She devised what she hoped would prove a plausible explanation but was happily not obliged to try it out, being able to stow it quickly under one of the low sofas before the older woman came through to greet her. Farah looked at the red slippers and sniffed.

'Why you make such a fuss about that cobbler is beyond me,' she remarked. 'They're good, yes, but you could have as good a pair made here if you'd only take the trouble to explain what you want.'

Latifa smiled sweetly. 'But you see, this little man doesn't have to be explained to. He *knows*. What's more, he doesn't patronise me, or palm me off with an apprentice, or keep me kicking my heels like they do here.'

'That will stop as soon as your mistress is married. You'll find you go to the top of the line then. Perhaps that's a thought that could spur you into persuading her to do something about it. She listens to you.' Farah sighed. 'She was arguing again today, over something which *she* said could be interpreted two ways and the *mullah* said couldn't, that was a fault of the translation. I couldn't follow the argument at all, and I couldn't see that it mattered, anyway.'

Latifa nodded. 'She is very argumentative. She used to contradict her father quite often. I was always amazed that he didn't beat her for it, but he didn't—he just argued back. I hope she doesn't argue with the King.'

Farah raised her eyes to the heavens. 'By the grace of Allah,' she said with feeling.

Latifa had to wait until Farah had left for her own bed in that part of the harem set aside for past concubines before she dared rouse Ferelith and bring out the parcel.

Wrapped up in the rather splendid piece of heavy silk was a white *serouel*, the baggy trousers whose legs reached only to mid-calf, a loose white shirt, a man's brown, lightweight *djellabah*, distinguished from a woman's by opening only as far as the chest and slit just halfway to the knees. There was also a rough woollen turban of the sort Zaid customarily wore and a pair of dull brown *babouches* that only a man would be seen in. Because all the garments were intended to fit loosely, they fitted Ferelith quite well and the length of the *serouel* and *djellabah* were exactly right, having been selected with Zaid in mind.

Ferelith looked at herself in the mirror and giggled. 'How shocked Papa would be to see me dressed like this,' she said.

'I don't think Moulay Ismail would be overjoyed,' Latifa said drily. 'Still, it will do to get you out of the palace.' She produced a woman's black robe and matching headkerchief, or *chador*. 'Once we've got them looking for a boy, we can transform you back into a woman. The only thing wrong now is your colour. We can disguise that with walnut juice but once it's done it will have to stay until it wears off, and that won't be overnight. We have two choices. Early tomorrow or early the next day. Which is it to be?'

'The sooner, the better,' Ferelith said without hesitation.

'That's what I thought you'd say. Now—listen carefully.'

CHAPTER TWELVE

By the time the dawn came up, only someone with a deeply suspicious mind or reason to look very closely indeed would have recognised the pale-skinned, auburn-haired Ferelith. A carefully painstaking application of walnut juice had stained all visible skin so that she looked as if she had acquired the sort of tan that only a hay-making English peasant would be prepared to be seen with. Latifa had no means of dyeing that give-away hair, so she tied it up and back as tightly as she could and crammed it into the peasant's rough turban before pulling the hood of the *djellabah* over it. She painted Ferelith's eyebrows and lashes with charcoal and decided, when she stood back to scrutinise the effect, that her eyes could easily be mistaken for the light ones of a Berber. It was unfortunate that Zaid had the brown eyes of an Arab, but that couldn't be helped. All in all, she prided herself that she had done a good job. If they were caught, it would lead to her death.

'Ready?' she asked her mistress.

Ferelith nodded.

'Then, for the love of your God and mine, be careful.'

It was still too early for anyone to be about—an important matter, since Zaid, young as he was, had no business within the harem. Ferelith took no chances, however, and darted from pillar to pillar, sending up a small prayer of grateful thanks that Moorish architecture abhorred a wide-open space. People would be stirring soon, and they must get outside the women's quarters before that happened. Ali would be one of the first to be about and neither of them suffered from the delusion that they would be able to hoodwink him. The two tired guards outside the main harem doors, coming to the end of their long stint, were an easier proposition.

237

The women reached the doors, Latifa clutching a parcel and Ferelith hiding behind a pillar to one side of the doors.

'Now?' Latifa said softly.

Ferelith nodded. 'Now,' she whispered.

Latifa turned the huge, but happily well-oiled key and pulled back the equally well-oiled bolts. The guards outside would hear it because that was what they were there for, but she hoped there would be no one else within earshot inside to come asking awkward questions.

She pulled one heavy door towards her and stuck her head round it, looking to right and left.

'Drat that boy. Isn't he here yet? I *told* him first thing.' She stepped out, taking care to convey the impression that, as an unaccompanied woman, she was ready to dash back in if the guards stepped out of line. 'Have you seen Zaid?'

They shook their heads. 'No sign of him. No sign of anyone, if it comes to that.'

'I told him yesterday I wanted to be out and back before madam wakes up. I didn't think he was listening, and it's so important. Look, would one of you go down to the end of the corridor and see if there's any sign of him?' She pointed in the direction she meant, since he could go either way, and stood beside the other guard, watching. When she glanced round, 'Zaid' was waiting a little way off, having apparently approached from the other end.

'And about time, too,' Latifa exclaimed. 'No, don't make excuses. I don't want to know—I haven't the time. Come on, we need to hurry.' She turned back to the guard. 'Isn't that just like a child—to sneak up on you from the wrong direction without a word? But thanks for your help. I expect you'll be gone by the time we get back.'

The man nodded. 'Our relief ought to be here soon,' he said.

Latifa took Ferelith none too gently by the arm and hurried her away, scolding all the time as they hastened through the palace courtyards towards one of the smaller

entrances. There were plenty of people about now and
the biggest risk they ran was of actually bumping into
the real Zaid or, more probably, someone who had only
just seen him somewhere else. Their luck held, however,
and they were finally out of the palace and then out of
the Bab en Nouara and within sight of the trees that
bordered the *oued*.

'We'll take a short cut along here,' Latifa announced
for the benefit of anyone who might be watching them,
hoping that it crossed no one's mind to wonder where
a short cut that was intersected by a river was supposed
to lead.

They were very quickly by the water-course and,
glancing back, Ferelith could see that they must be virtually invisible among the gnarled trunks and low
branches of the olive trees. Now Latifa hesitated, taken
aback. She had expected people to emerge from behind
trees and rocks, yet they seemed to be alone. She could
see no one.

'What's the matter?' Ferelith asked. 'What's gone
wrong?'

'I don't know. Nothing, I hope, but I expected to be
met. Now I've no idea whether we should go upstream
or down.'

'Which way is north?' Ferelith asked practically.
'Tangier is north so we may as well head in that
direction.'

Latifa shook her head. 'The river runs along the city
walls. We'd be seen and once they find we're missing—
which won't be long—word will soon get back. Besides,
that's the way they'll expect us to go. No, we'll head
south. Come on.'

They half walked, half ran and it was not until they
were completely out of sight of the fortifications, thanks
to a convenient bend in the river, that they realised they
were no longer alone. Two men, Berbers, stepped out
of the shadows cast by a huge boulder and stood before
them.

'Come,' one of them said, indicating with his head
the direction in which they should follow.

He led the way at an uncomfortably fast pace until they reached a grove where the olives were older and thicker and had been left untended until they now provided even more cover than hitherto. So effective was this cover, in fact, that neither woman realised there were some half-dozen horses and men waiting within it, mounted already so that they could take instant flight if they were discovered by the wrong people.

As soon as the foot-party's identity was clear, one of the men swung himself down from his horse and came towards them. He cast Latifa a cursory glance and caught Ferelith's hands. Her heart leaped when she saw it was Hassan Benani, the man she had thought never to see again. She remembered the recent coldness in his manner. If he was helping her to escape, she was grateful, but he must be doing it because her father had died in his care. She longed for there to be another reason but dared not allow herself to hope.

She withdrew her hands. 'I thought you'd been banished to the mountains,' she said.

'So does the King. Are you all right?'

There was no warmth in his voice, none in his eyes. Ferelith felt her heart bleeding to death.

'Yes, thank you,' she said politely. 'I think Latifa is some kind of genius.'

'She certainly possesses a degree of ingenuity that could be very uncomfortable. But come, we have more urgent business than to discuss your maid's character. We must needs be gone. I have horses for you.' He took her hand again, led her to her horse and threw her unceremoniously into the saddle before mounting his own.

The little party crossed the river and headed east, away from Meknes, towards the multiplicity of rivers and streams that ran out of the Atlas Mountains to the south and across the great plain in which the capital sat. Their goal was to reach the great city of Fez before the gates shut for the night. Long before they came within sight of its walls, they split into twos and threes and entered the old capital through different gates. Once within its narrow, twisting streets, they could disappear until morning with less likelihood of discovery than would have been the case had they camped in the relatively open countryside beyond.

Both Ferelith and Latifa went with Hassan. He led them to the small house of a Berber weaver who had set up in business in the city and was happy to extend hospitality to the son of his tribal chief and his companions. If it struck him as at all odd that Benani should bring with him a Sudanese woman and an Arab boy, he was too polite to refer to it, but he knew a man with a small stable tucked away down a neighbouring alley, who fortunately owed him a favour. He apologised profusely for the fact that he had no separate women's quarters in so small a house, but perhaps it would be satisfactory simply to divide the principal room—which was not itself very large—by means of some rugs?

Hassan indicated that that would do very well. It was an ideal solution because, while their host would undoubtedly expect the Arab boy to share Benani's half of the room, he would have no idea that he was actually spending the night in Latifa's. Ferelith was particularly glad: it avoided the embarrassment she would feel at being alone with Hassan once more in case he thought she would expect a repetition of their previous night together. She need not have worried. Quite apart from the arrangements he had made, he gave no sign, by look or word, that such an expectation had so much as crossed his mind. Ferelith felt more dispirited than ever.

Hassan made sure both women were awake before their host discovered the unconventional nature of their sleeping arrangements, and when the weaver brought in a simple breakfast of bread, sheep's cheese and dates, with ewes' milk to wash it down, he also brought some news.

'They say a messenger from Meknes arrived at first light. He seeks audience with the governor of Fez. Two women are missing from Ismail's harem, they say. A Sudanese and an Englishwoman. The rumour is that they head for Tangier on foot, the latter disguised as a boy. But the King leaves nothing to chance so we are warned.'

He glanced at Latifa. 'I have a son her height but his clothes are Rifi.'

Hassan shrugged. 'No matter: we, too, have slaves—and she is from southern Egypt, taken from a galley. Still, we're in a hurry and would prefer not to have to answer unnecessary questions. Thank you, my friend.'

'The rest of your party will be leaving by different gates?'

'The details of our departure are already arranged.'

The weaver nodded. 'Good.' He glanced at the breakfast. 'Might I suggest that speed becomes of the essence?'

'We shall be on our way as soon as the slave is dressed.'

A man and two boys, one of them very tall, left the weaver's little house less than ten minutes later and were soon mounted and threading their way through the maze of densely packed, winding streets to the Bab Guissa, the north-facing gate that led on to the cemetery of the former Merinid Kings. They headed north from here, making for the mountains where they would be less easily followed, and they were out of sight of the city before the first of their escorts rejoined them, to be followed within an hour by the rest. From now on they avoided settlements. Their destination had been guessed and it could not be much more than a day before someone realised they could no longer be on foot. The mountains, familiar ground to their Berber escort, represented their safest route, but time was not on their side and they pushed their horses as much as they dared. The rough terrain and the need to survey the surrounding landscape left no opportunity to converse. It left all the more for thought.

Ferelith found it unbearably painful to be so close to Hassan, yet to know he was unreachable. Their present situation precluded their being alone and she supposed that was just as well, for she wasn't sure she could bear with composure his clear indifference. Yet what more could she possibly expect? She had no doubt that he had at one time been as attracted to her as she to him but then she had given herself to him outside of marriage and, though he had been happy to take her, his indifference had dated from that occasion, a fact which spoke more clearly than anything else could have done. He had warned her about Ismail and she had chosen to ignore his warning, putting her father's welfare first. Her father had died in spite of her efforts and the warning had proved entirely justified. How could she even consider ever being close to him again? Even if he still wanted her, would he dare be associated openly with the woman his monarch had intended to marry? Ferelith suspected that to do so would be treason.

She must make plans accordingly. Once back in England, she would distance herself from all further acquaintance with those who had known her here—for they would certainly speculate upon what might have happened in the course of her absence—and live retired in some quiet market town.

As they drew closer to Tangier, the Berbers' vigilance increased. They guessed that at least some of the men sent after them by the King would probably have gone straight on to the English-held city by the shortest possible route, so that there would be a reception party to prevent Ferelith actually reaching her own people. There was a good chance Ismail's men would be no more than a day ahead of them, especially if they had set out still believing the two women were on foot. If that was so, they would not have felt under any particular pressure to hurry. It was with that in mind that Hassan announced that there was something to discuss before they turned in for the night.

'By tomorrow evening we shall be within sight of the city and must go carefully,' he said. 'That will certainly be no time to stop and talk. We all know there is a considerable degree of risk, which can only increase as we get closer. The fewer of us that are exposed to it, the better. Latifa, do you wish to enter Tangier with your mistress?'

'No,' she said bluntly and without pausing to consider. Latifa, too, had had plenty of time for thought in the last few days. 'It means returning to captivity. On the other hand, I suppose I'd rather be captive but alive than free and dead, and, once Ismail's men catch up with me, death will be inevitable.'

'I can try to persuade the governor to send you home with me,' Ferelith suggested.

Latifa grimaced. 'You're very kind, madam, but for one thing you can't guarantee it and for another I'm not sure I'd want to go. Even Tangier is too cold for my blood and they say England is worse. No, the only real choice I have is captivity or death. I'll opt for captivity because there's always a chance it will come to an end. It isn't what I want to do, but it's the only real choice I've got.'

'There is another,' Hassan said. 'I don't know that you'll necessarily like it any better, but you could come back to the Rif with us. You'd be free and if you don't decide to marry a Rifi first we may eventually find a trader who will take you back to the Sudan.'

Latifa snorted. 'Or sell me on the way, more like. Can you guarantee my liberty in your village?'

'I vouch for it. My father will undertake your protection as if you were his daughter.'

Latifa turned to Ferelith. 'What say you, madam? If I accept Benani's offer you will have to face your fellow countrymen alone and that won't be easy.'

'I'd have to do that, anyway,' Ferelith told her. 'I couldn't take you everywhere with me. Besides, I once promised you your freedom and so far you've benefited very little from it. No, if returning to the Rif under Benani protection is what is in your best interest—and, I feel bound to say, it seems so to me—then that's what you should do.'

Ferelith caught a brief, approving smile on Hassan's face which lifted her spirits somewhat but was poor compensation for the loss of the woman she had come to think of as a friend.

'That's settled, then,' Hassan said. 'At dawn you will return with the rest of my men to our village and I shall continue with Mrs Durliston.' He turned to Ferelith. 'I must ask you to trust me, madam. By sending the rest of them back to the mountains, I limit the risk they undergo. I hope you will be willing to go on alone with me tomorrow, and tomorrow night. My plan is to bring you to the Catherine Gate as they open it at dawn.'

Ferelith smiled fleetingly. 'It would be churlish to mistrust you after you have done so much on my behalf. As many as possible must be safeguarded. By all means let them leave by first light.'

Both women felt the parting deeply and each was close to tears as they hugged one another and wished each other well, but once the horses were ready the Berbers interrupted the leave-taking, knowing that time thus spent was time wasted and a risk increased. Ferelith had only a few moments to watch Latifa and her escort retrace their steps before Hassan insisted that they, too, set off. She glanced back over her shoulder several times but it wasn't long before a bend in the tortuous path and an outcrop of rock hid the other party from view. She was alone with Hassan and was unsure whether to be glad or sorry.

In fact, that day was very little different from its predecessors. They rode in single file, Hassan continually on the watch for any indication that they were not as alone as they seemed. Every so often he held up one hand, a silent signal to draw rein while he listened and looked before deciding it was safe to continue. When they paused in the shadow of the rocks while the sun was at its hottest, they dismounted but the horses remained saddled, ready to be ridden off at the slightest hint of danger. Hassan spotted none and was unsure whether to be glad or deeply suspicious. It was not like Moulay Ismail, who was nothing if not thorough, to have left the approaches to Tangier unwatched.

Anxious to betray no hint of their presence, they forwent a fire that night, a sacrifice accentuated by the pinpricks of light emanating from the city in the distance, for they were high enough to be looking down over the walls, though from a great way off. Closer were the outlying forts, and between the two, well lit up, the fort of Whitehall, a fort in fact in times of battle but at others the place where soldiers and civilians alike caroused and gambled with the tacit permission of the governor, who punished such excesses when they took place within the city walls.

Ferelith and Hassan made do with their cloaks and blankets, huddled under the lee of a rocky outcrop. Ferelith added the robe and *chador* and earned an approving nod from Hassan.

'It is more fitting,' he said.

Ferelith chuckled. 'Warmer, too,' she told him.

If there were other watchers they, too, were managing without fire.

'Are you asleep?' Hassan asked quietly after they had sat in silence for some time, their spartan supper of bread, soft cheese and water long since finished.

'No, I've been watching the lights. It seems strange to be so close after being away so long, especially when I didn't expect to see it again.'

'What will you do?'

Ferelith sighed. 'Face Colonel Kirke, I suppose.'

'Not a good man.'

'No, but there are worse.'

'And what will you do when you get back to England?'

'I've been thinking about that. I shall buy a house in some small market town where no one knows me and just live quietly. Perhaps I'll have a dog for company— a little spaniel.'

'A dull life for a young woman,' he remarked and lapsed into silence for a long time. 'And then remarry, I suppose,' he said suddenly.

'I don't think so,' Ferelith said.

'Whyever not?' He seemed surprised. 'You're young and healthy. Why throw the rest of your life away on a little spaniel?'

Ferelith was uneasy at the direction the conversation was taking. His questions were natural but they cut too close to the bone and she was unsure how best to answer. 'I don't think I shall love again,' she said at last, truthfully.

'And if you did?'

'It makes no difference. I still couldn't marry.'

'Why not?'

Ferelith moved uncomfortably under her blanket, but it was discomfort of the mind rather than the body. 'Because I would have to...to explain. To tell him about Tangier...and Meknes. About what happened on the road there and being in the harem, knowing that he would always wonder if perhaps there weren't some details I had kept to myself. It would be unfair—dishonest, even—not to tell him the truth but he would never be entirely sure that I had done so.'

'Many women would simply lie about it.'

'Perhaps, but I'm not one of them.'

'Would it be so difficult to convince a man you love—and whom you believe to love you?'

'I think it could never be easy and to face seeing his regard diminish as suspicion took its place—that would be beyond bearing.'

'Why should his regard diminish? Your evident integrity should surely convince him.'

'I'd like to think so, but I doubt it.'

'You don't have a high opinion of the love of men.'

'I've little experience of it—only my husband's, and even he... No doubt his Christian charity would have been stretched to its limits. Oh, he would have said it made no difference, and believed he meant it, but I think his love would have withered.'

Hassan said nothing. It was not for him to question the depth of another man's love for his wife. He did not speak again for a long time, so long that Ferelith wondered whether he had fallen asleep and wished she could follow suit, but sleep had never been further from her. Tomorrow held no lures. If she was lucky, she would be facing Piercey Kirke's lustful eyes and then the nudges and whispers of her compatriots. If she was unlucky she would be hauled back to Meknes for unceremonious execution. Either way, she would never see Hassan again. She would have liked to have found comfort in the fact that he was at least exhibiting some curiosity as to what she would do but it was probably only to make conversation and now it seemed that, curiosity satisfied, he had dropped off to sleep without any of the heartache that beset her.

His voice broke into her thoughts, proving her assumptions wrong. 'Have you never loved but the one man?' he asked.

The question was so entirely unexpected that, instead of a carefully phrased reference to the duty of a widow to the memory of her husband, she was startled into saying simply, 'One other.'

'Before or since?'

She hesitated. 'Since.'

'Then why are you not married to him?'

'Perhaps because he didn't ask me. Besides, there would have been problems.'

'There always are. Would these have been insuperable?'

Ferelith thought about them. There had been duty, and honour, religion and customs, language and expectations. 'No, none of them,' she said.

She thought he nodded. When he spoke it was to change the subject. 'Get some sleep. We don't have far to go tomorrow but we'll need our senses about us the whole time.'

Ferelith must have slept eventually because Hassan had to shake her awake. He pointed to the east, where the first hint of a lightening sky heralded the brief dawn. Then he pointed to the west. Ferelith could see nothing.

'Beyond Anne Fort,' he said. 'Where the old trench leads to Kendal. Watch there.'

Ferelith did and at first could still see nothing. Then, as the sky behind them lightened still further, the rim of the rising sun caught something that gleamed. One gleam and then another, close by.

'What is it?' she whispered.

'Steel,' he replied. 'Toledo steel, in all probability. That's where Ismail's men are.' He helped her to her feet and they stood well back against the cliff, still wrapped in the brown blankets that had kept them warm that night, blankets which also rendered them invisible from a distance against the rock. Hassan slipped his arm round Ferelith's shoulders. 'In a quarter of an hour the gate will be open. It will take us ten minutes to cover the space between. We shall have just two minutes' start at the most over Ismail's men. Do you want to do it?'

Ferelith looked up at him, surprised. 'I have no choice,' she said.

'You have a choice,' he replied. 'It lies between a quiet market town in England and a little spaniel—preceded by the attentions of Colonel Kirke and the gossip of the good citizens—or a return with me to the Rif.'

She stared at him, oblivious to the sunrise. 'Return with you?'

'Is the prospect so dreadful?'

'No...yes. I mean, I'm not quite sure...' Her voice tailed away.

He smiled and the warmth of the sun's glowing sphere was echoed in his voice. 'You said the problems were not insuperable,' he reminded her.

'But I didn't know... I didn't think...'

'You didn't think I knew who else you had loved?' He swept her to him, crushing her with the force of his embrace. 'I am only disappointed that you doubted the depth of my feelings for you. I promise you, they equalled yours—perhaps surpassed them, though on that I fancy we'd not agree.'

'But you were so...so cold, so indifferent after that night on the road to Meknes.'

'What choice had I? You had pledged yourself to bargain for your father's freedom and had placed your trust in me. A trust I betrayed that night when you could so easily have been lost forever. It was my ardent prayer that Ismail would reject your offer and then, when your father died, I'm ashamed to say I was almost glad because I knew, if I could only reach Meknes in time, he would be honour bound to release you. When I saw you, I thought I was too late.' He kissed her gently. 'You don't know how close I came to killing myself then. All that stopped me was the knowledge that it would do nothing to help you, and that became my priority.'

He was touching on sensitive matters. Ferelith longed to sink her head into his shoulder, to have the comfort of his arms around her while she told him exactly what had transpired in Meknes, but she could not bear the thought that if she did she might find herself gently but firmly put aside when she had finished. Yet it had to be done. She withdrew from his hold and turned her head away so that she did not have to see the welcome warmth in his eyes turn to an icy chill.

'Enough,' she said. 'Ismail's is a name I would willingly never hear again, much less speak, but I must. Hassan, I'm not sure how much you offer me and how much is my own wishful thinking but, whatever the truth of that, I must first tell you...' she paused and took a deep breath to give her the courage to go on '...Ismail did not take me but I was saved from that fate only by the fortuitous arrival of a messenger.'

Hassan caught her to him, turning her so that he could kiss her lips. 'I know what Ismail is,' he said. 'I'll always bless the arrival of that messenger, but had he not come it would have made no difference. Forget the King. That interlude is over and, I promise you, you'll find me a very different man. As to what I offer you, marriage is what I had in mind.' He chuckled. 'Do you realise that if I had followed my heart in the first place we'd have been married these many months? What a fool I was to hesitate!'

'"These many months"? What do you mean? You could hardly have married me from the governor's ball.'

'No, though it crossed my mind to abduct you then and there when I observed the conduct of the governor. No, I meant before that. When you were lost in Lisbon, in fact, and I found myself looking into the most bewitching green eyes I'd ever seen.' He laughed. 'The only green eyes, as a matter of fact. My impulse was to snatch you then and be out of Portugal before you were missed. I've regretted that lost opportunity even since. That was why I volunteered to accompany Benabdala to Tangier— I wanted to see you again.' He kissed her once more and then grew serious. 'If you marry me, it has to be on my terms—the terms of a Berber. I undertake to make only one concession to your own beliefs.'

'And what is that?'

'I'll never take another wife so long as you live,' he said and Ferelith reached up to kiss him.

'An undertaking, indeed,' she said. 'You father won't be very happy about it: you are the chief's son, after all.'

'I suspect he will be only too pleased to have me settled at all,' Hassan told her. He looked over her head. 'The gates are open and the sun is up. If we ride to Tangier now, the enemy will no longer have the sun in their eyes. Do we go? Or do you marry a heathen?'

'We go,' Ferelith replied, 'but to the Rif—so that you may marry an infidel.'

LOVE'S PAROLE
Elizabeth Lowther

Take in a French prisoner of war?

Mr and Mrs Kingston had never accustomed themselves to a lower standard of living. So they had no idea what a burden they placed upon their daughter Olivia in feeding a paroled man – an enemy from the Napoleonic Wars.

But Captain Miles Gilbert, an American captured aboard a French ship, who was charming and humorous, reminded Olivia painfully of the fiancé she lost during her father's difficulties. For a sailor, Miles had remarkably little knowledge of the sea – and pursuing *that* little nugget led more than Olivia's heart into danger . . .

TWO
HISTORICAL
ROMANCES

Masquerade historical romances bring the past alive with splendour, excitement and romance. We will send you a cuddly teddy bear and a special MYSTERY GIFT. Then, if you choose, you can go on to enjoy 4 more exciting Masquerades every two months, for just £1.99 each! Send the coupon below at once to – Reader Service, FREEPOST, PO Box 236, Croydon, Surrey CR9 9EL.

&

TWO
FREE GIFTS!

--- **NO STAMP REQUIRED** --- →

Yes! Please rush me my 2 Free Masquerade Romances and 2 Free Gifts! Please also reserve me a Reader Service Subscription. If I decide to subscribe, I can look forward to receiving 4 Masquerade Romances every two months for just £7.96, delivered direct to my door. Post and packing is free, and there's a free Newsletter. If I choose not to subscribe I shall write to you within 10 days - I can keep the books and gifts whatever I decide. I can cancel or suspend my subscription at any time. I am over 18.

Mrs/Miss/Ms/Mr _____ EP04M

Address _____

_____ Postcode _____

Signature _____

The right is reserved to refuse an application and change the terms of this offer. Offer expires December 31st 1991. Readers in Southern Africa please write to P.O. Box 2125, Randburg, South Africa. Other Overseas and Eire, send for details. You may be mailed with other offers from Mills & Boon and other reputable companies as a result of this application. If you would prefer not to share in this opportunity, please tick box. ☐